A Murder of No Consequence

James Garcia Woods

Table of Contents

Part One

Madrid 10–15 July 1936

Chapter One

Madrid, that summer, was a city suffocating under a blanket of heat and a dark cloud of fear. Armed gangs roamed the streets like packs of rabid dogs. Shots cut through thick night air; the rattle of machine-gun bullets punctuated the usual afternoon calm. Anarchists shot fascists, socialists killed communists. In the first week of July alone, eleven young men were murdered for their political beliefs. And the Minister of the Interior sat in his office on the Puerta del Sol, and let it happen.

*

The driver of the stolen black car, which was heading along one of the wide, tree-lined avenues towards the centre of Retiro Park, knew all about the killings, and regretted that some of them had happened. But there were other deaths, he was convinced, which were necessary; and for one of these, he himself had been responsible only the night before. He had killed without hesitation or remorse, and now, as he drove past the artificial lake and the equestrian statue of Alfonso XII – the last king to rule an empire – he held his left hand up in front of his eyes to see if it was still steady. He could find not even the slightest hint of a tremble. He congratulated himself. There were not many men who could have done what he'd done and still be so calm, he thought smugly.

In the distance he could see the Crystal Palace, topped by its glass dome. A little further into the park, he told himself, and he could complete his previous evening's work. He brought the stolen car to a halt beside a clump of trees, and looked around him. The avenue he had driven up was deserted, as he'd expected it to be at that time of the morning. Leaving the engine idling, he got out of the car and opened the boot. Inside it was a long, thin bundle wrapped in a piece of sacking. He picked up the bundle as if it weighed nothing, and headed into the trees. When he re-emerged, a few seconds later, he had only the sacking in his hands.

Chapter Two

The park keeper studied the two men walking towards him. One was a little taller than average, had a tight, compact frame, and moved with the grace of a man who was fully aware of his body's potential. He wore a pin-striped blue suit – which looked like it had been chosen without much thought, but was good on him anyway – and he was clean-shaven. The other man was a little shorter than his *compañero*, but probably weighed around thirty kilos more. He had a bushy black moustache, and his suit had the appearance of having been bought second-hand from a stall at the Sunday morning *Rastro*. The keeper was not sure whether or not they were policemen, but he certainly hoped they were, because he was finding the responsibility of looking after the girl's body a considerable strain.

The two men drew level with the keeper, and came to a halt. The thinner one reached into his jacket pocket, pulled out a leather wallet and flicked it open to show his warrant card.

'Inspector Ruiz,' he said, speaking with the accent of a country boy who had lived in Madrid for a considerable time. 'And this is Constable Fernández. Are you the one who found the body?'

'Yes . . . I . . .'

'Take us to her.'

The keeper turned and led the two detectives through the trees into a small clearing, where a second keeper was standing guard. The victim was lying sprawled, face upwards, among the roots of a mature elm. She was a pretty girl. Her nose was slim, without being pinched, the wide eyes seemed more astonished than afraid. Beneath her oval chin was a line of ugly black bruises.

'Oh, God!' Paco Ruiz gasped.

His partner, Fat Felipe, raised a surprised eyebrow. 'Something wrong, *jefe*?'

Paco shook his head. 'No, nothing wrong at all.'

But there was. His first sight of the girl had shocked him. Not because she was so young or pretty, nor because of the nature of her death. It was something else entirely. Though he would swear he'd never seen her before, he had an overpowering feeling that he knew her.

'*Jefe* . . .?' Felipe said tentatively.

Paco took a deep breath, and turned to the man who had discovered the body. 'What time did you find her?' he asked.

'Must have been half an hour ago. Maybe a bit more.'

'This spot's a bit isolated. What brought you here?'

'I . . . I was taking a short cut to the head keeper's office.'

'And once you'd found her, what did you do then?'

'I looked around for help. I saw Augustin coming up the *paseo* . . .'

'I was just reporting for duty,' the second keeper explained.

'. . . and I told him to telephone you. Then I came back here to watch over her.' He looked down at the girl again. 'She's very young, isn't she?'

'She's about as old as anybody ever gets,' Paco said. 'Was there anyone else around at the time?'

'No one. It's about the quietest time in the whole day. Most people are in the bars, taking their mid-morning break.'

That was true enough, Paco thought. 'You can go,' he said.

'Go?' repeated the keeper. 'Just like that?'

'Just like that,' Paco agreed. 'I'll send someone round to take your statements later.'

The two keepers made their way back to the *paseo*. They seemed reluctant to leave, but that was often the way it was with civilians – violent death repelled them, yet at the same time it held a horrible fascination.

Paco lit a Celtas, took a deep drag, looked down at the girl again, and felt a small, involuntary shudder run through his body.

'You want *me* to examine her?' asked Fat Felipe, who had noticed Paco's reaction, just as he always noticed everything that his boss said or did.

Paco grinned. 'No, I'll do it,' he said. 'If you get on the ground, it'll take a bloody crane to raise you up again.'

Gritting his teeth, he bent down and placed the back of his hand against the girl's cheek.

'Is she cold?' Felipe asked, over Paco's shoulder.

'Very.'

The peace of the park was suddenly shattered by the sound of gunshots in the distance. Though he'd been under fire many times in Morocco, Paco still felt his stomach churn, and despite the fact he could already feel the weapon pressing against him, he automatically checked his pistol was in his shoulder holster.

More shots.

'Do you think we should go and see what's happening?' Fat Felipe asked.

'No! Public order's not our job,' Paco said.

He turned his attention back to the girl. She was around twenty or twenty-one, he guessed. He, himself, was thirty-six, and had been for more than ten hours. He wondered if he should celebrate his birthday, and decided there wasn't much to celebrate.

There was a third burst of shooting in the distance. Paco took the hem of the girl's blue dress between his finger and thumb, and rubbed softly. He was no expert, but it felt like silk to him.

'Do you think she was killed here, *jefe*?' Felipe asked.

Paco straightened up and looked at the dusty ground around the dead girl. 'No. There isn't any sign of a struggle, and even if she'd not been able to do anything else, she'd have lashed out with her feet and left heel-marks in the dirt.'

'Could have been killed somewhere close and brought here,' Felipe suggested.

Or murdered miles away, Paco thought.

From their right came the sound of a siren wailing. It grew louder and louder, until it was almost ear-shattering. Then, through a gap in the trees, they saw a speeding car containing four *Guardias de Asalto* – the new police force that the government had created because it did not trust the old-established *Guardia Civil*.

'Here come the guts-and-glory boys,' Fat Felipe said sourly.

The car screamed past the copse. Paco lit another cigarette, then cocked his head to look at the girl from another angle. He felt a slight stabbing pain, and wondered why he couldn't summon up his usual professional objectivity – wondered, in fact, why he seemed as morbidly fascinated with her as the park keepers had been. 'Does she remind you of anyone, Felipe?' he asked.

'Somebody I know, do you mean? Or somebody famous?'

'I'm not sure,' Paco admitted.

Fat Felipe shrugged his heavy shoulders. 'Can't say she does.'

Paco bent down again, opened the girl's bag and laid the contents neatly on the grass in front of him. There was not much – a handkerchief, some cosmetics, a purse, a few hair clips. And a colour postcard of the Virgin of somewhere-or-other.

'A good Catholic,' Felipe said.

Yes, and that's rare enough these days, Paco thought. He opened the purse. It contained a few coins, a metro ticket and a cardboard religious calendar. 'I know nobody pays much attention to the law any more, but it *is* still an offence not to carry your DNI on you, isn't it?' he asked sarcastically.

Fat Felipe nodded. 'Identification papers must be shown to any officer of the law who wishes to see them,' he quoted, taking the question at face value.

'Then where's this girl's identification card?'

Fat Felipe shrugged again. 'Maybe the killer took it.'

'And why should he want to do that?'

'To slow down the investigation. We can't very well work out who'd be likely to kill her when we don't even know who she is.'

That made sense. Yet even in a big city like Madrid, the murderer couldn't imagine that it would take them long to come up with a name. Everybody had family and friends – a grey-haired grandmother or worried father – who would report to one of the police stations that Pili, or Mariluz, had gone missing.

The *Asaltos* car passed them again, heading back for the city. It contained the same officers as before, but now, between the two on the back seat, was another man – wearing a blue shirt which was soaked in blood.

Fat Felipe scratched his backside reflectively. 'Ever get the feeling we're wasting our time, *jefe*?' he asked, as the sound of the siren faded away.

Paco ground his cigarette butt under his heel. 'Wasting our time? What makes you say that?'

'The country's going to hell,' Felipe said. 'The murder rate's at an all-time high, the detection rate at an all-time low. And it can only get worse. So, when you think about it, does it really matter whether we find the killer in this case or not?'

Paco looked down at the girl again and tried to imagine her as she would have been in life. Those eyes might once have looked kind and hopeful. The generous mouth must have produced some radiant smiles. Maybe by the time she'd reached thirty-six, *she'd* have felt sorry for herself too – but she'd never been given that opportunity to make that choice.

'Yes, it matters,' he said. 'Even if nobody else gives a damn, it still matters to me.'

Chapter Three

Captain Hidalgo swivelled in his chair, and looked up at the photograph hanging on his office wall. There were two men in the picture, one a lieutenant and the other a corporal. They were posing, perhaps a little awkwardly, in front of an adobe fort.

The lieutenant was a broad, square-headed man. His face – big nose, wide mouth, and eyebrows like scrubbing brushes – looked oddly unfinished, as if it had been carved by a sculptor who had got bored half-way through and given up.

The corporal was younger. His hair was dark, and his eyes shone with intelligence. He had a long straight nose, a pleasant mouth and a chin which suggested either determination or stubbornness.

The captain sighed. 'When was that picture of us taken, Paco?' he asked.

'June 1921, I think.'

Hidalgo turned to face his inspector. '1921,' he repeated. 'Fifteen years ago. When we were young.' He sighed again. 'Still, they were great days, weren't they?'

Paco, who was standing in the at-ease position, shifted his weight slightly. 'Great days? Do you really think so?'

'But of course they were. What times we had in Morocco! What sights we saw. What things we did.'

A thin smile came to Paco's face. 'Sometimes, when I hear you describing it with so much enthusiasm, I think we must have been in different armies,' he said.

'Different armies! What rubbish you can talk!' Hidalgo snorted, missing the point. 'Why, weren't you by my side all the way through the siege of Melilla? And thank God you were there – or I wouldn't be sitting behind this desk today.'

'And I probably wouldn't be a policeman.'

'You'd always have been a policeman, whether you'd met me or not,' Hidalgo told him. 'You were born to be a policeman.' He clasped his big hands together. 'Yes, I still miss Morocco,' he confessed. 'Life was a lot less complex than it is here. For a start, you always knew who your enemies were.' He paused. 'Now, tell me about this new murder of yours.'

Paco filled him in on the details. 'It's almost certainly a domestic case,' he said when he reached the end.

Hidalgo raised his scrubbing brush eyebrows a fraction of an inch. 'Isn't it rather early in the investigation to be making such an assumption?'

Paco shrugged. 'What else could it be but a domestic? If it had been political, she'd have been shot, not strangled. Sexual, and she'd have been naked, or at least had her clothes disarranged. Robbery, and the murderer would have taken her purse, even though it only contained small change.'

The captain nodded. 'Very well, treat it as a domestic killing. But keep me informed of developments.' He reached across his desk for the stack of papers he had been putting off dealing with. 'That will be all, Inspector.'

'How many men can I have for this investigation, sir?' Paco asked.

'Fat Felipe was with you in the park, wasn't he?'

'Yes.'

'Then use him.'

'And the rest of the team?'

'There is no rest,' Hidalgo said.

'But sir—'

'If it's as simple as you claim, two men should be enough to wrap it up.'

'I don't even know the girl's name,' Paco protested.

'Are you saying you can't solve this case without a bigger team?' Hidalgo asked challengingly. 'If so, perhaps I'd better put another investigator onto . . .'

'I can solve it,' Paco interrupted, 'but it could take days. Now if you'd give me just a couple more men . . .'

Hidalgo's eyebrows rose again, this time in an annoyance which was not far from anger. 'The department is stretched to the bloody limit,' he said. He picked up the sheaf of documents and shook them in the direction of his inspector. 'Do you know what all these are?' he demanded. 'Case notes on political murders! We have to investigate each and every one of them – even though we know they're random killings, so there's no chance of making an arrest. And you want more men? *Joder*, inspector, you should be kissing my arse for even giving you Fat Felipe.'

'If we allow the trail to go cold—' Paco persisted.

The captain raised a hand to silence him, then swung round in his chair so that he was looking out of the window. Almost as if he'd arranged for it

14

to happen, an open car, filled with blue-shirted Falangists, chose that moment to drive by on the other side of the square.

'Look at that!' he said. There were six young men in that car, each – apart from the driver – waving a machine-gun above his head. 'You get the message?' Hidalgo growled.

'"We have the weapons – and we can use them any time we want to"?'

'Exactly. Now why do you think we let them get away with displays like that?'

'Because they have friends in high places?' Paco guessed.

'No! It's not because they have friends in high places. It's because, much as I'd like to throw their aristocratic backsides straight in gaol, much as it offends every instinct I've ever had as a policeman to see them carrying on like that, arresting that lot would be like lighting a few sticks of dynamite and then stuffing them down our own pants.'

'You arrested their leader,' Paco pointed out.

Hidalgo shook his head, as if he despaired of his inspector ever learning anything about the reality of the situation. 'It was February when we arrested José Antonio,' he said. 'This – in case you haven't noticed – is July, and the situation has deteriorated very badly in the last few months. If we were to lock up those young gentlemen, it would be like declaring war on the Falange – and before you had time to fart, Madrid would be nothing but a bloody battlefield.'

The captain reached for his packet of cigarettes, took one himself, and offered the packet to Paco. The inspector shook his head. He wanted a smoke, but somehow – perhaps because of his Moroccan days – he never felt comfortable lighting up in the presence of a superior officer.

'I know what's going on in that head of yours,' the captain continued. 'You're saying to yourself that our job is to enforce the law, not to play politics. Am I right?'

'More or less,' Paco admitted.

'We don't have any choice but to play politics, because no other organization seems to have the will or the ability to stop this country tearing itself into shreds.'

'So the only way we can keep the police force together is to stop behaving like policemen?' Paco asked.

Hidalgo took an angry puff on his cigarette. 'What makes you such a good detective is your single-mindedness,' he said. 'You're like a dog that's got its teeth clamped on some poor bastard's leg, and won't let go whatever happens. But no one, Paco, not even you, can stay blinkered for ever.'

'I just want to do my job.'

'I give up on you,' Hidalgo said. 'I really do. All right, Inspector Ruiz, you're dismissed.'

Paco clicked his heels together in the approved military manner. 'At your orders, sir,' he said.

Then he turned and marched smartly out of the room.

*

Dr Muñoz stood over the dissected body of the victim. 'She was killed around eighteen hours ago, as nearly as I can guess,' he said. 'Cause of death – asphyxiation.' He looked down at the corpse and laughed dryly. 'Apart from being dead, she's in really excellent physical shape.'

Paco lit a cigarette and inhaled a mixture of nicotine and formaldehyde. 'Anything else you can tell me that might be of use?' he asked, though not with much hope.

'Like what?'

Paco shrugged. Like what, indeed? 'I don't know,' he said. 'Scars from an unusual operation? A distinctive birthmark?'

The doctor shook his head. 'Nothing like that.' He looked down at the girl again. 'Would you say the dress she was wearing when they brought her in was expensive?'

'Very.'

'So she wasn't a street walker?'

'What makes you ask that?'

'Even today, it's very uncommon to find a girl from a good background who's lost her virginity.'

'And this one has?'

'Yes. She's had sex in the last few days.'

'Voluntarily?'

'If you're asking me if she's been raped, I'd have to say no.'

'Maybe she was married,' Paco speculated.

The doctor lifted up the dead girl's limp hand for Paco to inspect. 'No wedding ring,' he said. 'And no sign that there's ever been one.'

Paco looked at the girl's face again, and wondered why it was that she had seemed so familiar from the first moment he'd seen her. And then, suddenly, he knew. Shock coursed through his body. He could taste the dry heat of the desert. He could smell the overpowering odour of the camels.

16

He felt as if he'd been kicked in the stomach. It was hard to breathe, and there was a pounding in his head.

'Is anything the matter?' the doctor asked. 'You look as if you've seen a ghost.'

'I have!' Paco gasped.

After all those years, she had come back to haunt him, to remind him of his failure. He felt his cigarette drop from between his fingers. On this day of all days – what a present. 'Happy birthday, Paco,' he said to himself.

Chapter Four

The Puerta del Sol – the Sun Gate – was the heart of Madrid, and hence the heart of Spain and all things Hispanic. Once, it had been nothing more than its name suggested – the gate on the edge of a city through which the first light of day shone. But as the city had grow, the walls had come down, and now Sol was a huge irregular oblong of a plaza, absorbing the traffic which was spewed into it from twelve different streets.

It was a strange mixture of the civic and the political. *Madrileños* eating cakes at the famous outdoor café at one end of the square could watch the comings and goings of important personages at the Ministry of the Interior. Then, while they sought shelter from the sun under the awnings of the shops on the north side of Sol, they could let their gazes fall on the *Asalto* barracks. A little further along, they would come to the symbol of Madrid – the bear standing on its hind legs, eating from the strawberry tree. And even if they knew that strawberries did not grown on trees – and how many had failed to take the Strawberry Train to Aranjuez and see the strawberry cultivation for themselves? – it did not stop them taking pleasure in the idiosyncrasies of the animal chosen to represent the spirit of their city.

All the major roads of Spain started in Sol, and when the peasants in the far-flung villages heard the chimes of the new year over their wirelesses, they were listening to the clock on top of the Ministry of the Interior, right in the centre of the plaza.

Sol had both seen history, and made it. Angry mobs congregating there had caused governments to topple and kings to abdicate. It was in Sol that the revolt against the Emperor Napoleon had begun, a revolt led by men and women from the poorer *barrios* of the city, armed with no more than knives, shovels and axes. Ill-equipped as they had been, they had still put up astounding resistance. People had even fought from their homes, pouring boiling water from their balconies and throwing tiles from their roofs down on the confused French and Egyptian troops. The uprising had failed, as it was bound to, and there had been terrible retribution, chronicled so graphically by Goya in his paintings *The Second of May* and *The Third of May*.

Paco thought about the revolt as he and Felipe crossed the square. It had been both so heroic and so hopeless, and that, he supposed, was what had made it so typically Spanish. He wiped his hand across his forehead. It was two hours before the sun would reach its zenith, but the air was already suffocating. Enough of history and the weather, he told himself, it was time to think about the murdered girl. And though he didn't will it, he found he was not thinking of one murdered girl, but of two.

*

The shop at which the two detectives came to a stop was on the fashionable Calle Alcalá, half-way between the Puerta del Sol and the Cibeles fountain. Alcalá was one of Madrid's favourite streets, where the rich came to buy and the poor came to look. This particular establishment was called *Moda de Paris*, and though it had a large plate-glass window, there were only three dresses on display between the dried flowers and freshly cut ferns.

'Who are we today?' Fat Felipe asked.

Paco thought about it. 'In a place like this, we'd better try the big, ignorant lout and his long-suffering companion.'

'And I suppose I get to be the big, ignorant lout,' Fat Felipe complained.

Paco laughed. 'That's right.'

'Why is it always me?'

'Because you're so good at it.'

Fat Felipe nodded to acknowledge the truth of the remark, and turned his attention back to the shop window. 'You get more choice than that down the second-hand clothes market,' he said, slipping effortlessly into his assigned role.

Felipe opened the door and the two detectives stepped inside the shop. A bell rang in a back-room – not with the harsh jangling sound of shop-bells in Paco's own *barrio*, but with a softer, more musical tone. Paco looked around him. There had been only three dresses in the window, but there was none at all in the shop. Instead, groups of gilt-painted chairs had been gracefully arranged around low, onyx coffee tables.

'Funny kind of shop,' Fat Felipe muttered.

The door to the back-room opened, and a woman emerged. She was around forty, Paco guessed. Her hair was composed into an elaborate structure held in place by pins, and she was wearing a long black dress. She looked more like a customer than a shop assistant.

19

She gave the two men a quick inspection, and the expression which came to her face said that whatever her standards were, they both fell well below them.

'Can I help you?' she asked, without much conviction.

'This is supposed to be a frock shop, isn't it?' Fat Felipe said. 'So where are all the frocks?'

The woman laughed, lightly and patronizingly. 'All our dresses are made to order. The client selects the pattern of her choosing from our extensive catalogue, and then our dressmakers produce exactly what she requires.'

'Can't be cheap,' Fat Felipe said.

The woman's face, never very welcoming, now became positively hostile. 'No, it isn't cheap,' she admitted. 'So if you were thinking of ordering a dress yourselves . . .'

Paco laughed, as if he and the woman were sharing a joke. 'Of course we're not thinking of buying a dress,' he said. He slipped his hand into his pocket, and produced his warrant card. 'We are extremely sorry to disturb you,' he continued, 'but we are policemen, and you may know something which could advance our investigation.'

The woman took two steps forward, just enough to enable her to read Paco's warrant card from a distance. 'We're not used to seeing the police here,' she said, somehow managing to make it sound much more like a complaint than a statement of fact. 'And I can't think of any way I could possibly be of assistance to you. Perhaps if you wished to question one of our dressmakers . . .'

She broke off, and watched with fascinated horror as Paco put the bag he was carrying onto the coffee table, opened it, and took out the blue silk dress. 'This has your label in it,' he said. 'I wondered what you could tell us about it.'

'Why should the police be interested in one of our dresses?'

'We are not at liberty to reveal the nature of our enquiries,' Fat Felipe said. 'Look at it, please.'

The assistant reached out and relieved Paco of the dress. Her right hand touched his left for the briefest of moments. Her skin felt both cold and dry.

With neat, backward steps, the assistant retreated a safe distance before stopping to examine the dress.

'Well?' Fat Felipe asked.

'Yes, it does have our label inside,' the woman admitted. 'But I can tell from the cut that it's not this season's.'

'So when would you have sold it?'

'I would guess at about this time last year.'

'Who did you sell it to?'

The assistant stiffened. 'We pride ourselves on our discretion here,' she told Paco.

'And we're conducting a very important investigation, señora,' Fat Felipe said.

The woman hesitated, as if deciding whether or not to tell him to go to hell. 'I'd have to check my records . . .'

'Then please do so,' Paco interrupted.

'. . . and I'm rather busy at the moment.'

'You do it, or we'll do it,' Felipe said.

The woman shot the fat detective a look of pure loathing. 'It may take some time.'

Felipe made a great show of scratching his backside. 'We'll wait,' he said.

Horror fought with outrage on the woman's face, then both were replaced by panic as she realized that a customer might come in any minute and see what she'd just seen. She dropped the dress on the nearest chair, turned, and fled to the back-room.

'That really was a very good show you put on,' Paco said.

'Show?' Fat Felipe replied innocently. 'What show?'

*

When the assistant emerged from the back-room a couple of minutes later, she was carrying a large leather-bound ledger. 'The dress in question was commissioned by Doña Mercedes Mendéz Segovia,' she said breathlessly, as if she'd been running.

The name sounded vaguely familiar to Paco. Was she famous in her own right? Or only by association, because of who she was married to? He'd read somewhere that in most other countries, a woman took her husband's surname instead of retaining both her mother's and her father's after marriage. It seemed to him to be an extremely sensible system which probably made police work a great deal easier.

'And she is married to . . .?' he asked, stabbing in the dark.

The assistant smiled her superior smile, as if just selling the dress to Mercedes Mendéz Segovia put her in the same class as her client. 'Doña Mercedes' husband is Don Eduardo Herrera Moreno,' she said.

Of course! That was why he recognized her name. So that was who had bought the dress – the wife of one of the most powerful right-wing politicians in the whole of Spain.

Paco remembered seeing photographs of her in the newspapers, standing by her husband's side – grainy photographs of an elegant woman in her thirties looking up at a distinguished-looking man in his late forties. She was too old to be the dead girl in the park.

'Did she order the dress for herself, or was it for someone else?' he asked.

The assistant consulted the leather ledger. 'For herself. She had several fittings.'

'Thank you for your help,' Paco said, stuffing the dress back in his bag.

'Is . . . is Doña Mercedes in any kind of trouble?' the assistant asked worriedly.

'Now how could anyone as important as her possibly be in trouble?' Paco replied, walking towards the door.

*

While he was still visible through the dress shop window, Paco walked up Alcalá at an amble, but once out of sight he increased his pace to almost a run.

'What's the hurry?' Fat Felipe asked, as he struggled to keep up.

'I want to get to a phone before that bitch in the dress shop decides to ring up Doña Mercedes Mendéz and warn her to expect a call from the police.'

Felipe swerved to avoid two unemployed matadors, who were standing around hoping that somebody would recognize them and offer to buy them a drink. 'But why should you care if she *is* warned?' he asked his boss.

'When you're dealing with a political case, you need every advantage you can grab,' Paco said.

'Political!' Felipe repeated. 'But half an hour ago, you were convinced it was a domestic murder.'

'That was before I knew Eduardo Herrera Moreno was involved.' Paco pointed across the street. 'There's a phone box over there.'

They crossed the six lanes of traffic, avoiding the trams which were rattling furiously up and down, earning the curses of car drivers who were forced to slam on their brakes.

'You can't say for certain that Herrera is involved,' Felipe said, when they were safely on the opposite pavement. 'All you can be sure of is that the dead girl was wearing his wife's dress.'

'He's part of it,' Paco said with conviction. 'I just *know* he's part of it.'

They had reached the phone box. Paco flicked impatiently through the phone book.

'You don't think that maybe you're going off the deep end on this one?' Felipe asked.

'No,' Paco said. His finger had located the number he wanted. He dialled it rapidly.

It rang five times before someone picked it up. '*Si? Quié e?*' A woman – a young one – with a thick Andaluz accent, and an uncertain telephone manner.

'This is the police,' Paco said. 'Who am I speaking to?'

There was a sharp intake of breath, followed by a pause, and then the woman said, 'I am Paulina.'

'You work there?'

'Yes, I am one of the maids.'

'Please tell your mistress that I wish to speak to her.'

'She . . . she is not here,' Paulina said stumblingly. 'None of them are here.'

The maid sounded as if she had a guilty conscience, Paco thought, but that didn't prove a thing. If she was a country girl, then her only contact with authority would have been through the *Guardia Civil*, so it was hardly surprising that she was worried. And her fear was to his advantage. A more sophisticated girl might have asked for proof he really was who he said he was, whereas this one was frightened enough to tell him anything he wanted to know.

'Who else lives in the apartment besides your mistress?' Paco asked.

'There is Luis, the master's valet, Señora Cora, she is the cook . . .'

'The family,' Paco interrupted – because servants didn't wear expensive silk dresses. 'I'm only interested in the family.'

'Well, there's the master himself . . .'

'Anyone else?'

'The mistress's younger brother, Don Carlos.'

23

'Children?' Paco asked.

'There are no little ones.'

'Is there perhaps a teenage daughter? One who might be taken for a little older? Say twenty or twenty-one?'

'There are no little ones of any age.'

Paco tried a different tack. 'You said they are not there. When will they be back?'

'I don't know for sure, but the mistress said not to expect them back before two o'clock in the morning.'

And there was no chance of questioning them at that time of night. 'Damn!' Paco said.

'What was that?' the maid asked.

'I'll ring again tomorrow,' Paco told her.

'Am I to tell the mistress that you called?'

She would anyway, whatever he said, so it was best not to put Mercedes Mendéz on the defensive. 'If the opportunity arises, by all means tell your mistress,' Paco said, trying to suggest by his tone that the call was of so little importance that it really didn't matter one way or the other. 'Thank you for your help, Paulina.'

'*De nada, señor.*'

Paco replaced the phone on its cradle. 'As I thought, the dead girl isn't one of the family,' he said.

Fat Felipe shrugged. 'So Doña Mercedes gave the dress away to the daughter of one of her friends. That presents no problem. We have only to ask her who she gave it to, and we'll have the identity of our victim.'

Paco shook his head. 'I don't think it's going to be that simple,' he said. 'It never is with politics.'

'Politics!' Felipe snorted. 'First you want nothing to do with them, *jefe*, and now you've got them on the brain.'

Chapter Five

To anyone looking in through the front window of the *Cabo de Trafalgar* bar that night, it would have been obvious that, of the three men sitting at the table closest to the door, two were engaged in a heated argument and the third was bored by the whole proceedings.

'You left-wingers will be the downfall of the country,' Ramón was saying as he skewered a piece of octopus from the plate in front of him and popped it into his mouth.

'We socialists will be Spain's salvation,' Bernardo countered hotly. 'It is the UGT who'll rid our homeland of the priests and monarchists who have been sucking it dry for so long.'

It hadn't always been like this, Paco reminded himself. When they'd first become friends, eleven or twelve years earlier, they'd talked about other things. Women and food – two of the Spaniard's great loves – had featured regularly in their conversations. And during the season, there had been much to say about the bulls. But now, Ramón and Bernardo – in common with most of the population of Madrid – seemed to live and breathe nothing except politics.

Paco examined his two companions with a policeman's eye. Ramón was a small man with a neat moustache and slicked-back hair. He worked as a minor clerk in one of the ministries, which, like the octopus he was eating, seemed to have tentacles everywhere – all of them securely bound up in red tape. He probably didn't earn much more than a mechanic or a barman, but when he went to work every morning he carried a briefcase, and by the standards of the neighbourhood, that entitled him to some measure of respect.

Bernardo presented a complete contrast. He was a huge man with thick arms and a barrel chest – a market porter and the secretary of the local branch for the *Unión General de Trabajadores*, the union closely allied to the socialist party.

'Since February – since this so-called liberal government was elected – one hundred and sixty churches have been burnt to the ground,' Ramón complained in his thin, clerk's voice. 'Think of that! One hundred and sixty!'

'Is it any wonder, when the Catholic Church is such a force for reaction?' Bernardo asked. He pulled a well-thumbed pamphlet out of his pocket.

Ramón groaned theatrically. 'Not that old chestnut again!'

But Bernardo was not to be put off. 'I have here the catechism,' he announced. 'Let me read you a little. "Question: What kind of sin is committed by one who votes for a liberal candidate? Answer: Generally a mortal sin".'

'The churches are not being burned down by people who are outraged by what they read in the catechism,' Ramón said. 'Most of the arsonists are ignorant peasants who can't read at all!'

'There's more,' Bernardo persisted. '"Question: Is it a sin for a Catholic to read a liberal newspaper? Answer: He may read the *Stock Exchange News*". That's your priests for you! Hand in glove with the capitalists.'

Paco let his eyes roam around the bar. In the far corner were the wooden wine casks. Even without labels, it was easy to tell the red from the white, because under the tap on the barrel of red the floor was as stained as if a ghastly, bloody murder had been committed there.

His eyes moved to the zinc counter, against which Nacho, the barman, was resting his ample belly. Spread along the counter was a feast of seafood: oysters glistening in the light of the overhead lamp; plump grey crabs struggling ineffectually against the cords which bound their claws together; fried calamar rings; pink mussels covered with a garnish of green pepper and cucumber; shrimps lying on a bed of crushed ice.

What a wonderful display, Paco thought – and all the more remarkable when you considered that the city was hundreds of kilometres from the sea!

It was like magic, and, as with most tricks, there was a great deal of careful planning behind it. The fresh seafood arrived by train every morning, from both the Mediterranean Sea and the Atlantic Ocean. The fish trains were always ensured a smooth passage. So what if that meant a passenger-train full of people sweated away in a railway siding for a couple of hours? How could their business possibly be as important as the delivery of the marisco?

'Three more wines, Nacho!' Ramón called to the barman. Then, turning to Bernardo, he continued his attack. 'Do you realize there have been one hundred and thirteen general strikes since February?'

Statistics! How people like Ramón, with their neat clerical minds, loved statistics. This many people killed, these many strikes, that many priests assaulted. You didn't need statistics to know the country was falling apart – you only had to look out of your own window.

Paco wondered for a moment whether the situation would improve if the military took over, and decided it wouldn't. True, the government was making a mess of things, but from what he'd seen of the army's incompetence and corruption while he was serving in Morocco, it seemed unlikely that the generals could do any better.

'The peasants in Extremadura are taking over the large estates . . .' Ramón said, his outrage increasing with every sip of wine.

'And why shouldn't they?' Bernardo demanded belligerently. 'Most of the land they've seized has been lying idle for years.'

'This gutless government can see outright robbery, but doesn't have the will to step in and stop it. Now if Calvo Sotelo or Herrera were in charge . . . .'

It was interesting to hear the two men referred to in the same breath. Calvo Sotelo was a prominent monarchist, and Ramón, who knew about such things, was putting Herrera on an equal footing with him. Paco hadn't realized that the man was quite so important.

He ran his mind over all the questions which were still unanswered. Just what was Herrera's connection with the dead girl in the park? Why, when she had been missing for over twenty-four hours, hadn't some concerned relative reported her disappearance to the police? And who had she been to bed with only days before she was murdered?

'What do you think, Paco?' Ramón asked, as Nacho placed the three fresh glasses of wine in front of them.

'Think? About what?'

'About the political situation, of course.'

Paco shrugged. 'I'm a policeman. I arrest criminals. I don't have opinions about politics.'

'Then you must be the only cop who doesn't!' Bernardo said. 'The *Guardia Civil* is riddled with right-wingers . . .'

'With men who love their country with all their hearts,' Ramón corrected him.

Paco knocked back his drink in two swift gulps. How many wines had he drunk that evening? he wondered. Six? Seven? He reached into his pocket, pulled out some change, separated out a couple of pesetas, and slid the coins across the table.

'The drinks are on me tonight,' he said.

'You're leaving, Paco?' Bernardo asked, astonished. 'But why? It's still so early.'

'I have a headache,' Paco lied.

Or maybe it wasn't a lie at all. His head did ache – ached from all the heated arguments and pointless rebuttals. Was he the only man in Spain who didn't think he had all the answers to the country's troubles? Wouldn't it be better if there were a few more people like him, who only wanted to get on with their jobs? Maybe if there were, the troubles would go away of their own accord.

He stood up.

'See you tomorrow?' Ramón asked.

'Of course.'

Why not? They had met at the same table in the *Cabo de Trafalgar* almost every night for a decade. Why should a little thing like politics get in the way of that?

Chapter Six

It was well after midnight when Paco left the *Cabo de Trafalgar*, but the narrow Calle de Hortaleza still throbbed with life. Men lounging on street corners called out a greeting as he passed. Women, sitting on the small, low chairs which are specially designed for use on the pavement, waved to him. People were entering bars or leaving them, finishing their restaurant dinners or just beginning to attack the first course. There was nothing unusual in any of that. During the summer – which often lasted from the beginning of June to the end of September – Madrid hardly slept. And when the air was as hot as it was that night, the city didn't sleep at all.

Paco reached his own front door and clapped his hands loudly. A few moments later the *sereno* appeared, the front-door keys to every house in the street jangling noisily from his belt.

'Good evening, Don Francisco,' he said cheerfully, as he inserted his key in the lock and opened the door for Paco. 'Have you heard the latest news?'

'Is it political?'

'What news is not political these days? It seems that—'

Paco held up his hands. 'If it's political, I'd rather not know,' he said. 'If that's all the same to you.'

The night-watchman shrugged his flabby shoulders. His belly wobbled and his keys jangled even louder. 'I was only making conversation,' he said.

'Then why not talk about the bulls?' Paco demanded. 'Why not tell me about the wonderful new bar you've found? Must it always be politics, politics, politics?'

The watchman twisted his keys nervously in his hands. 'I'm sorry, Don Francisco. I only—'

'No, I'm the one who should be apologizing,' Paco said, feeling a sudden rush of shame. He reached into his pocket, fished out a twenty-five *centimo* coin, and put it into the watchman's hand. 'See you tomorrow, José.'

'I'll be here, Don Francisco. You can rely on that.'

Paco stepped into the bare hallway and looked up at the wooden stairs. Some blocks on the street had lifts, but his was not one of them, and, since he lived on the third floor, he had seventy-two steps to climb before he reached his apartment.

It was as he was starting to ascend that he realized that, as from that day, it was two steps for every year of his life. He wondered if he would still be making the climb when the correspondence was one to one. He grinned ruefully. Yes, probably he would – with his bad luck he might well live into his seventies.

He had almost reached the second-floor landing when the door of the apartment on the left opened, and he saw the woman standing in the doorway. It was her hair he noticed first. She was a *rubia* – a blonde – almost as rare in Madrid as a black face. She was in her early twenties, he guessed. She had blue eyes, high cheekbones and a generous mouth. Definitely the sort of woman to turn heads wherever she went.

'Señor Ruiz?' she asked, and even from just those two words, he recognized that she was foreign.

'Yes, I'm Ruiz.'

'My name's Cindy Walker. I'm your new neighbour.' She pronounced her first name 'Thindy', as if she thought that would make it easier for him to get his Spanish tongue round it.

'Are you from the United States?' he asked.

'That's right. I'm American.'

It annoyed him that she spoke, as so many of her countrymen did, as though she owned the title. 'There are many Americans,' he said. 'Everyone from the Arctic Circle to Tierra del Fuego can call themselves by that name.'

The girl flushed, and Paco felt another stab of shame. First he'd picked on José the *sereno*, and now he was having a go at this girl. As if it was their fault everything was in such a mess – as if they were responsible for the dead girl in the park. 'Look, I'm sorry . . .' he began.

The girl held up her hand to silence him. 'No, you're quite right,' she said. 'We *Yanquis* are too presumptuous by far. I won't make the same mistake again.'

After his outburst, he felt it incumbent on him to say something more, to express an interest he didn't really feel. 'Have you been in Madrid long, Señorita Walker?' he asked.

'I've just arrived,' the girl said. 'I'm going to be studying for an advanced degree at the university . . . and . . .' she looked down at the bare floorboards, as if she was slightly uncomfortable with what she was about to confess, '. . . and I'm hoping to write a novel while I'm here – about life in Spain.'

Why did Yanquis nearly always turn out to be aspiring authors, Paco wondered. And why did potential novelists invariably feel that there was a novel just waiting to be wrenched out of Spain?

He was now standing close to her. Far too close. He could smell her perfume, which seemed to him to be a delicate mixture of several wild flowers. He could see deep into her blue eyes – which he found disturbing.

He held out his hand. 'Welcome to my country,' he said formally. 'I hope you enjoy your time here.'

She took the hand. Her skin felt smooth and cool, and the contact sent a series of small electric shocks through him. 'There's a letter for you,' she said.

'A letter?'

'You were out when the postman came. He had a certified letter. I said I'd sign for it.'

'That was very kind of you.'

Cindy realized that their hands were still touching. She pulled hers awkwardly free. 'It's on the table in the salon.' She gazed down at her hand, as if she expected it to be changed in some way. 'The letter, I mean. I'll get it for you.'

She turned and disappeared into the apartment, re-emerging a couple of seconds later and handing him the letter. He looked down at it. Even in the dim light of the hallway, he recognized the handwriting and the Valladolid postmark. Pilar, his wife, had never been one to take the chance that her rebuking letters might not get through to him.

Now she'd handed over the letter, Cindy Walker seemed unsure of what to say next. 'I thought my Spanish was pretty good until I arrived in Spain,' she said finally, 'but now I see how much work I'm going to have to put in just to keep my head above water.'

It was a statement which clearly invited comment, perhaps even a compliment. Paco wondered what she meant about keeping her head above water. Maybe it meant something in her native language, but translated, it made no sense at all. He almost asked her to explain, but pulled back at the last instant. 'I have to go now,' he said.

31

Cindy squiggled slightly, as some people do at embarrassing moments. 'Of course, you must be tired. But if . . .' She stopped.

'If what?'

'If you find that you have a few minutes to spare over the next few days . . .'

'Yes?'

'I really would appreciate it if you could tell me a little about Madrid. It seems such a confusing city.'

'Not once you get to know it,' Paco said, promising nothing. 'Good-night, Señorita Walker.'

'Good-night,' the girl said, with just an edge of disappointment in her voice.

Paco turned and started to climb the remaining twenty-four steps to his apartment.

*

The Ruiz apartment, like many of the apartments in the older part of the city, sounded very impressive on paper. Seven rooms! Yes, but then you had to consider that each room was tiny – that some bedrooms had barely enough room for a bed, that in order to cross the living-room it was necessary to edge your way between the table and the wall.

Yet even so, the apartment seemed huge to a man who was living in it alone.

Paco went over to the cabinet, poured himself a stiff brandy, and settled down in his armchair to read the letter from Pilar.

'Dear Francisco,' it began – Pilar had never called him Paco, not even in the early days of their marriage – 'I am afraid I do not know when I will be returning to Madrid. My nerves, though much improved, are still bad.'

They would be, he thought. She was a highly strung woman – which was another way of saying that she had been spoiled as a child and now became almost hysterical if everything didn't go her own way.

'My parents have been very kind and understanding . . .' And so they should be. They had always doted on their daughter, and must have been delighted to have finally prised her away from her unsuitable husband.

'There is a new priest at our parish church. He is young, but very devout. I wish that you could meet him. Perhaps after a few minutes with Father Ignacio you would see the error of your ways and return to the Church.'

The Church! What did that mean to him? In the village where he had been brought up, not one peasant in twenty had gone to Mass, because they had seen how the local priest had hobnobbed with the rich landowners and knew – without being told – whose side God was on.

'At any rate, I pray nightly for your redemption', the letter continued. She'd had a religious streak in her when they married, but at least it had been under control then. It was when she'd learned she could never have children that the Church had really got its claws into her. Now she was a fanatic, always on her knees praying to one virgin or another.

When they'd still been living together – before this unstated, but clearly understood, separation – she'd fed him religion his every waking hour. *Come to mass, Francisco. I'm begging you.* There'd been tears at least once a day. *I can't bear to think of you damned, burning in hellfire for all eternity.* God had even come between them in bed. *How can you concern yourself with things of the flesh when your mortal soul is in such danger?*

They'd married too young, he thought. Much too young. And maybe if he hadn't been fresh out of the village, he would never have fallen for this city girl so easily. The marriage had been begun on shaky foundations – but religion certainly hadn't done much to shore it up.

There was a great deal more to the letter, but since it was all bound to be in a similar vein, he didn't feel up to reading it at that moment. He laid the letter aside, stood up and walked over to the window. Across the well, one floor down, he could see Cindy Walker working at her table under the window. A pretty woman by any standards, and she'd seemed attracted to him. But he wouldn't allow it to go any further – there were enough complications in his life already.

Behind him, the phone rang. He crossed the room, and picked it up. 'Speak to me,' he said.

'Inspector Ruiz?' asked a male voice.

'Yes.'

'My name is Carlos Méndez Segovia.'

The man spoke uncertainly, as if not quite convinced of his own identity, and for a second, the name meant nothing to Paco, either. Then he made the connection. Carlos Méndez Segovia was the brother of Mercedes Méndez and, according to Paulina the maid, shared the apartment with his sister and brother-in-law.

'Are you still there?' Méndez asked.

'Yes. What can I do for you, Señor Méndez?'

A slight pause. 'I understand you wish to talk to my sister,' Méndez continued.

'That is correct,' Paco said cautiously.

'And she, for her part, is more than willing to co-operate with you in any way she can. When would you like to see her?'

Now! Several hours ago! 'I'd like to see her as soon as I can,' Paco said.

'My . . . my sister wondered whether, instead of her going down to the police station, you could come to the apartment. Would that be possible?'

Why did he even need to ask? Didn't he realize that women of Doña Mercedes' importance simply didn't report to police stations like ordinary members of the public? Perhaps he was only being polite.

'I could come to the apartment,' Paco said.

'That's very good of you. Shall we say, nine o'clock tomorrow morning? If that's convenient.'

'It's convenient.'

'And you have the address?'

'I do.'

'In that case, we look forward to seeing you then.'

The line went dead. Paco replaced the receiver in its cradle, walked over to the cabinet, poured himself another brandy, and glanced out of the window again. Cindy Walker's *salon* was in darkness, which probably meant she'd given up studying, and gone to bed. He wondered what she looked like naked.

He returned to his armchair and took a sip of brandy. Méndez's phone call had been disturbing, and for two very good reasons. The first was that the man was being blindly co-operative. When people learned that the police wished to talk to them, their immediate reaction was to want to know why. Yet Méndez, who had a perfect right to ask what it was all about, hadn't done so.

Which led onto the second thing bothering Paco. The dress shop assistant had given his identity card the most cursory of glances, and he had not identified himself at all to Paulina, Doña Mercedes' maid. So how the hell did Carlos Méndez know that he was the man to ring?

Chapter Seven

The water carts had just finished their morning's work – moving slowly up the narrow streets and spraying the cobbles with their cooling jets – and now, on the tiny wrought-iron balconies, housewives watered the flowers which sprouted from clay plant-pots and old olive-oil tins.

Paco wound down the window of his 1932 Fiat Balilla – the only thing of any value that he actually owned – and breathed in deeply. He loved the early mornings. In the summer, they were the only time of day when it was really cool, the one short period when the smells of the city – geraniums, horse dung and roasted coffee – were not smothered by the thick, hot air.

He turned to look at his passenger. 'You know, Felipe, I should never have left the village,' he said.

Fat Felipe cupped his hands over his belly. 'What's wrong with the town?' he asked.

'Life is so much more complicated here than it is in the *pueblo*. You don't get many murders in the villages, but when there is one, everybody immediately knows who did it.'

'If Madrid was like that, we'd be out of a job,' Felipe said philosophically.

'Villages are so straightforward. You have your land, you cultivate it – and that's all.'

'And you earn twenty-five pesetas a month – and that's in a good month,' Felipe pointed out. 'You couldn't run a fine car like this on five *duros* a month.'

'True,' Paco admitted. 'But if I still lived in the village, I wouldn't really need a car, would I?'

They had been driving up the Paseo de la Castellana, the widest street in Madrid. Now Paco made a right turn, and looking out of his side window, thought how different this area was to his own *barrio*. Downtown, the apartment blocks looked like dominoes, standing on end and huddled together, with only the occasional side-street to break the monotony. In the Barrio de Salamanca, the buildings were wider and had a sweeping grandeur which was missing from the cramped dwellings in the centre.

There were other differences, too. Where a downtown block would have a solid wooden door which led into a narrow hallway, these blocks had expensive glass doors through which could be seen plush foyers watched over by uniformed doormen. While a thin layer of plaster and a couple of coats of paint was considered sufficient decoration for the outsides of houses downtown, here the plaster was moulded into elaborate curlicues, flowers and heads, which ran all along the frontage.

'That's where Calvo Sotelo lives,' Felipe said, pointing to a block they were just passing.

'How do you know that?' Paco asked.

Felipe grinned. 'I show an interest in politics,' he said.

'And I don't,' Paco agreed.

He wanted nothing at all to do with any of the factions which were screaming at each other in parliament, or fighting it out on the streets. He was neutral. Yet despite that, the further he drove into the Barrio de Salamanca, the more he felt he was getting deeper and deeper into enemy territory.

*

The doorman was dressed in a scarlet uniform, complete with a peaked cap as ostentatious as an admiral's. He gave the two detectives a sweeping glance, but did not speak.

Paco produced his warrant card. 'We're here to see Doña Mercedes Méndez Segovia,' he said.

There were places where showing the card would have had an immediate effect, with everyone rushing around getting the policeman whatever it was he wanted. The doorman in the scarlet uniform merely looked down his nose and said, 'Do you have an appointment?'

'Yes. For nine o'clock.'

The doorman shrugged, as if to say that if Doña Mercedes wanted to waste her time talking to policemen, it was no business of his. 'Go down the corridor and take the first lift,' he said. 'The señora and her family live on the third floor.'

As the two detectives walked down the corridor, Paco felt a knot tightening in his stomach. This was not his territory at all. He was used to investigating cases in seedy bars downtown and in cramped workmen's blocks to the south of the city. He didn't like working under these conditions – didn't like the fact that, though he'd agreed to it, he was having to go and see Mercedes Méndez, instead of telling her to come and

36

see him. Put simply, he resented having to tread on alien ground and, in all probability, playing the game by the other people's rules. Yet what choice did he have? When you were dealing with important people, you had to be prepared to eat a little shit.

The lift was almost the size of Paco's living-room, the fitted blue carpet on the third-floor corridor so thick that Felipe's heavy boots made virtually no sound.

'How are we going to play this?' Felipe asked when they reached the door of the apartment. 'Am I the big, ignorant one again?'

Paco shook his head. 'It wouldn't work. Not with these people.'

'So what will I be?'

'You'll be quiet,' Paco said, forcing himself to grin.

He rang the bell. The door was opened, almost immediately, by a plain girl with a weather-beaten face, dressed in a maid's uniform. 'You are the police?' she asked.

'Yes, we are the police,' Paco confirmed. 'And who are you? Paulina?'

The girl nodded, then said. 'You must follow me.'

Christ! Paco thought, in this building even the maids think they have the right to order us around.

Paulina led them through the main door and down a long corridor even more plushly carpeted than the one outside. At the end of the corridor, the maid stopped and knocked lightly on an impressive oak door.

'Enter,' called a woman's voice from the other side of it.

The maid opened the door, then stepped aside to let the two policemen go in.

Paco glanced quickly around him. The room he had just entered was a large one which looked out onto the street, or would have done if the long velvet curtains hadn't been drawn to exclude the morning sunlight. The sofas – two of them – were covered in velvet, too, as were the armchairs. The largest coffee table Paco had ever seen – made of inlaid teak – dominated the space between the seats. A huge crystal chandelier hung down from the ceiling.

'It's the police, madam,' the maid said to a woman who was sitting on one of the sofas.

So this was Doña Mercedes Méndez Segovia. She was in her late thirties, Paco guessed. Her hair was purest black, her eyes arrogant, her whole expression haughty. She was wearing a long, green silk dress which revealed a firm figure – and probably cost as much as a police inspector earned in a couple of months. Paco found himself taking an instant dislike to her, but even seen through the eyes of prejudice, he had to admit that she was a very handsome woman.

Doña Mercedes was not alone. Next to her was a man perhaps ten years younger than she was. The overall impression he gave was one of thinness. Thin nose. Thin lips. Thin, artistic hands. His resemblance to the woman was striking, though there was nothing the least effeminate about him. He was there, Paco thought, as a witness; so that if Doña Mercedes wanted to make a complaint later, she would have someone to back her up.

'You can go, Ortega,' Doña Mercedes told the maid in a voice which was as imperious as her general demeanour. Then she turned to the detectives and said, 'You may sit down if you wish,' in just about the same tone.

Felipe, who never needed that kind of invitation twice, immediately plopped down into one of the armchairs. Paco, at a more leisurely pace, sat down on the second sofa.

'I understand you wish to ask me some questions,' Doña Mercedes said.

Instead of answering her, Paco turned his attention to the young man. 'Am I to take it that you're Don Carlos?' he asked.

The other man jumped slightly. 'Yes . . . yes, that is correct. I am Carlos Méndez Segovia.'

'And it really was you who phoned me last night?'

A nod. 'Correct again.'

'Then perhaps my first question should be to you. How did you know I was the one to call?'

'Señora Umbral phoned . . .'

'Who is Señora Umbral?'

'She owns a dress shop on Alcalá.'

'I see. Go on.'

'She phoned to say that the police had been making enquiries.' Don Carlos waved his slim hands. 'Once we knew that, the rest was easy.'

'Easy?' Paco repeated. 'In what way?'

'My husband is a man of considerable influence,' Doña Mercedes interrupted. 'He simply called the Ministry of the Interior.'

Which puts you in your place, Ruiz, Paco thought. But aloud, he said, 'The other thing that puzzled me at the time, Don Carlos, was that you didn't ask me *why* I wanted to see Doña Mercedes.'

'But we already knew – and from the same source,' Don Carlos explained. 'A woman was found murdered in Retiro Park, yesterday morning. She was wearing a dress which perhaps once belonged to my sister.'

'Almost definitely belonged to her,' Paco corrected him. He turned to Doña Mercedes. 'Could you tell me how the dead girl came to acquire the dress?'

'It was a blue dress with a neckline like this, wasn't it?' Doña Mercedes asked, tracing a pattern round her own throat with her slim, aristocratic fingers.

'Yes, it was,' Paco agreed.

'Then I have no idea how she got it. I gave it away to the rag-and-bone man some months ago.'

Paco raised a sceptical eyebrow. 'It was an expensive dress,' he said. 'Silk.'

'It was last season's fashion,' said Doña Mercedes, managing to lard her words with contempt at the inspector's ignorance. 'It, and all the other clothes in the same style, simply had to go.'

'Do you always give away your clothes after only a year?' Paco asked, pretending not to notice her tone.

Doña Mercedes shook her head. 'Not always, no. I have certain items – my riding clothes, for example – which stay in style for much longer than a year. But if you were to look through my wardrobes,' she continued, making it plain that this was not an invitation, 'you wouldn't find many dresses more than a few months old.'

'This rag-and-bone man,' Paco said. 'Can you describe him to me?'

Doña Mercedes laughed, 'You surely don't imagine I handed it over to the *chatarro* myself, do you?'

'Then who . . .?'

'I instructed one of the servants to do it.'

'Which one?'

'I really can't remember.'

'In that case,' Paco said, 'I'll have to interrogate them all.'

Doña Mercedes looked outraged at the very suggestion. 'I cannot possibly permit such a thing,' she said.

The knot in Paco's stomach tightened another couple of twists. She – or her husband – probably could prevent him from talking to the servants if they really wanted to. 'I'm afraid you don't have any choice over the question of interrogations, señora,' he bluffed. 'A serious crime has been committed and one way or another, I *will* talk to the servants – even if it takes a judge's warrant.'

Brother and sister exchanged the sort of glance that passes between people who know each other so well that they no longer need words to communicate. 'Surely, if you put your mind to it, you could remember which servant you gave to,' Don Carlos suggested.

Doña Mercedes closed her eyes and made a show of searching her memory. 'I think it was Paulina,' she said after some seconds had passed. 'Yes, I am almost sure she was the one. Go and find her, Carlos.'

Don Carlos sprang to his feet, like an eager office boy. 'I'll come with you,' Paco told him.

'You'll wait here,' Doña Mercedes said firmly.

Don Carlos opened the door and disappeared into the corridor.

'I would offer you some refreshment,' Doña Mercedes said, coldly and unconvincingly, 'but I expect that you are eager to finish your work here and be on your way.'

'Quite,' Paco agreed.

In the corner of the room was a grandfather clock in a walnut case. Paco fixed his eyes on the large brass pendulum and watched it swing from one side to the other. Click . . . click . . . click. . . .

A minute passed, then two, then three. 'Your brother seems to be taking a long time to find the girl,' Paco said.

'Perhaps he's trying to calm her down,' Doña Mercedes suggested.

'And why should he need to do that?'

Doña Mercedes' face showed fresh contempt at his apparent naivety. 'She's a country girl. Anything that isn't covered in animal dung frightens her.'

It was another five minutes before Don Carlos returned. 'The girl is ready to see you now,' he said.

Paco stood up. 'Where is she?'

Don Carlos seemed surprised by the question. 'In the kitchen, of course.'

Of course! Her room would be too small to contain three people, and, as a mere maid, she couldn't very well be allowed the use of one of the family rooms, even for something as potentially serious as an interrogation by the police.

'Where is the kitchen?' Paco asked.

'I'll show you.'

Paco turned to Doña Mercedes. 'Goodbye, señora.'

The woman inclined her head, more in a gesture of dismissal than farewell. Felipe forced himself to rise from his comfortable chair, and the two policemen followed the young señorito out of the room.

Chapter Eight

The kitchen was a long narrow room. White tiles covered the walls, many of them cracked. The work surfaces were chipped, and the only natural light came from a small window almost at ceiling level. The place was only twenty steps away from the luxurious salon they had just left, yet it was in a different world. But then it didn't really matter how run-down it looked, Paco thought, because it was only the servants who saw it.

Paulina was sitting at the table, her elbows on the rough board, her hands clenched together as if in prayer. It was not until Don Carlos touched her lightly on the shoulder that she even looked up.

'These gentlemen wish to ask you their questions now,' Don Carlos said soothingly. 'You must answer them truthfully, as I've already explained. Do you understand that?'

'Yes, sir,' the girl replied, her eyes wide with something approaching terror.

Don Carlos turned to Paco. 'Do you wish me to stay?'

'That will not be necessary, señor.'

'But when you wish to leave . . .?'

'Paulina will show us out.'

'Well, if you're sure there's nothing more I can do . . .'

'There isn't. Thank you, sir.'

Don Carlos nodded and stepped into the corridor, closing the door behind him. Paco pulled out a chair and sat down opposite the maid. 'Where are you from, Paulina?' he asked softly.

'El Soto del Principe,' the girl said in a whisper.

Paco smiled. 'I'm not sure I know exactly where that is,' he said. 'Is it a big place, like Madrid?'

Paulina laughed, as he'd intended her to. 'No, it's only a village,' she said.

'And what does your father do?'

'He has a little land.'

'But not enough to support his entire family, eh?'

'No,' Paulina agreed. 'Not enough for that.'

Paco held out his packet of cigarettes to the girl, and when she shook her head, he lit one up himself. 'Your mistress told us she instructed you to give some of her clothes away to a rag-and-bone man,' he said. 'Is that correct?'

The girl gave a barely perceptible nod of her head.

'What kind of clothes were they?'

'There . . . there was a blue silk dress.'

'What else?'

The question seemed to confuse the girl. 'I don't understand what you're asking.'

'Doña Mercedes said she gets rid of a lot of clothes that way. What else was there with the dress?'

The natural red of Paulina's face was intensified by a fierce blush. 'There was . . . a . . . I don't remember,' she stuttered.

Or to put it another way, Paco thought, her peasant imagination was incapable of conjuring up any imaginary clothes without help. 'Is it always your job to give the clothes away?' he asked.

'I . . . no . . . it was the first time I'd ever done it.'

'And the last?'

'Yes.'

'So on just this one occasion, your mistress entrusted you with that particular task, and it's never been repeated?'

'That's right.'

'Who normally gives the clothes away?'

'I don't know. You'll have to ask the other servants.'

Paco sighed. If only he could do that. But he'd been pushing his luck to get as far as he had. 'Tell me about the rag-and-bone man,' he said.

'What about him?'

'Did he come here, to the apartment, or did you have to go out looking for him?'

'I heard him in the street. You know what they're like. They drive their carts slowly along the road and shout *chatarrero* at the tops of their voices. They're so loud that you can hear them even from the back of the apartment.'

'So you heard him and you took the dress – and the other clothes which you can't remember now – down to the street.'

'That's right.'

'Did he pay you anything for them?'

'No, he . . . he just took them.'

'The silk dress alone was worth a lot of money. Why didn't you ask him for a few *duros*?'

Paulina gazed down at the table. 'I just didn't think to,' she mumbled.

'What did he look like?' Paco asked.

'He was a gypsy.'

'Most of the rag-and-bone men are. Was he tall or short?'

'About the same height as you.'

'His hair colour?'

'The same as yours.'

'Did he have a moustache?'

'I don't remember. It was weeks ago.'

'What about his cart?'

Paulina shrugged. 'It was just a cart.'

'Was it pulled by a horse or a donkey?'

'I don't know.'

Paco stood up.

'Is that all?' the girl asked, the relief evident in her voice.

'That's all,' Paco confirmed. 'You can show us out now.'

*

The traffic ahead had been reduced to a crawl, and Paco – who would have liked to make some speed, if only to relieve his frustration – was forced to shift down to second gear.

'Do you know what really pisses me off about that stuck-up bitch back there?' he asked Felipe.

The fat constable scratched his belly. 'No,' he said. 'What does piss you off?'

'That she's so confident of their own position – her own superiority – she didn't even bother to come up with a half-way decent lie.'

Felipe wormed his finger through his bulging shirt and scratched his belly button. 'You don't believe that the rag-and-bone man exists?' he asked.

'If he does, Paulina never saw him.'

Ahead of them they could see what was causing the delay. A mule train, half a dozen or so teams of the animals each pulling a bright blue cart painted with vines and flowers, was progressing slowly down the street.

'They should keep mule trains out of Madrid,' Paco growled.

'If they did, where would we get our charcoal, olive oil and wine from?' Felipe wondered.

It was true, Paco thought. Without the mule trains, so many goods would never be moved. It was strange. Spain prided itself on being a modern, European country, but in so many ways, it hadn't changed since he was a child. Enough of abstract speculation – he was right behind the mule carts now, and he signalled to overtake.

'What makes you so sure that Paulina never saw the rag-and-bone man?' Felipe asked.

'I'm sure because she comes from the same peasant stock as I do,' Paco said.

'You're being – what's the word – enigmatic,' Felipe said.

Paco grinned. 'Sorry, I wasn't meaning to be. Your mother was a washer-woman wasn't she, Felipe?'

'That's right,' the constable agreed. 'I was brought up by the side of the river.'

'So you're a city boy, through and through. And you can't have any idea how a peasant thinks.'

Felipe stuck an exploratory finger in his left ear. 'How does a peasant think?'

'A peasant has a nose for a deal. They're all born with it. Sometimes, it's the only thing they've got in their favour.'

'So?'

'So it's simply inconceivable to me that a girl like this Paulina would hand over an expensive silk dress without expecting something in return.'

Felipe removed his finger from his ear, and inspected the wax on the end of it. 'Maybe she did get something in return, and simply lied about it,' he suggested.

'Then there was the animal,' Paco continued, ignoring the implication because it didn't fit in with his theory.

'What animal?' Felipe said.

'I asked her whether the car was pulled by a horse or a donkey. She said she didn't remember. I wasn't surprised when she couldn't describe the rag-and-bone man, but a girl from the country would remember the beast he had with him.'

'So what you're suggesting, *jefe*, is that the family instructed her to lie?'

'Of course I am. That's why Don Carlos – who seems to be little more than his sister's errand boy – was out of the room for such a long time. He was briefing the poor, frightened kid on what she should say to us.'

Felipe attacked his right ear with the same methodical approach he had adopted with his left. 'Are you sure you're not letting your personal prejudices cloud your judgement?' he asked.

'Personal prejudices!' Paco repeated, as he turned off Velazquez and narrowly avoided a collision with a truck full of live pigs which was coming from the other direction. 'What personal prejudices?'

Felipe shrugged his fat shoulders. 'You'll admit you don't like Doña Mercedes won't you?' he asked.

'I don't like anybody who immediately treats me as if I was an insect that's just crawled in under the door,' Paco replied.

Felipe nodded. 'And because you don't like her, you automatically assume she's lying, and got her brother to tell the maid to lie, too.'

For some reason he couldn't explain, Paco was starting to feel defensive. 'That seems a reasonable assumption to me,' he said.

Felipe examined the results of his labours on his right ear. 'Reasonable, yes,' he admitted. 'But only because you haven't left yourself open to considering the alternatives.'

'And what exactly are they?'

'Say, for the sake of argument, that Paulina wasn't lying to save her employers. Say she was lying to cover her own back.'

'And why should she do that?' Paco asked, though he already had an inkling of where Felipe was going.

'Put yourself in Paulina's place,' Felipe said. 'Doña Mercedes gives her a dress which she could never afford herself, and tells her to throw it out. You say peasants are good at sniffing out deals – well, maybe she did. But she knows she can get a better deal than the one offered by the rag-and-bone man.'

'So she sells it to someone else?'

'Or gives it away to a friend. It doesn't really matter, because, either way, when Don Carlos tells her the police want to talk to her, she flies into a panic.'

'Go on,' Paco said.

'She can't tell us she's disobeyed her mistress, because she might lose her job,' Felipe continued. 'On the other hand, she can't describe the rag-and-bone man, because there never was one. Perhaps that's why Don

Carlos was out of the room for so long. Maybe Doña Mercedes was right, and you were wrong. Isn't it possible that he really was trying to calm her down?'

They had reached the Plaza de la Cibeles, the end of the fashionable side of Alcalá. To their right lay the gothic Palace of Communications, which was so impressive that tourists often mistook it for the world-famous Prado Museum, and wandered in to find no masterpieces, but scores of clerks selling stamps and registering parcels. Was Felipe right? Paco wondered, as he swung the steering wheel round. Had Don Carlos been doing nothing more than helping a country mouse get over her nervousness before she met the big, bad policemen?

The statue of Cibeles herself lay ahead of them now, sitting in her chariot pulled by two powerful lions, surrounded by the fountains which spouted in her honour. Paco looked into her carved face, almost as if he thought that would give him inspiration. But the Mother of All the Gods merely stared stonily down at him, each haughty line of her features suggesting that the death of an unknown girl in Retiro Park was far too insignificant an event to merit her attention.

Which was pretty much the attitude Doña Mercedes adopted, too, Paco said to himself.

He tried to put himself in Paulina's shoes, and decided that Felipe's reconstruction of her actions and motives made a lot more sense than the idea that the wife of one of Spain's leading politicians would lie about what she'd done with her dress.

'Well, what do you think?' Felipe asked.

'I think I hate you,' Paco told him.

Felipe grinned. 'Being hated, now and again, is what partners are for. But can you honestly tell me, *jefe*, that everything I've said since we left the Herrera apartment has been a load of shit?'

'No I can't,' Paco admitted in disgust. '*Joder*! Another good theory gone out of the window.'

Chapter Nine

When Felipe announced that the new bar he'd discovered was close to the Montaña barracks, Paco's first reaction was to suggest that they should go somewhere else. Then he told himself he was being stupid. It was nearly half a lifetime since he'd finished his military service, he argued, and it should surely be possible to confront the ghosts of his past without flinching. Yet as they sat at the pavement table, waiting for the *raciones* Felipe had ordered, he found his eyes slowly and reluctantly climbing the grassy slope up to the barracks. And when those eyes finally settled on the Montaña itself, he felt a shudder run through his body.

The barracks squatted malevolently on the crest of the hill. Its windows seemed to gaze down disapprovingly at Paco, and the slanting roof above them looked like one long, disapproving eyebrow.

'*Papa knows an important official who can get you an exemption,*' Pilar had said, all those years ago when he'd received his call-up papers.

'*I don't want exemption. It's my duty to serve,*' the young Paco had replied, with the idealism of youth. '*Anyway, I should have thought he'd be glad to see the back of me.*'

'*Papa just wants me to be happy.*'

And wasn't that the truth? He wanted her to be happy, and not just eventually, but at the very moment she wanted it. Which was why he agreed to give into her tearful demand that she be allowed to marry the young engineering student from the country who had just enrolled at the University of Valladolid. It would have been better for all of them, Paco thought, if Pilar's father had been firmer.

He ran his eyes along the lower wall which enclosed the drill square he had marched endlessly up and down as a raw recruit, and wondered if he'd have given his wife the same answer if he'd known then what he knew now. Probably. His time in the military had changed his life for ever – and not for the better – but his sense of duty was still with him, hanging like a great weight round his neck.

A waiter arrived, and placed two earthenware dishes on the table. One contained kidneys cooked in sherry, the other calamar rings in batter. They were accompanied by two hunks of bread the size of small mountains.

'Now this is what I call a good snack,' Fat Felipe said enthusiastically, spearing one of the juicy calamares and popping it into his mouth.

Paco forced himself to turn away from the barracks. You may be able to face your ghosts, he thought, but you can't alter what they've made you into.

'Why don't you have something to eat while it's still hot, *jefe*?' Felipe urged him.

Paco tried one of the kidneys. It was good – very good – but he didn't really feel like food at that moment, and when he'd chewed the kidney for a few seconds, he swallowed it as if it were an indigestion pill.

'No one else on earth eats the way we Spaniards do,' Felipe said, attacking his fourth or fifth calamar. 'If it was an Olympic event, we'd win the gold medal every time.'

Paco broke off a small section of bread and rolled it moodily across the table until it was the shape of a pellet. 'I'm going to go back to that apartment,' he said.

Felipe stopped munching. 'You're going to do *what*?' he asked.

'Go back to that apartment.'

The fat constable laid his fork on the table. 'Tell me it's not the Herrera apartment you're talking about,' he said.

'You were right when you said I let my prejudices against the family influence the way I handled the interrogation,' Paco told his partner. 'This time, I'll make sure I do it right.'

'You were pushing your luck the first time. Try it again, and Doña Mercedes will complain to her husband. And then Herrera will get his pals at the Ministry to roast you alive.'

'Doña Mercedes won't even know I've been there,' Paco argued. 'Paulina will answer the door, and I'll walk her down the corridor and say what I should have said this morning.'

'And when she tells her mistress . . .'

'If she's any sense, she won't do that – because if she does, she'll be landing herself in trouble.'

Felipe looked down at his food, and then back at Paco. 'Well, they say that the condemned man always enjoys a hearty breakfast, don't they? So if you wouldn't mind giving me a few more minutes to finish off this . . .'

'I said, I'm going back to the Herrera apartment,' Paco told him. 'You're not coming with me.'

Felipe narrowed his eyes and looked suspiciously at his *jefe*. 'Why are you leaving me behind?' he asked. 'Is it because you don't want to drag me down into the shit with you?'

'There'll be no shit . . .'

'Well, then?'

'. . . but it's always better to be safe than sorry.'

*

Paco had noticed that the corridor carpet was blue on his last visit, but now he realized that it was exactly the same shade of blue as the Falangists' shirts. He wondered whether it was just coincidence. It didn't seem likely.

He reached the apartment door, rang the bell, and waited for Paulina to appear. It would all work out just as he'd promised, he told himself. He'd take Paulina down the corridor, and within a minute she'd be telling him whether she'd sold the dress or given it away. Whichever was the case, it wouldn't be long before he had the name and address of the dead girl.

The door opened, and Paco's heart sank as he looked at the complete stranger in a maid's uniform. How much chance was there now of talking to Paulina without Eduardo Herrera finding out? And when the politician did, would he, as Felipe had predicted, be so furious that he'd get on to his friends at the Ministry and demand that heads roll?

'Can I help you, señor?' the maid asked.

His best course of action would be turn around and walk away, Paco thought. That was certainly what any sane, sensible man would do. 'I'm from the police,' he said briskly. 'Go and tell Paulina that I want to see her immediately.'

'Paulina?' the girl repeated, pronouncing the word as if it were in some kind of foreign language.

'Paulina Ortega. Don't act as if you don't know who I'm talking about. She's one of the maids.'

The girl bit her lower lip. 'But . . . but she's . . .'

'She's what?'

'She's . . . she's . . .'

'Out with it, girl!'

The maid, her eyes fixed firmly on the ground, was already backing away. 'Wait here,' she mumbled. And then she closed the door behind her.

Paco checked his watch, then lit a cigarette. He had almost smoked it down to his fingers when the door opened again. This time, he found himself looking at a large, dark-complexioned man of about thirty-five who was wearing a red and white striped waistcoat and black trousers with red fluting. 'I am Luis, Don Eduardo's valet,' he said, his tone suggesting that he expected Paco to be impressed, and his accent parodying the upper-class speech of his mistress. 'One of the maids has just been to see me in a very distressed state. She says you claim to be a policeman.'

'I am a policeman,' Paco told him. 'I was here earlier in the day.'

'I know nothing of that,' Luis told him, 'and before I say any more, I want to see some identification.'

Paco took out his warrant card and handed it to Luis. The valet made a great show of studying it. 'So what business do you have here?' he asked curtly, giving the card back.

'I wish to speak to Paulina Ortega,' Paco said.

'That is not possible.'

'Why?'

'Because she isn't here.'

'Then where is she?'

The valet shrugged. 'Who knows? It's her day off. She could be anywhere in the city.'

'Her day off?' Paco repeated.

'That's what I said.'

'Then why was she here when I called earlier?'

'Because she knew that you wanted to speak . . .' Luis began, before seeing the trap that the policeman had led him into.

'I thought you didn't know I'd been here before,' Paco said.

'I . . . I remember now,' Luis answered unconvincingly.

'And Paulina was in her working clothes. She didn't know I wanted to talk to her. Even *I* didn't know until after I'd talked to Doña Mercedes. So let's cut the crap. Where is she?'

'It's like I told you, it's her day off,' Luis said, starting to pull himself together again.

'We've already established that she was working this—'

'None of the servants ever have the whole day free. She was on duty until noon.'

Who was the valet covering up for? Paco wondered. Paulina? No, he wouldn't stick his neck out so far for a mere maid. So it was back to the family – which meant that his first instinct had been right, and the girl's murder was somehow political.

'You're lying to me, aren't you?' Paco said accusingly.

The valet had recovered enough to allow a thin smile to come to his lips. 'Am I?' he asked.

Like his mistress, he was so bloody sure of himself, Paco thought – so convinced that as long as he was under the protection of Eduardo Herrera, no harm could come to him.

'Why won't Doña Mercedes let me talk to Paulina?' Paco said. 'What's she afraid the girl's going to tell me?'

The smile on Luis's face had become a full-blown smirk. 'The mistress is afraid of nothing Paulina or anyone else might tell you,' he said, 'because *she* is a great lady of Spain, and *you* are a mere inspector of police.'

'What about you?' Paco asked.

'Me?' the valet said.

'Do you know what happened to the dress? Can you tell me the identity of the dead girl in the park?'

'Of course not,' Luis replied, and Paco was almost – but not quite – certain that he was lying. The valet took a step backwards. 'You had your chance to talk to Paulina this morning,' he said. 'Now, as far as this household is concerned, the matter is closed.'

'The matter's far from closed,' Paco said hotly. 'A young woman has died, and somebody is going to have to pay for it.'

'Perhaps somebody will,' Luis agreed. 'But it will not be anyone from this family.' He took a further step backwards into the apartment. 'Goodbye, Inspector. If your career matters to you, it would be wisest for you not to come here again.'

For several seconds after Luis had gone, Paco stood staring at the thick oak door which separated him from the truth. He would be back, he promised it. Oh yes, he would be back.

Chapter Ten

The message had said that Captain Hidalgo wanted to see him urgently, but now that Paco was actually in his chief's office, Hidalgo seemed in no hurry to talk – seemed, in fact, absorbed by the pile of reports he was shuffling in his big hands.

'The bloody thing must be somewhere amongst this lot,' he said agitatedly, without bothering to explain exactly which bloody thing he was looking for.

Paco, standing to attention, shifted his weight slightly, and wondered what could have reduced his boss to this nervous state. He remembered Hidalgo advancing under fire, as cool as if he was taking an afternoon *paseo* to work off his lunch. He recalled the captain facing down a general who wanted to put his unit at unnecessary risk. This man raking his fingers through his grey hair was a completely different person. What the hell had happened to him?

Hidalgo extracted one of the reports from the wad. 'This is it,' he said, scanning it quickly. 'There's been a shooting incident near the socialist headquarters in the *casa del pueblo*. Two of their militiamen were gunned down from a passing car.'

'What's that got to do with me, sir?' Paco asked.

'We have to stop these political killings,' Hidalgo said woodenly, as if he were a very bad actor reading a hastily written script. 'And the only way we can do that is by bringing some of these young thugs to justice.'

'We both know that's almost impossible,' Paco reminded him. 'The killers don't even know their victims, so, unless we catch them in the act, there's nothing to connect them with the murders.'

'Exactly,' Hidalgo agreed. 'That's why, if I'm ever to get an arrest, I'm going to have to put my best investigator on it.' He smiled, but without much conviction. 'And my best investigator is you.'

'I'm already working on a case,' Paco said.

'From what you told me yesterday, that seems to be a pretty straightforward domestic investigation that anyone could handle,' Hidalgo said. 'No point in wasting my best man on that.'

'Yesterday, I thought it was straightforward,' Paco told him. 'Today, I think I could be dealing with a whole can of worms.'

'Even if the case isn't as simple as it looks, it's far less important than the new one I'm assigning you to,' Hidalgo argued.

Paco's head was starting to pound. 'Suppose I refuse to be reassigned,' he said.

He was expecting his chief to explode, but instead Hidalgo only sighed. 'The police force isn't some kind of democratic debating society,' he said. 'You have your orders, Inspector. Your only option is to carry them out.'

Paco took a deep breath. It made him feel a little calmer. 'I've lost count of how many tribesmen I killed in Morocco,' he said, 'but I do remember one of them in particular. He had you in his sights at the time. At that range, he couldn't have missed.'

Hidalgo looked down at his desk. 'I remember that, too,' he said. 'And I'll always be in your debt for it.'

'I never asked for a favour in return. I never expected any special treatment.'

'No,' Hidalgo admitted. 'You didn't.'

'I'm asking a favour now, *jefe*,' Paco said. 'Please let me stay on this case.'

Hidalgo spread his big, beefy hands helplessly in front of him. 'I can't.'

'You're the captain . . .'

'Which gives me a little power, but not much.'

'It's because I went back to the Herreras' apartment, isn't it?' Paco demanded.

'I don't know,' Hidalgo said. 'The order to put someone else on the case came directly from the Minister's private secretary. People like him don't bother to explain things to people like me. Besides, even without a direct order from the top, I'd probably have removed you from the investigation.'

'Why?'

'Because of the whispers I've been hearing.'

'What kind of whispers?'

Hidalgo shook his head. 'I can't tell you that. Just take it from an old comrade that though it might not look like it, this is for your own good.'

'I shall lodge a formal protest,' Paco said.

It had taken a long time for the signs of anger to reach to Hidalgo's eyes, but they had finally come, and the eyes blazed. And yet even now, it was not so much anger at Paco as at the situation. 'You'd be a fool to make a protest,' he growled. 'No one would listen to you, and it would count against you in the future.'

He was right, Paco thought. It would count heavily against him. 'May I go now?' he asked.

'Yes, you may,' Hidalgo said. 'And where you may go is to the *casa del pueblo*, where you will investigate the murders of the two socialist militiamen. Is that clearly understood, Inspector?'

'At your orders, sir,' Paco said.

*

By the time Paco and Felipe reached the Calle de San Mateo, the bodies of the two murdered militiamen had already been removed, and – apart from the group of young boiler-suited men talking excitedly by the main door of the *casa del pueblo* – there was nothing abnormal about the street.

Paco pulled out his warrant card. 'Did anyone see anything?' he asked.

Several of the youths started talking at once, then they all fell quiet and a thin boy with steel spectacles stepped forward.

'I saw it,' he said. 'I was walking just behind them when it happened.' He shuddered. 'I couldn't have been more than three or four metres away from them.'

'And what happened?'

'I heard this car behind me. It was going slowly at first, then suddenly it accelerated. Then it was past me, and I heard this cracking sound – like fireworks it was – and Julio and Martin, they . . . they just sort of started jerking, first this way and then that, and there was blood everywhere, and I . . . I . . .'

'Did you see what make of car it was?' Paco asked.

'It was a big black Fiat.'

Of which there were thousands in Madrid. 'Did you get the number?' Paco said.

'No, it was covered with a piece of sacking.'

Not that the registration number would have been much use anyway. Chances were the car had been stolen just before the murders, and dumped immediately afterwards. 'What about the people who did the shooting?'

'I think there were three of them in the car,' the boy said.

'Yes, three,' another boy agreed. 'The driver and the two with guns. They were Falangists.'

'How do you know that?'

'Because they were all wearing those blue shirts.'

'Did you get a look at their faces?'

Both boys shook their heads. 'They were wearing masks,' the one with the steel spectacles said.

Paco looked around the group. 'Has anyone got anything to add to what these two have just said?' he asked. 'Any little detail they might have left out?'

Some of the young men shook their heads, others looked down at the ground as if they were ashamed they couldn't be of more help. 'Collect the names of everyone who was a witness,' Paco told the boy with the steel spectacles. 'My constable will be round in the morning to talk to you all.'

*

'What did you mean when you said *I'd* be questioning them in the morning?' Felipe asked, when they were comfortably seated in the nearest bar.

'I meant just what I said,' Paco told him. 'You *will* be questioning them.'

'And what will you be doing?'

'Look, I'll tell what I think about this case,' Paco said. 'We'll never be able to link the car to the killers, and we have no description of them. Even if, by some incredible stroke of luck, we did happen to get some clue which led us to them, you can bet your last *duro* that they'll all have alibis.'

Felipe took a sip of his wine. 'So?'

'It's a waste of time investigating this case, and there's no point in wasting two people's time.'

'You still haven't answered my question,' Felipe pointed out.

'And what question was that?'

'What will you be doing?'

Paco lit a cigarette. 'The captain's assigned Inspector Matute and Constable Zabala to the Retiro murder. Zabala's all right, but Matute's the one in charge, and he doesn't know his arse from a hole in the ground.'

'I still don't see . . .' Felipe began. And then, suddenly, he did. 'You're not dropping the Retiro case, are you?'

'No,' Paco agreed. 'I'm not.'

'Even after the captain warned you.'

'*Because* the captain warned me. He said I was his best investigator, and that wasn't just flattery. If anybody can solve the case, it's me.'

'You don't know who you're tangling with,' Felipe said.

'Do you?'

The fat constable shook his head. 'No, but I've got sense enough not to try and find out,' he said.

Chapter Eleven

'Tell me what you know about Eduardo Herrera Moreno,' Paco said to Ramón as they sat drinking wine at their customary table in the *Cabo de Trafalgar*.

Ramón ran a finger through his neat, bureaucratic moustache. 'Herrera?' he said. 'Why would I know anything about him?'

'He's a politician, and you work in a ministry. Besides, you're an incurable collector of information – any information.'

Ramón smiled, as if he took that as a compliment. Then the smile was replaced by a look of suspicion. 'Why this sudden interest in Don Eduardo?' he asked.

Because someone must have had a hell of a lot of influence to make the captain take me off the case, Paco thought – and Herrera's the only name I can come up with.

'Well?' Ramón said. 'What is your interest?'

'I was reading about him in the paper this morning, and I just wondered what kind of man he is.'

'He's a great political visionary,' Ramón said enthusiastically, 'a man in whose hands Spain would be—'

'I'm not interested in his politics,' Paco interrupted. 'I'm not interested in anybody's politics, as you well know. What's he like as a person?'

'He's extremely wealthy,' Ramón said.

'Where does he get his money from? Did he inherit it?'

'Oh no. His father owned a small barrel-making company in Jerez. It was almost bankrupt when Don Eduardo took it over, but by hard work and diligence he built it up into an empire. Now he's part-owner of a shipyard in Bilbao, he deals on the Madrid Stock Exchange, he has banks, distribution companies – you name it, and he's probably got his finger in the pie.'

'What about his wife?'

'Her family's one of the oldest and most respected in Jerez.'

'And are they rich, too?'

'They used to be,' Ramón said. 'They were in sherry, but they lost most of their money in the Twenties.'

'So both Doña Mercedes and her brother are dependent on Herrera,' Paco said thoughtfully.

Ramón shot him another suspicious look. 'How did you know about her brother?'

'It must have been in the same article,' Paco said hastily. 'What's Herrera like as a person? And please keep away from all the political crap, if you possibly can.'

'He's a very confident man,' Ramón said. 'Makes decisions on the hoof and sticks to them – which is good, because those decisions are usually the right ones. He used to be an excellent horseman . . .'

'Used to be?'

'As far as I know, he doesn't ride any more. Probably can't find the time. Where was I? Ah yes, he's also good at languages – speaks English, French and German. He seems to have the energy of ten men and—'

'You disappoint me,' Paco interrupted.

'Disappoint you? In what way?'

'I ask you to tell me about a real, flesh-and-blood man, and all you do is give me a long, boring list of virtues. You aren't making him live for me. Tell me something to humanize him. Does he have dandruff? Bad breath? Is he involved in any scandals?'

Ramón looked shocked. 'Scandals? Certainly not!'

'He must have some faults, mustn't he?' Paco coaxed. 'Don't you know what they are? I'm beginning to suspect you don't know half as much about people as you pretend to.'

Ramón seemed stung by the remark. 'Well, he does have one weakness,' he conceded, 'but it is a weakness that's shared by many other rich men.'

'And what is it, exactly?'

'He can be irrationally mean on occasions.'

'For example?'

Ramón leant forward, as if he were about to divulge a state secret. 'He's fanatical about waste. I've heard that he has his servants take all the old candle stubs and make a new candle out of them. And he re-uses envelopes. I know that for a fact, because I've handled some of them. Imagine it: a man as rich as he is sending out important documents in second-hand envelopes.'

Yes, it did seem incredible, but it didn't get Paco any closer to discovering why Herrera had used his influence to block the investigation.

'What else can you tell me about him?' he asked Ramón. 'Does he gamble? Does he drink to excess? Is he faithful to his wife?'

There was a loud crash behind them, as the street door was flung open and Bernardo stormed into the bar. The big porter's face was almost black with anger. He saw Ramón sitting there, and stopped in his tracks. 'Have you heard the news?' he demanded across the room. 'Those fascist bastard friends of yours have killed two more of our boys today.'

'What if they have?' Ramón called back. 'It's nothing more than revenge for what those pigs in the Socialist Militia have done to the Falange.'

Bernardo strode over to the table. 'We didn't start it,' he said, wagging an angry finger at Ramón, 'but, by God, we're going to finish it!'

'Sit down, Bernardo,' Paco said firmly. 'Sit down and shut up. You shut up as well, Ramón. I've been listening to you two arguing for months. Now it's my turn to have my say.'

Bernardo hesitated for a second, then lowered himself grumpily into one of the free chairs.

Paco signalled Nacho for more wine. 'The three of us have been friends for years,' he said, 'and if even we let outside events tear that friendship apart, what the hell chance do you think the country's got of holding together?'

Ramón and Bernardo both looked a little shamefaced.

'Shake hands,' Paco ordered his friends.

Not entirely without reluctance, the two men reached across the table and shook.

'I'm sorry I lost my temper,' Bernardo said. 'I know it's not your fault the boys were killed, Ramón. But when I think of those innocent lives wasted . . .'

'How do you know they were innocent?' Ramón demanded. 'If they were militia, maybe they had blood on their own hands.'

Paco sighed. Loudly. It was going to be another one of those nights.

*

Paco climbed the wooden stairs up to his apartment, thinking, as he went, that he was a day closer to his age and the number of stairs reaching an equivalence. When he got to the second-floor landing, the door of the apartment on the left opened, and he saw Cindy Walker standing there.

She was wearing a white skirt with a hem that reached just below her knees, and a check blouse which, instead of being tucked into her waistband, hung loose. Her blonde hair spilled over her shoulders, and she was barefoot. Paco thought she looked about as unSpanish as anyone could.

'Is it always this hot at night?' she asked.

Paco laughed. 'This is just the beginning,' he said. 'Wait until we reach the end of the month.'

Cindy fanned herself with her hand, and Paco noticed that her fingernails were painted red. Her toenails, too. What a very strange race the *Yanquis* must be.

'I've made a jug of *sangría*,' Cindy said quickly, as if she was in a hurry to get the words out.

'I'm sorry?'

'I've made a jug of *sangría*. I've never done it before – I followed a recipe. I wondered if you'd like to try it, so I'll know whether it's any good or not.' She frowned. 'You do drink, don't you?'

'I'm a Spaniard,' Paco said.

'Well, then?'

'It's very kind of you, but . . .'

'And you did promise that when you had a moment, you'd tell me something about Spain.'

Had he made the promise? He didn't remember doing so. But it was still too hot to go to sleep, so why not spend a little time with Cindy? 'I'd be honoured to taste your *sangría*,' he said.

When she'd lived with Paco, Pilar was always buying things – a new coffee table, a set of traditional Castilian chairs, a floor-standing vase – and as a result the Ruizs' *salon* looked like a small, over-stocked, furniture store. Cindy's, in contrast, was spartan. All it contained was the table under the window, two upright chairs and a bookcase made of bricks and planks.

'The apartment came unfurnished,' she said, almost by way of apology. 'They're cheaper that way. I expect I'll pick up more pieces as I go along.' She pointed to one of the chairs. 'Please sit down, Señor Ruiz.'

Paco sat and looked out of the window across the well. Apart from his own, all the windows in the block were open. All the windows in Madrid would be open – with the summer heat, the apartments would have been unbearable otherwise.

Cindy disappeared into the kitchen and returned with a jug and two glasses. She almost filled the glasses with the red liquid, spooned a little fruit on top, and passed one of them over to Paco. She didn't start to drink her own, but watched, slightly anxiously, as Paco tried his.

The inspector took a sip. He could detect both brandy and Cointreau underlying the red wine, fruit juice and *gaseosa*.

'Is it good?' Cindy asked.

'Very good.'

Cindy took a swallow herself. 'Yes, I think I could get a taste for this,' she said. She put both her elbows on the table, and looked into his eyes. 'Just what's going on here?' she asked.

'In Spain?'

'Yeah. Everything seems so chaotic at the moment. I mean, I read about the political instability when I was back in the States, but until you walk around the streets for a while, you have no idea what it's really like. Why does everyone seem so angry?'

'Because they all want something different, so no one really gets anything,' Paco said.

Cindy grinned. 'That's a neat way of putting it,' she said. 'But it still doesn't tell me much.'

Paco drained his glass, and the girl filled it again.

'If we take the left for a start,' he said. 'The socialists want the government to control everything, the anarchists want the government to control nothing, and the communists want whatever it is that Moscow wants.'

'What about the right wing?'

'The Carlists, who are led by Calvo Sotelo, want a return to the last-but-one ruling monarchy. The Catholic parties want the Church to be part of the State like it used to be. The Falange wants a mass movement which will follow it unquestioningly, and the big landowners want the government to keep the peasants in line.'

'What about the army?'

'The army wants to see order. And the government – which is liberal – can't even keep itself in order.'

Cindy drained her *sangría*. 'Do you think the army'll try to take over?'

'I'm not sure myself, but most people think it will. It wouldn't be the first time in recent history. There was an attempt only three years ago, under General Sanjurjo.'

Cindy was looking at him strangely. 'You said all that almost without emotion,' she told him.

Her comment made him feel uncomfortable. 'You asked me for a summary of the situation, and that's what I gave you.'

'I know you did,' Cindy replied. 'And it was very clear. But I don't think I could be so cold if I was talking about my country going to hell in a hand-basket.'

Paco sighed. 'When I was younger, I was a conscript in the army. In Morocco.'

'What's that got to do with what we were talking about?'

'I learned a lot of things while I was over there, but the biggest lesson of all was that most of us – the ordinary people on the street – can't change the way things are. So what can we do? Well, the way I see it, we can carry out our duties and responsibilities to the best of our abilities. We can hope that if we each get our own bit right, the rest will just fall into place.'

The puzzled look in Cindy's eyes had deepened. 'What happened to you in Morocco?' she said.

'Why do you ask that?'

'Because you can be cold and detached when you're talking about Spain, but the moment you mentioned Morocco, a sort of wistfulness came over you.'

Paco drank the last of his *sangría*. 'There was a girl . . .' he began.

'And . . .?'

Paco looked up at his empty glass and the wine jug. 'And I think it's time I went to bed,' he said, standing up.

Chapter Twelve

The trees which lined the Calle Velazquez did a little to shield Paco's car from the morning sun, but even with all the windows rolled down, the inside of the Fiat was like a furnace.

Paco checked his watch. Ten past nine. He had only been sitting outside the Herreras' apartment block for just over an hour, but it felt as if he'd been there for days. He reached into his pocket, pulled out a cigarette, and lit it. The acrid smoke rasped against the walls of his lungs, but at least it gave him something other than the bloody heat to think about.

It was fourteen minutes past nine when a white Rolls-Royce Phantom, driven by a uniformed chauffeur, slid past Paco's Fiat and pulled up in front of the building. The chauffeur got out, and walked round to the back of the car. At exactly nine-fifteen, the doorman appeared, holding the door open and standing rigidly to attention. Two seconds later, a middle-aged man wearing a dark blue suit and – despite the heat – white silk gloves, stepped out onto the street and walked towards the car. The man was not alone. A male servant followed, an expensive leather briefcase in his hand.

Too important even to carry his own things, Paco thought in disgust. It had to be Herrera – the man who was screwing up his life. What was it Ramón had said about him? Rich, intelligent and decisive. He certainly seemed to fit the description. He was tall, with distinguished greying hair, quick eyes, a powerful nose, and a square jaw. Paco imagined him at the hustings, addressing the crowd in what probably sounded like the voice of God.

Herrera climbed into the car. The chauffeur took the briefcase from the other servant, placed it on the seat beside his master, closed the door, walked around to the driver's side, and got behind the wheel.

Herrera, as if he could sense Paco's inquiring gaze, glanced over his shoulder at the Fiat. The two men's eyes locked for a second. There was a questioning look in Herrera's, as if he didn't know what Paco was doing there, but suspected he was up to no good. Paco stared back, his own look challenging Herrera to leave the protection of his luxurious motor car and join him in the Fiat. Then the chauffeur engaged gear, and the Rolls-Royce was gone.

A bead of sweat rolled off Paco's forehead and landed with a plop on his cigarette. He looked down briefly at the discoloured tube, before throwing it out of the window in disgust. The car was becoming more unbearable by the minute. Paco began to wonder how much longer he would have to wait, and realized that, however uncomfortable he was, he would stay there for ever if that was what was necessary.

*

The girl who had answered the door the second time he'd visited the Herrera apartment emerged on the pavement at just after twelve-thirty. She was dressed in her maid's uniform, and had a wicker basket on her arm.

Going to the bread shop, Paco decided.

For most families, it was enough to buy bread once a day, but the Herreras, with their Rolls-Royce and their luxurious apartment, probably insisted on being served with fresh bread at every single meal.

Paco waited until the girl was a little way down the street, then got out of his car and followed her. She wasn't walking slowly, but neither was she hurrying – probably these excursions in the open air were the highlights of her day.

Paco increased his own pace, and caught up with her just as she had drawn level with a pavement café. When he tapped her on the shoulder, she jumped, then quickly turned around.

'Remember me?' he asked.

The girl's eyes were wide with fright, 'You're the policeman who came yesterday!'

'That's right.'

'W-what do you want?'

Paco put a hand on her shoulder. She stiffened, but did not try to pull away. 'What I want is to have a little talk with you,' he said. 'What's your name?'

'C-Concha.'

With his free hand, Paco pointed to one of the café tables. 'Let's sit down and have a coffee, shall we, Concha?'

The maid shook her head. 'If I'm out for too long, I'll get into trouble.'

'You're already in trouble,' Paco told her, deliberately hardening his voice. 'A lot more trouble than you could ever get into with your mistress. So why don't you sit down, and we'll see what we can do about it?'

Reluctantly the girl lowered herself onto one of the metal chairs. 'I . . . I don't know anything,' she stuttered. 'I'm only a servant.'

'Servants know more about their masters' business than the masters do themselves.'

'Not me. I'm just a simple country girl.'

A waiter appeared. 'Two coffees,' Paco said. 'I'll take mine black. And you?'

'With milk.'

The waiter nodded and left. Paco turned back to the girl. 'Yesterday, when I called, you told me that Paulina wasn't at home,' he said accusingly.

'I . . . I never. . . . I didn't tell you anything at all. I went and fetched Luis.'

'All right, so it was Luis who told me she was out,' Paco conceded. 'But it was a lie, wasn't it?'

Concha nodded. The waiter returned and placed their coffees in front of them. 'Anything else?' he asked.

'Nothing,' Paco told him.

The waiter moved on to another table, where two new customers had just sat down. Paco dropped his sugar cubes into his coffee. 'Why did Luis lie?' he asked.

'I don't know,' Concha said, studying the bubbles in Paco's cup as though they were the most fascinating thing she had ever seen.

'Where was Paulina when I called?'

'She was in her room.'

'Doing what?'

'Packing her things.'

Paco lit a cigarette. He offered the packet to the girl, but, as most country girls would have done, she shook her head.

'Why would Paulina want to pack her things in the middle of the day?' he asked.

'They told us . . .'

'Who is they?'

'Luis. Luis told us that her father had been taken ill, and she had to go home immediately.'

'But you didn't believe that?'

'No.'

'Why not?'

'Paulina comes from a little village north of Malaga.'

'I know. What's that got to do with anything?'

'I went to her room to say goodbye to her. I saw her railway ticket lying on her bed.'

'And . . .?'

'She was going to Badajoz.'

Which was almost as far from Malaga as it was from Madrid – but very convenient indeed for anyone wishing to slip across the border into Portugal.

'How did she seem?' Paco asked.

The question appeared to puzzle the maid. 'Seem?' she repeated. 'What do you mean?'

'Was she worried? Was she crying?'

Concha's brow pursed in concentration. 'I would say that she was worried, yes,' she admitted. 'But at the same time, she was very excited.'

'In what way was she excited?'

The maid searched around for a way to express herself clearly. 'Like I'd feel if I realized I had the winning ticket in the lottery,' she answered finally.

'Did she say anything to you?'

'Only that there were better ways of making money than being a servant.'

'What did she mean by that?'

'I don't know.'

'You didn't ask her?'

Concha shook her head again. 'I didn't have time.'

'Why not?'

'We heard someone coming down the corridor. It was Luis. He looked very angry. He shouted at me and told me I should get back to my work. Then he told Paulina that she'd better hurry, or she'd miss her train.'

The train bound for Badajoz, Paco thought. The train which would take her far out of his reach. 'Is there anything else you can tell me?' he asked.

'No.'

'You're sure that there isn't any little detail you might have missed out?'

'I swear by the blessed Virgin of my village, that I do not know any more.'

The blessed Virgin of her village – the wooden statue which was venerated above all else. For some of these country girls, swearing on that

67

was like swearing on her own mother's life. Paco sighed. 'Very well, you can go.'

'Am I still in trouble?' Concha asked.

'No,' Paco assured her. 'Go on – get on with your errand before they start wondering where you are.'

Concha gratefully rose to her feet. And stepped straight into the arms of Luis, the valet.

The big man effortlessly lifted her out of his way, then turned to Paco. 'You have no right to go questioning the servants,' he said belligerently, and though he kept his arms by his sides, his fists were bunched.

Paco stood up and faced him. 'Don't tell me what rights I do and don't have,' he said. 'What would you, a servant – another man's lackey – know about rights?'

Luis squeezed his fists into even tighter balls. The valet had about four centimetres and fifteen kilos on him, Paco estimated, but he thought he could take the man if he had to. And even if he couldn't, he'd at least like to give it a try.

'Keep out of the family's private affairs,' Luis said.

'Where murder's involved there's no such things as family privacy. I am a police officer pursuing an investigation into—'

'You haven't been involved in the case since yesterday afternoon,' Luis interrupted.

So Herrera had been responsible for his being re-assigned – otherwise the valet would never have known about it. Paco looked at the girl, who stood a metre away, trembling and too terrified to move – and felt his anger mounting. 'What will happen to Concha now she's spoken to me?' he asked. 'Will her father suddenly get sick, too? Will she have to take the train to Badajoz?'

'Perhaps,' Luis said.

'You're very good at frightening helpless girls,' Paco said. 'Have you ever thought of trying to bully someone who can fight back – or don't you have the guts for it?'

Luis's body tensed. 'I used to be a boxer,' he said.

'And now you brush your master's jacket and pick up his shitty underclothes after him,' Paco countered, thinking to himself, 'Take a swing at me, Luis. Just one punch – that's all the excuse I need.'

For a second, it did look as if Luis would lash out, then his body relaxed. 'I don't need to fight you,' he said, 'because you're already beaten. You see yourself as an important man, don't you? Well, let me tell you something, Señor Inspector – compared to the people you're dealing with, you're nothing.' He turned his back contemptuously on Paco, then took the girl roughly by the arm and half guided, half dragged her back towards the Herrera apartment.

Chapter Thirteen

Paco looked out of his office window, onto the bustling street below. How many of the people walking past had secrets they would rather keep hidden? Probably most of them. But few, if any, would have one as deep and black as the secret which was buried in the bosom of the man who dumped the murdered young woman in Retiro Park.

Behind him, he heard the sound of the door opening. He turned around. Felipe, an omelette *bocadillo* clutched in his hand, had just entered the room. 'Well?' the fat constable asked.

Paco shrugged. 'I lost her.'

'Paulina, you mean?'

'Of course I mean bloody Paulina. She took the train to Badajoz yesterday afternoon.'

Felipe bit a piece off the edge of his *bocadillo*, munched energetically for a few seconds, then said, 'Have you contacted the Badajoz police, *jefe*?'

Paco shook his head. 'How could I? What possible interest can I claim to have in her now I'm off the case? Besides, it would be a pointless exercise – she'll be in Portugal by now.' His eye fell on a cardboard box which was standing in the corner. 'Look at that!' he said angrily. 'Do you know what that is?'

'It's the dead girl's personal effects, isn't it?' Felipe said, chewing vigorously.

'Exactly. If I'd just been assigned to the case, it's the first thing I'd want to see. But Inspector Matute – who's supposedly been working on the murder for nearly twenty-four hours – still hasn't bothered to pick it up.'

Felipe pushed the last piece of bread into his mouth, and wiped his hands on his trousers. 'I don't see it makes much difference,' he said. 'We didn't learn much from her effects, so why should we assume Matute would?'

'That's not the point,' Paco told him. 'Matute couldn't know there weren't any clues until he'd looked for himself.' He walked over to the box and picked it up. 'And anyway, perhaps there really is a clue in here – a clue we missed the first time around because we were so busy chasing after Paulina.'

'Clutching at straws,' Felipe said softly.

'What was that?'

'Nothing, *jefe.*'

Paco took the dress out of the box, laid it on the desk, and placed the shoes and underclothes next to it. Just touching the dress brought an image of the girl to his mind – the wide, trusting eyes, the generous mouth. She may not have been a virgin when she died, but in some ways, he was sure, she had still been an innocent. 'Do the clothes tell us anything?' he asked Felipe.

The fat constable picked up one of the shoes, stuck his hand inside, then wiggled the heel to see how secure it was. 'These won't have been cheap,' he said. 'But I don't think they're in the same class as the frock.'

'I agree. And the underclothes?'

Felipe examined the rough-cotton knickers. 'Barely better than a peasant would wear,' he pronounced.

'It doesn't add up,' Paco said. 'It shouldn't be important for us to know how she got the frock, but if it isn't, why are so many people going out of their way to stop us finding out?'

He turned his attention to the contents of the girl's handbag. Handkerchief, hair clips, metro ticket. His eyes stopped on the colour photograph of the Virgin. Country girls really did take their Virgins seriously, he thought. Why, only an hour earlier, Concha, the other maid, had sworn on the Virgin of her village that she was telling him the truth.

He slapped his forehead with the flat of his hand. 'The Virgin!' he said aloud. 'Of course! What an idiot I've been! Why didn't I think of it earlier?'

'Think of what earlier?' Felipe asked.

'It's not any ordinary postcard she was carrying around with her. It's—'

The two detectives heard the door click open behind them. 'You have no right to be going through the evidence of a case which had been assigned to someone else!' said an angry voice.

Paco swung round. Standing in the doorway was a man who was somewhere between fifty and fifty-five. He was small, dapper and carried himself with an air of self-importance. It was almost like looking at a more successful version of Ramón.

'Who the hell are you?' Paco asked.

'I am the Minister's private secretary,' the man answered. 'And you, I assume, are Inspector Ruiz.'

'That's right,' Paco admitted.

'I am here to inform you, Inspector Ruiz, that as of now, you are suspended from duty.'

The hairs on the back of Paco's neck prickled, but it was no more than a mild irritation. Suspended? He couldn't be. That was insane. 'On what grounds has this decision been taken?' he asked.

The little man entered the room and stopped just short of the desk. 'What grounds? There are so many that they're almost too numerous to list.'

Paco gritted his teeth. 'For example?'

'Insubordination, unauthorized investigation, irregular interrogation, harassment of innocent citizens.' The secretary smiled maliciously. 'Any one of those is enough to hang you.'

'*You think you are an important man,*' Luis had said. '*But compared to the people you're dealing with, you're nothing.*'

'I will require your warrant card and pistol,' the private secretary told Paco.

The prickling sensation was becoming more acute, and Paco's head was starting to pound. His warrant card and his pistol! After more than twelve years as a policeman, those two things had become almost a part of him.

'I am waiting, Inspector,' the secretary said.

Paco reached into his pocket and forced himself to produce his warrant card. Then, with his free hand, he pulled his pistol from his shoulder holster. The secretary was holding out his own hand for them, but Paco ignored him and put both objects down on the desk. 'So what happens now?' he asked.

'You will leave this building immediately, and will not return to it until such time as you are summoned to appear before a disciplinary board.'

Despite the prickling sensation, the whole situation had, up to that moment, felt vaguely unreal, a little like a disturbing dream. Now, the words 'disciplinary board' hit Paco with the impact of a bucket of icy water.

He could lose his job. And if he wasn't a policeman, what was he? Nothing. He was experiencing a desperate need to talk to Hidalgo, to seek advice from the man who was both his boss and his old comrade from the wastelands of Morocco.

'Am I to be allowed to see my captain before I leave the building?' he asked.

The secretary shook his head. 'No, in accordance with the regulations, that cannot be permitted. In any case, there would be no point. This matter is now being dealt with at a level much superior to your captain's.'

Paco took a deep breath. He had powerful enemies ranged against him, he thought, but he wasn't beaten yet because he might – just might – have one little thing he could use to fight back.

He reached for the dress. 'Don't touch that!' the private secretary ordered him.

'I was only going to put it back in the box,' Paco said mildly. 'Leave things tidy.'

'Putting the evidence away will be entrusted to other, more competent, hands,' the private secretary said.

'Please yourself,' Paco told him, as he palmed the colour photograph of the Virgin into his back pocket.

Chapter Fourteen

The nun walked along the long, cool corridor with small, mincing steps, her hands clasped in front of her and her eyes fixed firmly on flagstones just ahead. She did not speak, nor did she give any indication that she was anything other than alone.

Walking a couple of steps behind her, and taking one stride for three of hers, Paco looked around him. It had been years since he'd entered an ecclesiastical building, years since he'd come into contact with religious statuary of the kind which now seemed to be waiting in ambush for him in half a dozen recesses in the walls.

He'd imagined he'd put his childhood dislike of school behind him, but now he discovered that he hadn't. The longer he was in the building, the more uncomfortable he felt. His neck was starting to itch again, and he found himself running his finger around the edge of his collar.

The nun stopped in front of a solid oak door, and gave the briefest of nods.

'Thank you,' Paco said.

The nun nodded her head a second time, then continued her journey down the corridor. Paco looked at the brass plate inscribed with the single word 'Headmaster', and knocked on the door.

'Come in,' said a rich baritone voice.

Paco entered the study and ran his eyes quickly over the man behind the desk, who had just stood up to greet him. He was a tall man, and very broad. His hair, which grew into a widow's peak, was starting to turn grey, but his eyes had an alertness which proclaimed that he still found life fascinating. It had been fifteen years since they last met, but Paco recognized him immediately.

'It's been a long time,' José Manuel Ordovas said.

'Too long,' Paco replied.

When they'd been at school, Ordovas has been a holy terror. Paco remembered the tricks they'd got up to together, the pranks they'd played on the Brothers who were entrusted with the almost impossible task of educating them. And then later, when they'd grown out of such childish things, there'd been the girls – the respectable young ladies they always saw in the presence of a chaperone, the jolly whores they'd visited in the Calle Echegaray when they had money in their pockets.

But that was all behind them. Paco was a married man, faithful in deed, if not in heart. And José Manuel was Father José, already an important figure in the Society of Jesus.

They shook hands. 'Take a seat, Paco,' Ordovas said, returning to his own chair.

'Thank you, Jo . . . er . . . Father.'

'José will do,' the Jesuit said.

Paco sat down. 'I have to admit that you're looking very well, José,' he said.

'And you look as if you're drinking far too much and sleeping far too little,' the Jesuit told him.

Paco grinned. 'There was a time when we both did that,' he said. He examined the study. Rows and rows of heavy, leather-bound books. A huge crucifix with a hanging Christ who seemed to manage to look down on José with approval, while at the same time showing disdain for his visitor. A second, smaller desk, where Ordovas's secretary probably worked. It was hard to reconcile any of this with the man he'd once known. 'Do you sometimes regret going into the Church, José?' he asked, before he could stop himself.

The Jesuit smiled. 'Did you ever hear the story about the rabbi and the priest?'

'No, I don't think I did.'

'It appears that the two of them are the only occupants of a railway carriage on the Avila train. For the first few minutes, they sit there in embarrassed silence, then the priest decides to get one over on his spiritual rival. "Tell me, Rabbi," he says, "don't you find it hard, when we have such fine pigs in Spain, never to eat pork?" The rabbi looks evasive. "We all have to give up things if we are to serve our God faithfully," he says. "But you must have tried pork," the priest persists, sensing a weakness. "Well, once when I was a young man, I did eat some sausages," the rabbi admits. The priest leans back in his seat, well pleased that he has uncovered a hypocrisy. "Tell me, Father," the rabbi says, "have you ever been to bed with a woman?" Now, it's the priest's turn to feel uncomfortable. "Not since I took holy orders . . ." he says. "But before then?" the rabbi asks. "When I was a student, yes," the priest begins. Then

75

he notices the broad smile on the rabbi's face, and asks, "What's the matter?" "Better than pork, isn't it?" the rabbi says.'

Paco threw back his head, and laughed. 'Better than pork!' he repeated.

'Whatever your chosen profession, you must give some things up by the very act of choosing it,' the Jesuit said, more seriously. 'I am happy with my life, Paco, happier – it would seem to be – than you are with yours.'

Paco nodded soberly. 'You're probably right about that, José,' he admitted.

The Jesuit smiled again. 'So what brings you to see me after so long? Are you here for spiritual guidance?'

Paco shook his head.

'I didn't think so,' the Jesuit said. 'So exactly what can I do for you?'

'I asked at the cathedral if they had an expert on local Virgins,' Paco replied. 'They told me nobody in the whole of Spain knew more about them than you.'

'If pride were not a sin, I'd have to agree with that,' the Jesuit said. 'In fact, I'm writing a book on the subject.'

'Why the interest?' Paco asked. 'Are Virgins really such a fascinating subject?'

'Indeed they are. And so are the people who venerate them. The Archbishop of Valladolid once said that while the peasants would willingly die for their local Virgin, they would burn that of their neighbours' at the slightest provocation. And it's true. You have only to see the processions during Holy Week. The members of a poor parish come down one street, their Virgin at their head, and reach the main square at the same time as the congregation from a rich parish arrive down another street, with their Virgin at their head. How the rich scorn the Virgin of the poor! And how the poor look with pure hatred on the lavish Virgin of the rich!'

Paco took the colour photograph out of his pocket, and slid it across the desk. 'Could you identify this Virgin for me?'

'Why should you want me to do that?'

'We found it in the handbag of a murdered girl. She had no identification on her.'

'And you think this is the Virgin of the place which she comes from?'

'Exactly.'

The Jesuit frowned in concentration. 'It is obviously from one of the poorer churches,' he said, 'and the style is that preferred by country folk, especially in Castile. But since you're looking for the name of a specific village, I'll have to do more research.'

'What kind of research?' Paco asked.

The Jesuit pointed to the bank of metal filing cabinets behind his desk. 'I have photographs of hundreds of Virgins in those,' he said. 'Your particular Virgin is not necessarily among them, but, God willing, she will be.'

They started with photographs of the Virgins in the villages closest to Madrid, and then worked their way outwards. They rejected scores of pictures before Father José finally said, 'Do you think that this might be it?'

Paco compared the photograph to the one he'd found in the dead girl's handbag. The former was in colour, the latter in black and white, and the two pictures had been taken from different angles. Still, it was the closest they'd come to a fit so far. 'Yes, I think it might be,' he said. 'Where can I find this Virgin?'

Father José took the photograph from him, and examined the notes he had made on the back of it. 'This particular Virgin's in the Church of San Francisco,' he said, grinning at the thought that the church and Paco should share the same name. 'It's in a village called Villaverde.'

'The name doesn't ring any bells with me,' Paco confessed.

'I'm not surprised,' the Jesuit told him. 'It's not a big place. In fact, my records show that there are only about 250 houses in the whole village.'

'And where exactly is it?'

'It's the other side of Navalcarnero. Just inside the province of Toledo.'

Which meant the village was probably no more than sixty or seventy kilometres from Madrid. Yet despite the relatively short distance, Paco knew from his own experience that it would be like another world, a world both frightened and fascinated by the thought of Madrid. Had the girl been the daughter of one of the two or three rich men you always found in villages like that? he wondered. Or had she, instead, been the daughter of some dirt-poor peasant, who had scraped together just enough money to buy her bus ticket to the capital?

If José's theory about the two Virgins being one and the same was right, the answer was only two hours' drive away.

Chapter Fifteen

The village of Villaverde lay huddled on a flat plain. It consisted of a single, slightly twisting street, which bulged in the centre of the village to form a square. From the mountain road – which was where travellers got their first glance of it – it looked like nothing so much as a long, white snake that had not yet fully digested its lunch.

Paco had left Madrid at nine o'clock that morning, and it was just before noon when he drove on to the village square. He stopped his car and looked around him. The place presented no surprises. It was just like hundreds of other villages in central Spain.

The biggest building, of course, was the brown-stone, baroque church. Beside it was the casino, the place where the more prosperous villagers would go to drink and play cards.

'Does your father go there, Dead Girl?' Paco said softly to the empty square. 'And will I have to go there, too, to tell the poor man that he no longer has a daughter?'

Next to the casino was the town hall. Paco looked up at the balcony. On election nights, the mayor would make his speech from up there. And when the village was in *fiestas*, and the square became a temporary bullring, the village notables would sit on that same balcony, fanning themselves and watching third-class matadors fight third-rate bulls.

Beyond the town hall there was the pharmacy, and after that there were houses which were only slightly grander than the mud-brick dwellings which made up the rest of the village.

Paco got out of his car and walked over to the church. He expected the main door to be locked – after the recent outbreak of sacrilegious attacks, many were – but when he turned the handle, it swung open.

He stepped through the door. His footsteps rang out on the stone slabs, and reverberated deafeningly around the ceiling. The smell of incense, which he'd never been able to tolerate, invaded his nostrils. He felt as uncomfortable in this church as he had in every other church he'd ever visited, but at least it was cooler in there than it was outside.

Though the light was dim, he could see the Virgin. When she was paraded around the village during the *fiestas*, she'd be dressed in a sumptuous cloak and wear a crown of imitation gold, but for the rest of the year she remained as she was now, a plain carved figure, standing in an alcove to the left of the altar.

Paco took the picture out of his pocket, and positioned himself where he calculated the photographer would have stood. The two seemed to match. He took a step closer. A piece of gold paint had been chipped off the carved Virgin's robe, and he could see that exactly the same piece was missing in the photograph. So now he had found the Virgin. All that was left to do was to find the victim's family. He turned round and walked back towards the door.

He had not been in the church long, but even so, his eyes had forgotten how bright it was outside, and for a second he could see hardly anything. Then his vision adjusted. The square was no longer deserted, as it had been when he arrived. A little, old woman, dressed in black, was hobbling painfully across it. Paco strode up to her. 'Excuse me, señora, I wonder if you could help me?'

The old woman raised her head, and narrowed her eyes. 'You're a stranger, aren't you?' she said accusingly.

'Yes,' Paco admitted. 'I'm from Madrid.'

The old woman clicked her tongue and shook her head. 'You've come a long way.'

'Yes,' Paco agreed. He took a photograph of the dead girl out of his pocket. 'Do you recognize this *muchacha*?'

The old woman took the photograph in her gnarled hands and angled it first one way and then another. 'It's María Sebastián,' she said. 'But I've never seen that look on her face.'

That's because you've never seen her dead, Paco thought. But aloud he said, 'You're sure it's her?'

'Of course I'm sure.'

'And does her family live in the village?'

The old woman clicked her tongue again, as if amazed at the depth of his ignorance. 'The family lives in the house next to the shop,' she said. 'Always has.'

'And where's the shop, señora?'

Was there no end to this man's ignorance? The old woman raised a shaky arm and pointed further up the street. 'Two doors beyond the bar,' she said. 'You know where *that* is, don't you?'

'I expect I'll find it,' Paco told her. 'Thank you for your help, señora.'

As he walked along the dusty street, Paco was conscious of eyes following him from behind every window grille. But that was only to be expected; in a place like Villaverde, strangers were always going to be suspect.

He reached the shop, which was no more than the front-room of an ordinary house. Cheap pans and brushes hung from nails outside, and through the open door he could see a few tins of canned food, each one looking uncomfortably isolated on the wide wooden shelves. You could tell how well a village was doing from the state of its shop, he thought – and this one wasn't doing very well at all.

He knocked on the door of the house next to the shop and waited. When a minute had passed, and still no one had replied, he knocked again.

'Marisol isn't there,' called a voice from across the street.

Paco turned around. A middle-aged woman, with thick peasant arms and legs, was standing in a doorway. 'Do you know where she is?' he asked.

'She and her daughter have gone to see her brother in Navalcarnero.'

'Her daughter? María?'

The woman shook her head. 'No, not María. She lives in Madrid. It's Paz I'm talking about.'

'Have you any idea when she'll be back?'

'She said she'd be on the one o'clock bus.'

Paco checked his watch. He had over an hour to kill. He might as well visit the village's one and only bar.

*

The bar was a square room with a rough wooden counter at one end. A dozen or so rickety tables lined the walls, a battered billiard table filled the centre of the room. Though it was the middle of the working day, the place was packed.

As Paco walked up to the counter, the place fell silent. 'I shouldn't have worn a suit,' he thought. 'Old trousers and a worn shirt would have fitted in better here.'

The barman was a fat man with copious hair growing out of both his ears and his nostrils. He looked at Paco with distaste. 'The casino's up the road, by the church,' he said.

'I know that. I've seen it for myself,' Paco replied. 'And I'd rather have a drink here.'

'Get back to your own kind!' someone shouted from one of the domino tables.

Paco turned round, and tried to work out which of the men had spoken, but all of them were staring at him with equal hatred. They were just looking for an excuse to pick a fight, to give vent to their frustrations by pounding hell out of the man who'd dared to enter their bar dressed like one of the enemy. They'd probably let him make it to the door, if he left now – and that would undoubtedly be the wisest course. But he didn't want to. He'd taken shit from Mercedes Méndez, and from that little arsehole of a Ministerial private secretary. It was time to draw the line.

'As I said to the barman, I'd rather have a drink here,' he told the hostile villagers. 'And as for being among my own kind, I already am. I was brought up in a village just like this one.'

'You don't look like one of us,' said another anonymous voice from the corner of the room.

Several other men growled in agreement, and it looked as if half a dozen of the peasants were on the point of jumping to their feet and rushing the intruder.

'It's not what a man wears, but what's in here,' Paco said, thumping his heart. 'I've tilled the fields just like you have, I've done the same stretch in the military—'

'Were you an officer?' interrupted a big man with dark hair and a weather-beaten face.

'No, I was a corporal.'

'Did you serve in Morocco?'

Paco shrugged. 'Who didn't?'

The big man took a sip of his wine. The eyes of all the other men were on him now, but like many natural leaders, he didn't seem to notice. 'When were you in Morocco?' he asked.

'Does it matter?'

The big man nodded. 'Yes, it does. At least to me.'

'I was there from 1919 to 1921.'

'Were you in the column which relieved Melilla?'

Why did that always have to come back to haunt him? Paco wondered. 'Yes, I was there,' he said.

The big man nodded. 'So was I.' He turned his attention to the barman. 'Give my comrade a drink, Jesus.'

The barman did not look happy. 'But Javier, how do we know he's not a spy for the *cacique*?' he asked.

'What if he is a spy?' Javier demanded. 'Have we all got so little spirit left in us that we no longer dare say what we think for fear it will be reported to Don Alfonso! Give the man a drink, I say. I will pay for it.'

Reluctantly, the barman poured a glass of rough red wine out of the goatskin. Paco picked up his glass, and made his way over to the man who had probably saved him from a severe beating.

There were three other men sitting at Javier's table, all of them with strong peasant bodies and leathery skin. Javier introduced them as Moncho, Kiki and Curro. They each grunted their own greeting to the man from the city.

'What shall we talk about?' Javier asked, and Paco noticed a cunning look had come into his eyes. 'Shall we discuss old times? The siege of Melilla, perhaps?'

Paco shook his head. 'That's something that I never talk about,' he said firmly.

Javier nodded. 'At first I thought you might have been lying about having been at the siege. But now I know you were telling the truth.'

'How can you be sure?' Paco asked.

'Because you refuse to talk about it. And that is how it should be. It is only those who have never seen true horror who have any pleasure in discussing it.'

Moncho had been looking at Paco suspiciously since he sat down. Now he said, 'Why are you here?'

Tell them he was a policeman, and all the goodwill he had built up with Javier would be gone in an instant. 'I'm just passing through,' Paco said.

'Passing through to where?'

'If he wishes to tell us his business, he will do so,' Javier said. 'If he does not, well, it is *his* business.' He turned to Paco. 'Isn't that so, comrade?'

'Yes, it is,' Paco agreed.

He looked around him. The domino players had resumed their games, and conversation had once again reached the level it had been at when he entered the bar. For the moment, at least, he was safe. 'Is the village in *fiestas*?' he asked Javier.

'Why do you ask that? Because we are all here?'

'That's right.'

The big peasant shook his head. 'No, we are not in *fiestas*. We are here because we have nothing else to do.'

'Careful, Javier!' Moncho warned.

'I will not be careful!' Javier said vehemently. 'We have been quiet long enough. Perhaps too long.' He turned his attention back to Paco. 'You must understand our history. Most of us here in the village are anarchists, and when the Republic was declared, we greeted it with enthusiasm. Now we could force the landowners to pay us decent wages, we said.'

Paco remembered his own village, and the two or three landlords who had acted as if they owned everything and everybody – which they almost did. 'The landlords refused to pay more?' he asked.

Javier nodded. 'We soon discovered that they would rather let their land fall into disuse than improve our conditions.'

'But surely you have land of your own which you could work,' Paco said.

'Some of us,' Javier admitted.

'Then why . . .?'

'Half of us lost it in the first year of the Republic. Don Alfonso, the *cacique* – the political boss – is also the village money-lender. When we started to cause trouble – as he saw it – he demanded that all outstanding debts be repaid in full. Those who couldn't pay had their land taken off them.'

'And the rest?'

'There is no point in growing things if you cannot sell them,' Kiki said gloomily. 'And who has the money to buy around here?'

'If you organized yourselves into a co-operative, you could hire a lorry and sell your products in Madrid,' Paco pointed out.

Javier laughed. 'The only lorry in the village is owned by Don Alfonso, and he has no wish to see us prosper.'

'Then hire one from someone else.'

'We did. We tried to hire from Escalona first, but Don Alfonso has political influence there, and no one in the town would do business with us. So we got one from Madrid. But Don Alfonso was one step ahead of us.'

Landlords usually were, Paco thought. That was how they managed to hold on to their positions. 'In what way was he one step ahead of you?' he asked.

Javier drained his glass. 'Do you know how the fruit and vegetable markets function in Madrid?'

'No, I don't,' Paco said, signalling to Jesus, the barman, to fill up everyone's glass.

'All the growers deal through allocators,' Javier explained. 'There's no other way.'

'How does that work?'

'The grower delivers the crop to the allocator, and he distributes it to the various stalls. Then, at the end of the day, he gives the grower the money he has made, minus his own commission.'

'Go on,' Paco said.

'We had a lorry load of green peppers. Beautiful green peppers. But every allocator we went to said there was no demand for peppers. It was a lie, of course, but there was nothing we could do but wait around until one of them decided there was a demand.'

'And did one?'

'At the end of the first day, an allocator came to us and said that he would buy the peppers outright. It was a pitifully small sum he was offering us, so naturally we refused. We hired warehousing for the peppers, while we slept on the street, like dogs. The next day, it seemed there was no demand for peppers either – even though we could see the allocators accepting them from other lorries. That night the same allocator returned and offered us even less for the peppers. Well, to be honest, they were worth less by then.'

'You refused him again?'

'We did. But by the end of the third day we knew that if we did not sell them, we would get nothing for them. So we let him have them practically as a gift. We only just covered the cost of the lorry and the storage.'

'And you think this Don Alfonso was responsible for that?'

'We know he was. He told us so himself. "You sell to me, at the prices that I am prepared to pay you," he said, "or you do not sell at all".'

'He's trying to starve us into working for low wages again,' Moncho said.

'Then there's the school,' Javier continued. He looked at Paco's suit, which the woman in the dress shop had examined with disdain, but which, to these villagers, identified him as a rich man. 'You must have gone to school,' he said.

'I did,' Paco replied, 'but I had to walk ten kilometres there and ten kilometres back every single day, because there was no school in my village.'

'There has never been a school here, either,' Javier said. 'But after the King left, the Republic offered us one. It was to be a fine building, with a playground in front. But before they could build the school, they had to buy the land. And the land they bought was so expensive that there was no money left for building.'

'It was Don Alfonso's land,' Paco guessed.

'Of course it was. But he'll pay for it in the end. When the day of retribution comes – and it is not far away – all the landlords will pay. That fat old priest, too.'

'The priest is not such a bad man,' Kiki objected.

'He drinks in the casino,' Javier pointed out. 'That makes him one of them, and . . .' he slid his finger across his throat as if it were a dagger, '. . . he will suffer the same fate as the rest.'

There was a rumbling sound which grew louder and louder, then an old bus passed the bar, rattling the windows. In a few moments it would stop on the square, and María Sebastián's mother and sister would get out of it, suspecting nothing.

Paco stood up. He was glad he'd had a drink before having to break the tragic news.

'You're leaving?' Javier asked.

'I have to,' Paco told him. He took a five peseta note out of his pocket, and laid it on the table. 'Have a drink on me.'

Javier scowled. 'Here, that will buy much more than one drink,' he pointed out.

'Then have more than one.'

The scowl still in place, Javier shook his head. 'We do not take charity in this village.'

'Between comrades, there is never any question of charity,' Paco countered.

Javier nodded. 'We will accept your money today,' he said. 'But the next time you come here, it will be a different matter. Then we will own the village and will be able to show you the true hospitality of Villaverde.'

They shook hands, and Paco walked to the door. In Madrid, just wearing a socialist armband or a Falangists blue shirt was enough to invite death, he thought. But the armband and the shirt could be discarded, and the threat removed. Out in the country, there was no such escape. Here, people were cloaked in a century of hatred, and when Spain finally fell apart – as it must – people like Javier would spill the blood of their enemies without a second's hesitation.

Chapter Sixteen

From his position in front of the bar, Paco watched the two women walk down the dusty street. One of them was in her forties, and dressed in widow's black. The other, who was little more than a girl, wore a faded green dress. Each, in her own way, reminded him of the photograph in his pocket.

The women reached their front door, and Paco made his move. The older woman watched the approach of the well-dressed stranger with alarm, her expression seeming to say that if he thought he had any business with her, he was sadly mistaken. Her daughter, in contrast, seemed mildly interested, as if any break in her dull routine would be welcome.

Paco drew level with them. 'Can we help you in some way, señor?' the girl asked.

'I believe so,' Paco replied. 'I'm a policeman and—'

'We haven't done anything wrong,' the mother said. 'I swear by the Virgin that we haven't done anything wrong.'

'I'm sure you haven't. I need to ask you some questions about your daughter.'

The woman looked anxiously at the girl in the faded green dress. 'Paz . . .?'

'Not Paz,' Paco told her. 'María. I've come from Madrid.'

'Is . . . is María in trouble?' the mother asked.

'I think it would be much better if we talked about it inside,' Paco said.

'She's always been a good girl. She's never done anything that might land her . . .'

It was pointless talking to the mother. 'It really would be better if we went indoors,' Paco said to the girl.

Paz nodded, turned the door handle and ushered her mother into the house.

The front door led straight into the main room. Running along the far wall was a cooking range, closer to the door a table and four straight-backed chairs. The only other furniture was a tall cabinet containing glasses and kitchen utensils, and a rag rug which covered about a quarter of the flagstone floor. Paco's first impression was shabbiness, but scrupulously clean shabbiness.

The mother seemed even more flustered now than she had been out on the street. 'Would you like a drink, señor?' she said, retreating into ritual. 'You must have a drink.'

'That's not necessary,' Paco told her.

'It's no trouble,' the woman insisted. 'Paz, give the gentleman some wine.'

The girl went over to the cabinet and extracted one glass and a flask of wine.

'Please sit down, señor,' the mother said – and because Paco knew it would make her sit down, too, he did.

The daughter placed the glass of wine in front of Paco. 'I don't like to drink alone,' he said. 'Why don't you bring a glass for your mother, too?'

'I don't want . . .' the mother began.

But Paz, who had read Paco's eyes said, 'The gentleman's right, Momma. A glass of wine would do you good.'

While she went to fetch the extra glass, Paco examined the mother. The woman was becoming more agitated by the second, and was now twisting her handkerchief tightly in both hands. She knows, Paco thought. They tell themselves they don't believe it, but somehow they always know.

Paz returned with a second glass of wine. 'What's happened to María?' she asked.

Paco took the photograph out of his pocket, and laid it on the table between the mother and daughter. 'Is this her?' he asked.

The mother squinted at the picture. 'Yes, it is,' she said. 'But she looks so . . . so . . .'

She twisted the handkerchief tighter, and Paco couldn't help thinking of the hands around María's throat.

'She's dead, isn't she?' Paz said.

'Yes, I'm afraid she is,' Paco replied, speaking as gently as he knew how to.

*

Paco heard the footsteps, and looked up. Paz was coming down the wooden stairs. Her face was pale and drawn, yet there was a determined look in her eyes which said that someone in the house had to manage to hold themselves together.

88

'How's your mother now?' Paco asked, as Paz reached the foot of the stairs.

'She's a bit quieter, now. Señora Gomez says that she will stay with her.'

'If you need more time with her . . .'

Paz shook her head. 'Señora Gomez trained as a nurse. She will make a better job of calming Mama down than I ever could.' She walked across to the table, and sat down. 'Besides, it is important that I answer your questions.'

'Yes,' Paco agreed. 'It is. Tell me just what kind of girl your sister was.'

A sad smile came to Paz's lips. 'She was the most wonderful older sister. So kind and so loving and helpful. Everybody liked her. I know people always say that about the dead, but in María's case, it really was true.'

'What made her go to Madrid?'

Paz shrugged. 'She'd always wanted to go there. Even when she was a little girl, she had her sights set on it.'

'When did she leave the village?'

'Just under two years ago.'

'And do you know if she was happy in Madrid?'

'She found it very hard at first. She got a job in a shirt factory. Sixteen hours a day she worked, and hardly earned enough to feed herself. She told me that several times she thought of giving up and coming home.'

'But she didn't?'

'No, because then she got lucky.'

'In what way.'

'The owner of one of the shops which bought the shirts noticed her, and asked her if she would like to work for him. And, of course, she said yes.'

'Where was this shop?'

'Somewhere in Madrid,' Paz said vaguely. 'In a very nice area. María said that all her customers were gentlemen, and it was a pleasure to serve them.'

'And I expect she was paid more, too.'

'Oh yes. At first she lived in a cheap hostel, but when she got the job in the shop, she was able to rent an apartment. It wasn't a very big one, she told me, but it was cosy. And the neighbours were mostly country-folk, like her, so she was very happy there.'

'Do you have the address of this apartment?' Paco asked.

'Yes, it's on her letters.'

'Could I see them, please?'

Paz went over to the cabinet, slid open the drawer, and brought out a sheath of letters tied up in a ribbon. 'María was very good about writing to us,' she said. 'We got a letter once a month, without fail – and after she got the job in the shop, there was always a little money in with it.'

She handed the letters to Paco. He slid one out of its envelope, and glanced at the address.

'Have you ever visited your sister?' he asked.

Despite her sorrow, Paz laughed. 'Me? No! I'm not like María. I'd be lost in the big city.'

Of course she'd never seen her sister's apartment. If she had, she couldn't possibly have described it as she did. A cosy little apartment? In a *barrio* inhabited mostly by country-folk like herself? The address at the top of the letter said María had lived in Calle Hermosilla, right in the middle of the Barrio de Salamanca. There were no country-folk there, and no small apartments either. It was one of the richest *barrios* in the whole of Madrid, and, as Fat Felipe had pointed out, it was a fascist stronghold.

*

Paco saw the two *guardias civiles* as soon as he reached the square. They were standing a few metres from his Fiat, and apparently, were in no hurry to go anywhere else. It had been a day for bringing back childhood memories, he thought. First there'd been the village itself – the dust, the smells, the faint sense of desperation – and now it was these two green-uniformed *guardias*.

He remembered the two who patrolled his own *pueblo* – how they used to swagger down the street, and how the villagers looked down at the ground when they'd passed. They'd been Galicians, almost foreigners to the people of La Mancha. And that was how it had been planned. No *guardia* was ever allowed to serve in his native province, among his own people. Nor did he live with the people he was sent to police. His quarters were in a *guardia* barracks, and that didn't change even if he married and had children.

The guardias' word was law in the countryside, and they knew, as did everyone else, that whatever they did, however brutal they were, they would probably not be punished for it. Was it any wonder then, that these policemen in their absurd, menacing three-cornered hats, were both hated and feared by the villagers? Paco asked himself. And was it any wonder that, even after so many years away from his childhood home, he should feel a shudder run through him at the sight of the old enemy?

The two policemen watched Paco's approach with obvious interest, then one of them, a corporal, leaned slightly towards his colleague, a private, and said something. The private nodded, unslung his rifle and held it out in front of him, so that the butt was resting in the dusty earth.

The village boy inside Paco told him to turn and run, while the sophisticated *madrileño* part of him said that he was not a peasant, and had nothing to fear. But it was an unequal battle, and, in the end it was only by force of will that he stopped himself scurrying away like a frightened rabbit.

He calculated the distance to his car. Another ten steps and he'd be there. Another two minutes and he'd be out of Villaverde altogether. If only the demons of his past would just give him the time to get clear. . . .

The two policemen stepped sideways, blocking his path. 'Is this your car, señor?' the corporal asked, pointing to the Fiat, even though it was the only vehicle on the square.

'Yes, it's mine,' Paco replied. 'Is there anything wrong with it, officer?'

'And you are Francisco Ruiz?' the corporal said, ignoring Paco's question.

Shit! The man not only knew his name, but felt under no obligation to put a 'Don' in front of it. Paco wondered just how much trouble he was in.

'I asked you if you were Francisco Ruiz,' the corporal repeated, menacingly.

There was absolutely no point in pretending. 'You know I am,' Paco told him.

'And could you explain to me exactly what you are doing in Villaverde?'

'Visiting friends.'

The corporal frowned. 'That is a lie,' he said. 'You have no friends – especially in this village.'

Paco looked from the private to the corporal and back again. He could neutralize one of them, he calculated, but with the two of them so alert, he had no chance of taking both. Very well, he would try to talk his way out. 'Look,' he said, 'as you know my name, you probably also know that I'm a policeman, and—'

'You are a policeman under suspension,' the corporal interrupted. 'And from what I've been told, even that is only a temporary state. Soon, you will be no kind of policeman at all.'

'So I'm not here in an official capacity,' Paco agreed. 'Let us say then, that I'm visiting the village as a private citizen. I still have a right to—'

The corporal held up his hand in what was almost a fascist salute, and then curled back three of his fingers so that only the index was pointing at Paco. 'Watch this finger, Señor Ruiz!' he said, making it an order, rather than a request.

Like a fool, Paco did. And he was still watching it, a split second later, when the private suddenly swung his rifle, and slammed it into his gut.

Paco was suddenly plunged into a world inhabited only by pain, a world where suffering was the only reality, and fighting against it the only reason for existing. He sank slowly to his knees. His stomach was on fire, his chest was crushed, and he did not think he would ever breathe normally again.

'Can you hear me, Señor Inspector?' the corporal asked mockingly, his words floating on a surreal sea of agony.

Paco nodded weakly. Even that caused him excruciating discomfort.

'What you have been given is only a warning,' the corporal said. 'It might hurt now, but you should consider yourself lucky . . .'

'You . . . son . . . of . . . a . . . bitch!' Paco gasped.

'. . . because it could have been much worse,' the corporal continued, calmly. 'If the orders from Madrid had been different, it *would* have been worse. I don't know who you have annoyed, Señor Inspector, but whoever he is, he can crush you like an ant, any time he feels like it.'

And having delivered their message, the two policemen walked away, leaving Paco on his knees, wondering just what it was going to cost him to stand up.

Chapter Seventeen

It was hard to say how he knew that something had changed in Madrid in the few short hours he had been away, but something definitely had. Even viewed through the windscreen of the Fiat, he could see that the people on the streets moved differently, gestured differently, had new, possibly frightened, expressions on their faces.

Had there been a military coup? Paco wondered.

No. A coup would have been followed by an ostentatious show of strength, tanks on the streets and soldiers on every corner. Perhaps the government had fallen – but it was doing so little anyway that its fall would cause no more than a minor ripple.

As he turned onto Calle Hortaleza, Paco changed gear and felt a pain shoot through his chest, a reminder – if he needed one – that the *Guardia Civil* had had a lot of practice at hurting people. The *Cabo de Trafalgar* was just ahead. Paco signalled that he was pulling in, and parked. Now that he was safely back in the city, he could have the drink he so desperately needed.

Ramón and Bernardo were sitting at their usual table. They were not alone. Occupying the third chair – Paco's chair – was the blonde *Yanqui* girl, Cindy Walker.

It was obvious even from the doorway that Ramón and Bernardo were arguing again, and Cindy was listening to them with a kind of interested confusion. Paco nodded to all three, pulled up a chair and, with only a slight jolt to his bruised ribs, joined them. 'Has something out of the ordinary happened today?' he asked.

'You could say that,' Ramón replied. 'Don José Calvo Sotelo's been killed.'

As a shock, it rated below the one delivered by the *guardia* civil's rifle butt – though not much. Calvo Sotelo couldn't be dead. Socialist militiamen and fascist foot-soldiers got killed; leading members of the *Cortes* – the Spanish parliament – were supposed to be above that sort of thing.

'How did it happen?' Paco asked.

93

Bernardo and Ramón both began talking at once –

'It was like this . . .'

'What really started it was . . .'

Ramón nodded his head to indicate that he was willing to let Bernardo tell the story. For the moment.

'A young lieutenant in the *Asaltos* was murdered yesterday afternoon, shot down in the street like a dog by four fascist gunmen . . .' Bernardo began.

'But what's that got to do with Calvo Sotelo's death?' Paco interrupted.

'You'll see if you just shut up and listen.'

Nacho arrived with fresh glasses of wine. 'Make mine a brandy,' Paco said, running his fingers gingerly over his ribs.

'The murder of the *Asalto* took place outside his home, which is close to the *casa del pueblo*,' Bernardo continued, 'so naturally, when his body was taken down to the *Asalto* barracks on the Puerta del Sol, a great many socialist supporters accompanied it.'

'Socialist riff raff, you mean,' Ramón murmured.

'Be careful how you talk about my comrades,' Bernardo warned. He turned back to Paco. 'You should have seen the procession. There were thousands and thousands of us. We filled Sol, right from one end to the other. We were so tightly packed together that none of us could move, but we didn't mind. Of course, it was a sad occasion, because we were mourning the death of the lieutenant, but at the same time there was a sort of joy there – a joy which came from seeing just how strong we were.'

Ramón had clearly had enough of Bernardo's version of events. 'They were out for revenge,' he cut in. 'Most of the rabble were all in favour of attacking any Falangist they could find, but then this captain – a treacherous man named Condés, who's left wing even if he is in the *Guardia Civil* – said to the people closest to him that instead of random violence, they should punish the leaders of the right.'

'José Calvo Sotelo,' Paco said, finally seeing where the story was leading.

'Gil Robles and Eduardo Herrera as well,' Ramón told him. 'But, as it turns out, Robles is away in Biarritz for the weekend, so they couldn't get at him.'

'And Herrera? Is he away, too?'

'Yes. He has a house in the mountains.'

'It's more like a stronghold, from what I've heard,' Bernardo interjected.

94

'Anyway,' Ramón continued, 'there they all were in Sol, in front of the Ministry of the Interior, plotting cold-blooded murder . . .'

'Half of what you're saying is no more than rumour,' Bernardo protested.

Ramón gave him a scornful look. 'You were prepared to believe that nuns were handing out poisoned chocolates to the children in the poorer *barrios*,' he said. 'That was rumour. This is fact.'

'There was clear evidence that the nuns were—'

'For God's sake, let's stick to the point,' Paco said firmly. 'Go on with the story, Ramón.'

'They arrived at Calvo Sotelo's flat shortly after three o'clock in the morning . . .'

'Who is *they*?'

'This Captain Condés I mentioned earlier, a couple of men from the socialist militia, several *Asalto* troopers, and two other men who have still not been identified.' He looked across the table at Bernardo. 'And this is not speculation. Calvo Sotelo's family have confirmed it. Why would they lie?'

'I would never trust the members of a fascist's family to tell the truth,' Bernardo muttered.

'Condés asked Calvo Sotelo to accompany him to police headquarters,' Ramón continued, ignoring Bernardo's comment. 'He did not have to go – parliamentary deputies are immune from arrest – but being the brave man he was, he agreed. About an hour later the bastards handed him over to an attendant at the East Cemetery. He had been shot twice through the back of the neck.'

'What will happen now?' asked Cindy Walker, speaking for the first time since Paco had entered the bar.

'The military will rise,' Ramón said. 'When the government cannot even control its own *Asaltos*, what other choice does the army have? Unless,' he lowered his voice, 'unless, of course, the government was in control all along.'

'Are you suggesting that the government was behind the murder?' demanded Bernardo.

'Are you taking its side?' Ramón countered.

Bernardo looked vaguely uncomfortable. 'I have no use for liberals,' he said. 'But I like to see fair play for everyone.'

'Then let us consider the evidence,' Ramón continued. 'Condés was dismissed for his part in the '34 revolt, and he has only recently been reinstated, at – it is widely said – the personal request of the Prime Minister.'

'Slander!' Bernardo gasped.

'Slander or not, you will find plenty of people, on both sides, who are willing to believe it.'

That was true enough, Paco thought. It had got to such a state of affairs that people would believe anything. He finished his brandy, and signalled to Nacho for another one.

*

The heat clung to the city like an overcoat which is three sizes too small. Women, on the small chairs outside their front doors, fanned themselves and ate slices of watermelon. Men leant against the walls, and jangled the change in their pockets. The excitement and hysteria which the murder of Calvo Sotelo had injected into the city had finally faded away. Now there was nothing to look forward to but a long, sticky night.

Paco and Cindy Walker negotiated their way along the route from the *Cabo de Trafalgar* to their apartment block, stepping off the pavement occasionally to avoid groups of people who had taken over the whole area between the buildings and the road. Neither of them spoke. They hadn't really spoken to each other all evening. Bernardo and Ramón had dominated the conversation, their argument about politics leaving little room for discussion of any of the more mundane aspects of normal life.

They reached their front door, and Paco clapped his hands to summon the *sereno* with his bunch of keys. 'How did you get talking to Ramón and Bernardo?' he asked Cindy.

She smiled. 'They said they were friends of yours and invited me to join them.'

'But what were you doing in the bar in the first place?'

'I was looking for you, of course.'

Her directness made him uncomfortable. 'Why were you doing that?' he asked.

Cindy looked him straight in the eye. He noticed how deep blue and how serious her eyes were. 'I was looking for you, because a big city like Madrid can be an awfully lonely place for some people,' she said.

'You'll get used to it in time,' Paco assured her.

'I wasn't talking about me,' Cindy told him.

96

Chapter Eighteen

The brandies he'd drunk in the *Cabo de Trafalgar* had helped to make the beating Paco had received earlier little more than a memory. Starting to climb the seventy-two steps which led to his apartment brought it back as a painful reality. He stopped and clutched the stair-rail.

'What's the matter?' Cindy asked.

Paco grinned, through clenched teeth. 'I had a disagreement with a *guardia* civil's rifle butt,' he explained. 'It turned out to be harder than my stomach was.'

'You mean, you were attacked?'

'The man who ordered it claimed it was more in the nature of a friendly warning,' Paco said, starting to climb again.

'But that sort of thing shouldn't happen to you. After all, you're a policeman yourself.'

Paco looked at her sharply. 'Who told you that?'

'Your friends. Bernardo and Ramón told me.'

'Did they indeed,' Paco said. Had they told her, or had she asked? he wondered. And if it was she who had asked, had there been other questions?

They reached Cindy's floor. Only twenty-four more steps to go and he would be back in his apartment. Paco stopped. He had escorted the woman that far, he might as well see her through the door. Besides, the way he was feeling, he could use the pause.

Cindy took her keys out of her purse, hesitated for a second, then said, 'Do you want to come inside and I'll take a look at it?'

'Look at what?'

'At whatever it was that the nasty policeman did to you.'

Paco's fingers automatically went up to his ribs. 'Are you a nurse?' he asked.

'Out in the boondocks, where I was brought up, everybody was a nurse. And a mechanic. And a veterinarian. The houses were so far apart that we didn't have much choice.'

It was strange the way people's perceptions worked, Paco thought. To him, the United States had always meant tall buildings and huge factories, yet he'd never had any reason to suppose that there weren't areas in it as remote as any to be found in rural Spain.

Cindy had opened the door. 'Well, are you going to let me have a look at it?' she asked in her blunt *Yanqui* way.

'Why not,' said Paco.

He had only been in her apartment once before, yet it seemed very familiar to him, as if he had been visiting it for years.

'Take off your jacket and sit yourself down on that chair,' Cindy said crisply.

He did as he'd been told. She knelt over him and started unbuttoning his shirt. He wondered whether he should tell her that he was capable of doing that himself, but it was really very pleasant, so he didn't.

She pulled the shirt free of the waistband of his trousers. Both of them looked down. A black wedge ran from just above Paco's navel to his ribs.

'That must have been some kind of blow,' Cindy said.

'The *Guardia Civil* have had a lot of practice,' Paco told her. 'Under the dictatorship, even belonging to a union was enough to get you beaten up.'

Cindy touched his stomach, and he winced.

'Still hurts, hey?' she said.

'A little,' Paco admitted.

'I'm going to check a few of your ribs,' Cindy said. 'Just to make sure they haven't been damaged.'

He felt her cool fingers pressing and probing. It was painful, yet at the same time he enjoyed it. Somehow, as she examined him, their heads seemed to move closer and closer together. Then they were kissing. It took Paco by surprise, even though, in a way, he'd been almost certain it was going to happen.

*

They stood in Cindy's bedroom, facing each other. For a few seconds, neither of them moved, then Cindy lifted her arms and began to unbutton her blouse.

'Would you like me to turn the light off?' Paco asked.

Cindy laughed. 'Why should I?'

'I just thought . . .'

'What I'd really like is to have you watch me undress.'

Though his hands had explored every inch of her increasingly unwilling body, Paco had never seen his wife naked. And now this girl was telling him that she actually wanted him to watch her undress. He felt as awkward as a virgin, as unsure of himself as a fumbling youth. He'd known whores act like this, but Cindy wasn't a whore. Where they were artful and calculating, she was merely natural and straightforward. He wondered whether all Americans were like her, and decided that it didn't matter, because she was the one he wanted – and he wanted her just the way she was.

Cindy discarded her blouse, and then her skirt. Now that she was half-undressed, she seemed a little less sure of herself. 'I think I've put on weight since I've been in Spain,' she said.

He ran his eyes up and down her body. Her legs were long and slim; her stomach had a slight, erotic bulge; her waist was narrow; and her breasts, still constrained by a brassiere he didn't think they needed, were like plump, firm peaches. 'You're beautiful,' he told her. 'You're perfect.'

She unfastened the brassiere, and he saw that he had been right about the breasts. She slipped out of her knickers, and he gasped as it revealed a patch of fluffy golden hair. Now she was naked, and, despite having no memory of undressing himself, he was too. Though he knew it would hurt him, he picked her up as if she were a baby, and carried her over to the bed.

'Don't!' she whispered into his ear.

'Don't what?'

'Don't treat me like some precious object you're afraid you might damage. Make love to me like you really mean it.'

He laid her down, and then his mouth was over one of her wonderful breasts – sucking and biting, biting and sucking.

'Touch me . . . touch me down there,' she groaned.

He had never done that to a woman before, but he knew that the stickiness he encountered said she was ready for him. He entered her, and she groaned again. He could have exploded right at that moment, but he held back, wanting to make certain that she was satisfied first. And as his buttocks rose and fell, a single thought – or perhaps merely an impression – flashed across his mind. And the thought was this: no one had ever had sex as good as this before, and no one ever would again.

*

99

They lay side by side, still naked. Paco was still experiencing some discomfort from his injury, but the rest of his body felt better than it had done for a long time.

'Tell me about the girl,' Cindy said lightly, as if the idea had come out of nowhere.

'The girl,' Paco repeated, seeing in his mind's eye the lifeless body of María Sebastián stretched out under the elm tree. 'How do you know about her?'

Cindy laughed. 'Don't you remember? You told me about her when you were here the other night. You know – the one you met while you were in Morocco.'

Oh, that girl?

Paco felt his stomach churn. 'You don't want to hear about her,' he said.

'Yes, I do, I wouldn't have asked if I didn't. We Yanks are like that, you know.'

'It was such a long time ago,' Paco said unconvincingly.

A smile played on Cindy's lips. 'But you remember it as if it were yesterday, don't you?'

'Yes,' he admitted. 'I do.'

'So tell me about her, for heaven's sake!'

Paco took a deep breath. 'Her name was Reyes. Her father was a missionary doctor. We met in Melilla, though she didn't live there – the family had a house next to one of the outlying garrisons, more than twenty kilometres from the city.'

The smile was still firmly on Cindy's lips. 'You met, and you fell in love.'

'That's right.'

'What was she like?'

He could close his eyes and see Reyes – smell her, almost feel her. Yet to paint a picture of her in words was an almost impossible task.

'I could tell you she was beautiful, but, in fact, she was no more than pretty,' he said. 'I could claim she was the most intelligent woman I ever met, but that wouldn't be true, either. She was warm and she was kind. And she made me laugh. I don't think I ever laughed so much as when I was with her.'

Cindy nodded her head, as if she understood. 'A classic case,' she said.

'What do you mean?'

'She was your first love, wasn't she?'

No evasions, no half-truths – Paco looked Cindy straight in the eye. 'I was already married by then,' he said. 'But yes, she was my first love.'

And my last, he added mentally.

Cindy became suddenly more serious, as if she sensed which way the tale was heading. 'Go on,' she said, encouragingly, though not without reservations.

'The army had been fighting the tribesmen for years – just skirmishes mainly – but in 1921 there were some real pitched battles. The generals' strategy was to pacify all the tribes at the same time, and then join the two halves of Spanish Morocco together. But it didn't work out that way. We started losing ground, then we were in a full-blown retreat. We gave up 5,000 square kilometres of territory – which God alone knows how much Spanish blood had been spilt to conquer – in only a few days.'

'What's that got to do with Reyes?' Cindy asked.

'I'm coming to that. We retreated as far as Melilla, the tribes hot on our heels. We hadn't been the only ones on the run, and the place was bursting at the seams with soldiers. They were conscripts, most of them – badly trained, badly equipped and totally exhausted. You should have seen them. Trying to hide their fear by getting drunk. Queuing outside the whore houses because it might be their last chance ever to have a woman.'

'Did you join them?' Cindy asked.

'No. I had much more important things to do. I wanted to find my Reyes.'

'She was in Melilla?'

'That's what I assumed. After all, why shouldn't she have been? All the other Spaniards in the area had fled to the town.'

Cindy bit her lip, as if she now definitely regretted having started the conversation, but was too far into it to stop. 'Reyes wasn't there,' she said.

'I met a friend of hers who told me that her father had refused to move. He'd done a great deal for the Moors, he said, and they would show their gratitude by harming neither him nor his family.'

'So what did you do?'

'I went to see my company commander. I didn't mention my relationship with Reyes . . .'

'Of course not.'

'. . . but I did say that I knew of a Spanish doctor who was stuck out in the middle of enemy territory. I suggested we send out a rescue column.'

'And what did he say to that?'

'He showed me a map. Reyes' father's house was in the shadow of one of the outlying garrisons. The soldiers would protect the doctor, he assured me.'

'And you believed him?'

'Yes, I believed him. I should have stolen a car, or a lorry, or anything, and driven out myself. Instead, I put my faith in the authorities.'

There was a hint of tears in Cindy's deep-blue eyes. 'She died?'

'She died.'

'Did you see the body?'

Paco laughed bitterly. 'It's only in romantic novels that the heroes are allowed one last tender moment with their dead loves. No, I didn't see her, but I did read the report. By the time the relief column from Tetuan got through, everyone in the garrison – and everyone in the house – was dead. They didn't even bring the corpses back to Melilla. After days of lying out in the sun, the only thing that could be done with them was to heap them in a pile and burn them.'

Cindy reached over and stroked Paco's arm. 'If you had stolen a truck and tried to reach her, you'd never have made it,' she said. 'And even if, against all the odds, you had succeeded, she was probably already dead.'

'I know.'

'So you've no call to go blaming yourself for her death.'

'I don't,' Paco said. 'Not all the time, anyway. But there's never a moment that I don't wish I'd at least *tried* to save her.'

'The other day, when you came in for a glass of *sangría*, you told me that you didn't trust people. Is that why – because of what happened way back then?'

'You misunderstood me,' Paco told her. 'People, I trust. It's organizations – the army, the political parties, the trades unions – that I don't have any faith in.'

'And why, exactly, is that?'

Paco sighed. 'The government will stay in power, or it will fall. If it falls, it will be replaced by another government, or the army, or the socialist and anarchist unions. And whoever is in control, there will always be someone to assure me that everything is all right, because if it isn't, what has he got to lose? Responsibility will be spread so thinly that he will only take a minute share of the blame.'

'Like your commander in Melilla?'

'Exactly. He promised me Reyes would be safe, but how was he to know the strength of the Moors, the resolution of the garrison or the length of time it would take the relief column to get through? So he can shrug aside the blame. But if I give *my* word – make *my* commitment as a man and a Spaniard – then whatever shame or honour comes from it is mine alone.'

Cindy shook her head. 'You were born at the wrong time or in the wrong place,' she said. 'You don't have the makings of a hard-boiled cop. You should have been a medieval knight like Don Quixote, chasing after windmills.'

'You're wrong,' Paco said. 'We are none of us born out of our time. We must merely learn to face our time on our own terms.'

'Quixote,' Cindy murmured, almost sleepily.

Well, maybe he was, Paco thought, but it was too late to change now.

Chapter Nineteen

It was early morning and the sun was still low enough to make walking just about tolerable as Paco made his way up Calle Hermosilla. It did not have the same sweep as grand streets like Velazquez, he thought. It was not nearly as wide, and the buildings were not half as majestic. But it was still a highly respectable – and expensive – neighbourhood in which to have an address.

He had reached the block in which, according to the address at the top of María Sebastián's letters, the murdered girl had lived. He looked up at the building. It was four storeys high, and instead of plaster mouldings – as there were on Herrera's apartment block – costs had been cut by hiring an artist to paint an elaborate design.

There were other ways in which it fell short of the Herreras' home, too, he noticed as he came to a stop in front of the building's double glass doors. The man sitting behind the desk in the lobby wore the blue suit of a porter rather than the scarlet uniform of a doorman – a clear indication that, as well as screening those entering the building, he would also be required to carry out minor repairs. And the lobby itself, while well furnished with leather easy chairs and pot plants, had none of the grandeur which had been evident in Herreras'.

Still, whatever its shortcomings, it was well beyond the budget of a humble police inspector. So how had a girl who'd spent her first year in Madrid working in a sweat shop been able to afford it?

Paco pushed the doors open and stepped inside. The porter, a balding man with sharp, calculating eyes, looked up from his newspaper. 'Can I help you, señor?' he asked.

'Police,' Paco said. 'I wish to examine one of the apartments in this building.'

He'd spoken brusquely, hoping to bluff his way into the place, but it was plain from the expression on the other man's face that the bluff wasn't working. 'I shall need some identification before I can allow you to see anything,' the porter said.

Paco reached into his jacket pocket, then feigned surprise. 'I seem to have left my warrant card at home.'

The porter gave a sigh. 'Without papers, a man is nothing. It's regrettable, but that's the way things are.'

Paco gave it one last try. 'I don't have time to go back downtown and pick my card up,' he said.

The porter scratched his bald head, thoughtfully. 'In that case, we'd better ring your police station. I am sure that someone there will vouch for you.'

'Listen,' Paco said, 'I am a policeman, but the case that I'm involved with at the moment is of what you might call an unofficial nature.'

The porter nodded understandingly. Everybody in Madrid had a racket – from the butcher's boy who trimmed a little off the meat and sold it himself, to the army general who received a generous gift from the military contractor. And if everyone else was on the take, his look seemed to say, wasn't it only fair that porters should get their share, too?

'This work you're doing, unofficially, is for a private client?' he asked.

'Yes.'

'A client who is paying you handsomely?'

'Adequately.'

The porter smiled. 'In that case, it would only seem fair that in return for my assistance, I should, how shall I put it . . .?'

'Be rewarded?' Paco suggested.

The porter's smile broadened. 'Exactly.'

'That seems fair,' Paco said. He thought of all the bribes he'd been offered over the years, and the contempt he'd always had for the men who'd offered them. And now here he was about to do the same thing. 'This is different,' he told himself silently. 'I'm doing it in the interest of justice.'

But even though he believed it really was different, he still had the taste of slime in his mouth.

'Which of the apartments did you wish to see?' the porter asked.

'Señorita María Sebastián's.'

'How long would you need to be in it?'

'About fifteen minutes.'

'And would you be taking anything away from it?'

'I'm not a thief,' Paco said, with a dangerous edge creeping into his voice.

'No, no, of course not,' the porter said soothingly. 'But even if you touch nothing, there is still a risk for me – a risk I could not possibly run for less than six *duros*.'

'If I pay you more than two, you'll be making almost as much as I will,' Paco said. 'And I'll be doing most of the work.'

'Say that Señorita Sebastián returns while we are still in her apartment?'

There was no chance of that, but if Paco told the porter the reason why, he'd never get into the place. 'If she does come back, you can always tell her I'm a building inspector,' he said. 'She has no reason to doubt your word.'

The porter shook his head. 'If she does not believe me, I could lose my job. Four *duros* is little enough compensation for that.'

'I've just been to a village where four *duros* would be considered a good month's wages,' Paco said. 'I'm offering you three for a few minutes' work.'

'Three, then,' the porter agreed.

Which was still a fair amount of money for a man who had just been suspended without pay, Paco thought as he followed the porter up the service stairs.

*

'How many rooms are there in this apartment?' Paco asked, as he and the porter stepped over the threshold.

'Let me see. There's the living-room and the dining-room, the main bathroom, a kitchen, two family bedrooms and the maid's room and bathroom.'

They entered the living-room, which had a large picture window overlooking the street. Paco remembered María Sebastián's simple home in Villaverde. She must have felt lost in luxury like this. 'She worked in a shirt shop, didn't she?' he asked.

'Worked?' the porter repeated.

'Works, then,' Paco amended hastily. 'She works in a shirt shop.'

The porter shrugged. 'If she does, she has very strange hours of employment.'

'What exactly do you mean by that?'

'Some days she never leaves the apartment at all. And then she's gone for a week at a time.'

Paco looked around the living-room. The furniture, which was cheap and mass-produced, just didn't fit in with this high-rent area. Paco wondered if María had chosen it herself.

It was then he noticed the scuffs on the parquet floor, two lines of them – lines such as might have been made by the shoe heels of a girl who was fighting desperately for her life. So María had been killed here, in her own apartment. Which meant that whoever her murderer was, she'd trusted him enough to let him in.

'Where does she go when she's away?' he asked the porter.

'I've no idea. All I know is that I see her leaving the block with her suitcase in her hand, then it's six or seven days before she turns up again.'

The two main bedrooms led off the living-room. In the first, the bed was stripped down to the mattress. Paco walked over to the wardrobe, and was not surprised to find it empty. In the second room, the bed was made up with satin sheets which must have cost a small fortune, but the wardrobe was as empty as the one in the other room had been.

'Didn't she . . . doesn't she have any other clothes than the ones she's wearing?' Paco asked.

The porter snorted. 'Don't be ridiculous. She has at least five or six expensive dresses.'

'So where are they?'

'I haven't a clue.'

'Could someone have broken into here and taken her things?'

The porter puffed out his chest. 'Not without being noticed by me,' he said.

But if he had not noticed a murderer, why should he have spotted a robber?

Paco checked the bathroom next. Bath, basin, shower, bidet. There was a fluffy towel hanging on the rail, and soap in the soap dish. There was no sign of any other toiletries. From what he had seen of the apartment so far, it looked just like a suite in a hotel, awaiting the arrival of its next guest.

'Does she live alone?' Paco asked, gazing directly into the porter's eyes.

'Yes,' the other man said, returning Paco's steady gaze with one of his own.

'What about visitors? Does she have many of them?'

The porter's eyes flickered for a split second. 'None. Nobody ever comes to see her.'

'Not even one person?' Paco coaxed. 'A special friend, perhaps?'

The eyes flickered again. 'Not even one person.'

Paco suddenly felt the impotence of his position. Only two days earlier, he could have dragged this man down to police headquarters and sweated the truth out of him. Now, although he knew the porter was lying, there was nothing he could do about it.

'Let's see the rest of the apartment,' he said, with a sigh.

It was in the maid's quarters – a cramped, airless space beyond the kitchen, with just enough room for a narrow bed, a night table and a closet – that he found what he was looking for. There was another picture of Villaverde's Virgin tacked to the wall, and a cheaply framed photograph of María's sister and mother on the night-table. So he'd been right about poor little María. The apartment had overwhelmed her, and though she'd had two perfectly good family bedrooms at her disposal, she had chosen to live here.

But if she didn't use the other rooms at all, what was the point of the satin sheets?

In the maid's bathroom – Turkish toilet and shower – he found her toiletries. And in the closet, he discovered the rest of her clothes.

Paco checked through the dresses. Most of them bore the label *Moda de Paris*, as he suspected that if he'd dared to check back at the dress shop, he would have found out they'd all been purchased by Doña Mercedes Méndez.

'It's time to go,' the porter said.

'What?'

'It's time to go. You've had more than the fifteen minutes you paid me for.'

Paco shrugged. Why argue? Without the help of a full team with hours at its disposal, there was nothing more to be learned from this apartment.

They were back in the living-room when they heard the doorbell ring. The porter went white. 'I told you this would happen,' he whispered.

'Keep calm,' Paco hissed back. 'It could be anybody.'

'I . . . I . . . it wasn't my fault. You made me bring you here,' the porter gibbered.

Paco had tried to intimidate the man earlier, and he'd taken it in his stride. Yet the sound of the doorbell had him almost on the point of collapse. Just who was he frightened of?

The bell rang again.

'Answer the door,' Paco said.

'I can't,' the porter gasped. 'I . . . it might be Don Ed—' He choked off the word in his throat, and looked down at the floor.

'Don who?' Paco demanded.

'Nobody. I . . .'

Paco grabbed him by the lapels of his jacket. 'You were about to say Don Eduardo Herrera, weren't you? Weren't you?'

The porter nodded. 'But if anybody finds out . . .' he mumbled self-pityingly, '. . . if they learn that it was me who told you . . .'

The bell rang for a third time. Paco let go of the porter's jacket, walked over to the door, and turned the handle.

'No!' the porter croaked behind him.

Paco opened the door. He half-expected to see Eduardo Herrera standing there, but instead there was only a young girl in a maid's uniform.

'Who . . . who are you?' she asked, tensing up.

'Owner's agent,' Paco said crisply.

'Agent?' the girl repeated the word fearfully, as if it had sinister implications.

'Yes, agent. There are certain repairs which need to be done in this apartment, and I was just making a note of the details.'

The maid relaxed. 'I see,' she said.

'And who might you be?'

'Belén, señor.' She gave a clumsy curtsey. 'I work in the apartment opposite.'

She turned to go. 'Just a minute,' Paco said. 'Why did you ring the bell?'

The girl started to redden. 'I beg your pardon, señor?'

'What was your reason for ringing the bell? Do you have a message to deliver from your mistress?'

The question seemed to confuse her; or perhaps it was her answer which was causing her trouble. 'No, I . . . I didn't have a message to deliver,' she stuttered.

'Well? Why did you ring the bell?'

'When I heard the door open a few minutes ago, I . . . I thought it was María . . . I mean the señorita . . . coming home.'

'And if it had been?' Paco asked. 'Why did you want to see her?'

Belén shrugged. 'To talk.'

'About what?'

Belén's confusion was growing. 'Just . . . you know . . . things,' she said.

Paco thought he understood. María – the country girl who only really felt comfortable living in the maid's quarters – would have nothing to say to the grand people who owned the apartments around her. But with a maid, a *campesina* like herself, she would be able to chat happily for hours.

There were a great many questions he wanted to ask this girl, but not while the porter was looking on. He smiled – so that the next time they met she wouldn't be so afraid of him – and said, 'If I were in your place, Belén, I'd get back to my work before my mistress noticed I'd gone.'

The girl bobbed down again. 'Yes, señor. Thank you, señor.'

Paco watched her disappear into the apartment opposite, then turned to face the quivering porter. 'Visitors!' he demanded.

'I've already told you—'

'You've already lied to me – about Don Eduardo Herrera. Was he the only one, or were there more?'

The porter hesitated. 'There . . . there is one more who calls occasionally.'

'Who?'

'I don't know his name.'

'Then describe him to me.'

'He's a big man. Around thirty-five.'

'Anything else you can tell me about him?'

'He moves well.'

'How do you mean?'

'He's got the kind of grace you see in men who've been trained as flamenco dancers.'

In his mind's eye, Paco could see Luis the valet standing outside the pavement café, fists clenched and balancing on the balls of his feet. 'Would you also say it was the same kind of grace as boxers have?' he asked.

'Yes,' the porter admitted. 'I suppose I would.'

Chapter Twenty

Just as they'd intended him to, Paco noticed the three young señoritos in blue shirts the moment he stepped out onto the street. They were standing on the pavement in a rough semi-circle, the middle one on the edge of the kerb, the two who were flanking him a little closer to the buildings. Paco turned to the left, and the boy on the left moved to the centre of the pavement, blocking him. He looked over his shoulder, and saw that the boy to the right had also shifted position.

The young man in the middle reached into his pocket, and extracted a photograph. He looked down at it, then up at Paco. 'Yes, this is the man,' he said.

It was pure theatre, Paco thought. They'd known who he was all along, and if they'd wanted to hurt him, they could simply have sneaked up and hit him from behind. But that would not have been enough for them. They had the power, and they wanted to celebrate it by reading the fear in his eyes.

'You were foolish to try and hurt the Falange . . .' the boy with the photograph began.

'I'm not interested in politics,' Paco interrupted. 'I'm investigating a murder.'

'. . . and you were even more foolish to ignore the last warning you were given,' the young man continued, playing his role for all it was worth, 'because now we have no choice but to silence you for ever.'

'Who sent you?' Paco asked. 'Eduardo Herrera?'

The boy looked genuinely surprised. 'It would be a great honour to work for Don Eduardo,' he said, 'but no, he was not the one who issued the order.'

Of course not. It would be one of his underlings who had issued it, and perhaps another who had passed it on to him, but Herrera would still be at the end of the chain.

Paco looked up and down the street. Shopkeepers were setting out their wares on the pavement. Maids were walking up and down with wicker baskets over their arms. A group of well-dressed ladies stood chatting on the corner of Calle Ayala. There was no one with the power to save him. Even if there had been, it was doubtful they would have tried. No one wanted to get into the Falange's bad books – and anyway, this *barrio* had fascist sympathies.

The young men had their weapons out now. A brass knuckle-duster on the leader's hand glinted in the morning sunshine. The boy on the left had produced a blackjack, the one on the right a knife. Passers-by, sensing what was about to happen, were making a wide arc around that section of pavement.

Paco thought of Maurico, the legionnaire who, in defiance of the legion's convention, had befriended him while he'd been in Morocco.

'When it comes to a fight, you're a bloody fool if you don't use every dirty trick I've taught you,' Maurico had told him – and Paco hoped he could remember a few of them now.

The leader of the Falangists studied Paco's face, and frowned. 'You don't look very frightened,' he said. 'Perhaps you don't fully understand what's about to happen to you.'

'I understand, all right,' Paco replied. 'And if I thought that begging you to spare my life would do any good, I'd beg. But it wouldn't, would it?'

'No,' the señorito agreed. 'It wouldn't.'

'Well, then, let's get it over with.'

If they all chose to attack at the same time, Paco thought, he was done for. But they didn't. It was the one with the knuckle-duster – the leader – who was to have the honour of bringing their enemy down, and until he had struck the first blow, his companions were content to be nothing more than spectators.

The young man took a step forward, and Paco felt his stomach tighten. What he did in the next two seconds, he told himself, would determine whether he lived or he died.

The boy feinted with his left, then brought his right hand into play. It was one of the first tricks Maurico had taught Paco, and he was ready for it. The knuckle-duster whistled through empty air, and before the boy even realized he had missed, Paco had grabbed his arm and was twisting it hard behind his back. There was a loud crack, like a rifle shot, and the boy let out a terrified and terrifying scream as he felt his arm being snapped in two.

From the corner of his eye, Paco caught the movement to his left. He swung the writhing boy round, using him as a shield against this new

112

attack. The blade of the knife flashed once in the sunlight, then the injured boy grunted and went limp. The young gentleman with the knife backed away. There was a look of horror on his face, and the blade of his weapon was blood-red.

'You've gone and killed him, Antonio,' sobbed the boy with the blackjack.

The one with the knife took a couple more staggering steps backwards, and then stopped. The knife fell from his hand and clattered onto the pavement. Paco spun the wounded – or maybe dead – boy around again, and hurled him at his friend with the blackjack. Without even waiting to see the result, he turned back to the knife-wielder. The boy was just starting to come out of shock. Paco swung his leg as hard as he could, and kicked him in the groin.

Paco's boot had only just connected when he heard the dull, crunching thud. For perhaps a split second, his shoulder burned with the pain of a thousand red-hot needles. Then his arm started to go numb, and though he tried to lift it, it would not obey. There was only the boy with the blackjack left to deal with – but Paco would be doing it one-handed.

He whirled round, two fingers of his right hand stretched out in a V. The Falangist with the blackjack was just raising his weapon to strike a second time. Paco's hand travelled in an upward arc. The V found the boy's nostrils and entered them. When he felt the tops of the fingers touch bone, he twisted his wrist as if he were opening a bottle.

The boy's scream was even louder than his friend's had been. Paco twisted again, this time the other way. He felt the strain on his wrist, and wondered what the pain was like inside the boy's nose. But he experienced no sense of pity; they would have killed him if he'd given them the chance.

He pulled his fingers free. The boy's eyes were streaming with agony. He dropped his blackjack, and tried to lift his hands to his nose. But the effort was all too much for him, and he crumpled to the pavement.

Paco had no time for the luxury of assessing his own injury, not until he was sure that his other two attackers were out of the game. He spun round and faced them. The one who'd had the knife was on his knees, fighting for air. The leader was sprawled awkwardly on his back across the pavement, his blue shirt stained by a rapidly growing patch of crimson blood, pumping out of the wound just above his belt.

Paco looked up and down the street. The maids, the gossiping housewives, and the busy shopkeepers, all stood in a frozen tableau of horror. But that would not last. Someone, soon, would snap out of it, and go searching for more Falangists. Though he knew even before he started that it would hurt like hell, Paco began to run down the street towards the Castellana.

Chapter Twenty-One

The bar was located close to the Puerta del Sol. It was one of the few still to have a cow shed in its cellar, and people who knew their Madrid history claimed it was already an old established business when Cervantes was writing *Don Quixote*.

From the threshold, Paco scanned the room. Fat Felipe was in the corner, his attention fully absorbed by a large dish of seafood soup. Most of the other customers were wearing the leather caps and jackets of cattle drovers. There was no one who looked like an official from the Ministry of the Interior, no one who seemed as if he might be a senior policeman. In other words, Paco thought, no one who could be a potential enemy.

He walked stiffly over to the fat constable's table, and lowered himself gently into the chair opposite his partner. Felipe looked up from his food. 'Something the matter, *jefe*?' he asked.

Paco shrugged, then, as a shooting pain seared across his shoulder, wished he hadn't. 'I got into a bit of trouble in the Barrio de Salamanca,' he said.

'What kind of trouble?'

'Doesn't matter. It's been dealt with.' Paco lit a cigarette. 'I think it'd be better if we didn't meet again for a while, Felipe.'

The fat constable frowned. 'Not meet? But if we don't see each other, how the hell can we carry on the investigation?'

'Forget the investigation,' Paco told him.

Felipe's eyes narrowed. 'Are *you* going to forget it?' he asked.

'No,' Paco admitted.

'Then I'm not, either.'

'I thought you didn't care about the case one way or the other,' Paco said.

Felipe gazed down into his soup. 'That was before the big boys started screwing you around,' he said. 'Besides, that poor kid who got killed didn't have much of a life. We should at least do right by her now she's dead.'

'Normally, I'd agree with you,' Paco told him. 'But after my bit of trouble this morning, I think you should drop out of the case.'

'That's the second time you've mentioned your bit of trouble,' Felipe said. 'Exactly what kind of trouble was it?'

'Three young Falangists attacked me on Calle Hermosilla. They said they were going to kill me.'

Felipe's mouth dropped open in surprise. 'They said they were going to do what?' he asked, recovering slightly.

'Kill me.'

'And what stopped them?'

'They were young and arrogant. And that made them careless.'

'Let me get this straight,' Felipe said. 'Three of them attacked one of you, and it was you who walked away from it?'

'That's not important,' Paco said. 'What does matter is that I'm a dangerous man to know.'

Felipe was smiling proudly. 'Three of them,' he said. 'And I'll bet they all had weapons!'

'For Christ's sake, get beyond that macho shit!' Paco said angrily. 'They've tried to kill me once, and they'll probably try again. And when that happens, I don't want you in the firing line.'

Felipe's smile melted away and was replaced by a serious expression. 'Being partners is like being married,' he said. 'However bad it gets, you're stuck with each other. Anyway, whether you like it or not, you need me. I'm your only contact with headquarters.'

It was true. Without Felipe, the job would be a lot harder, if not impossible. 'You can stay on the investigation if you really insist,' Paco said, 'but I don't want you taking any unnecessary risks.'

'I won't,' Felipe promised. 'Can we talk about the murder, now?'

'Tell me what's happening back at the station first,' Paco said.

Felipe trawled the thick soup and captured an *almeja* on his spoon. 'Ever seen a headless chicken?' he asked.

'It's as bad as that, is it?'

'Worse. Everybody from the top down is in a blind panic over Calvo Sotelo's murder. Captain Condés – he's the one who's supposed to have done it, remember – has gone into hiding. Our boys are trying to find him, but the *Asaltos* are doing everything they can to get in the way of the investigation.'

'They would,' Paco said. 'He's one of their own.'

116

'And it's not just headquarters that's panicking,' Felipe continued. 'Did you know that last night the socialists, communists and UGT sent a combined delegation to see the Prime Minister?'

'No, I didn't know,' Paco admitted. 'What did they want?'

'They demanded weapons for all the workers.'

'Why? What in God's name do they imagine that will achieve, except more bloodshed?'

'The way they see it, the army is about to stage a coup,' Felipe explained, 'and if it does, they want to be in a position to defend the Republic.'

Paco was already tired of talking politics – of discussing the big issues. It was enough for a man to do his job and take care of his friends. 'How are they treating you?' he asked.

Felipe laughed. 'They're treating me like I've got the plague. I told them it's not my fault I was partnered up with an idiot like you,' he winked at Paco, 'but shit sticks anyway, and they want nothing to do with me.' He plunged his spoon back into the soup. 'To hell with them! Apart from nearly getting killed, did you find out anything useful in the Barrio de Salamanca?'

Paco told him about the girl's apartment – the satin sheets in a bedroom she hardly ever used, and the slip the porter had made when the maid from the apartment opposite had knocked on the door. 'So what do we conclude from that?' he asked when he'd finished.

Felipe signalled for more soup. 'We conclude that María was Herrera's mistress,' he said.

'I should have worked it out earlier,' Paco reproached himself. 'My friend Ramón told me that Herrera was mean over minor things like candles and envelopes. What better example of that meanness could there be than that he gives his mistress his wife's cast-off dresses?'

'And so it's a simple domestic murder after all,' Felipe said.

'Except that it's complicated by the fact that Herrera has so much political power. And we still don't know who killed her.'

'Don't we?' Felipe asked. 'I should have thought it was obvious. Herrera finds out she's two-timing him, and kills her in a fit of blind rage.'

'But he doesn't find out who she's two-timing him *with*,' Paco said, 'or Luis wouldn't still be working for him.'

'True,' Felipe agreed. 'But apart from that, it seems straightforward enough.'

'Unless she did it.'

'Who?'

'Doña Mercedes. Say she found out about her husband's mistress. She wanted revenge, but she couldn't take it out on him because he controls the purse strings.'

Felipe shook his head. 'I don't think she's strong enough to throttle a fit, young girl. Besides, I can't see a lady like her . . .'

'I'm not suggesting she did it herself,' Paco interrupted. 'But she could have hired someone to do it.'

'You said she was killed in her apartment, so she must have known the killer,' Felipe pointed out.

'Probably knew the killer,' Paco said. 'But there's any number of ways he might have got into the apartment. He might have said he had an urgent message from Don Eduardo. Or maybe Doña Mercedes managed to get hold of the key, and he was lying in wait for her when she got home.'

'And if she did have María killed, would Herrera take the risk of protecting her?' Felipe wondered.

'What risk?' Paco asked. 'He's a powerful politician, and the only people really interested in the murder are two insignificant little cops. Besides, it would be a risk not to cover up for her. Can you imagine the scandal it would cause if she was arrested for murder?'

'So you're putting your money on her?'

'Or Luis,' Paco said.

'Luis?' Felipe repeated. 'Why would he kill her?'

'For the same motive you ascribed to Herrera. Jealousy. Say he really loved her, and couldn't bear the thought of his master touching her. He asks her to go away with him and she refuses. We're back to the blind-rage theory, only this time it's Luis who flies into it.'

'But the lads who attacked you this morning had to be working for Herrera, didn't they?'

'Not really,' Paco said. 'If Luis is involved with the fringes of the movement – and you'll admit that's likely – they might just have done it as a favour to him.'

'Herrera killed María. Doña Mercedes had her killed. Luis did it. I'm getting a headache,' Felipe said despondently. 'God, I hate this fucking case.'

A waiter appeared, carrying a large plate of *chorizo*. 'Fresh from the country this morning,' he told Felipe, with a smile on his face which said he knew he was about to make his customer's day.

'I'm not hungry,' Felipe said.

'Not hungry?' the waiter gasped.

'There are other things in life besides food,' the fat constable snapped. 'Take it away. Bring us some more wine.'

Shaking his head in amazement, the waiter walked back towards the kitchen.

'So, we've narrowed it down to three people, where does our investigation go from here?' Felipe asked.

Paco lit another cigarette. 'Until we have more evidence, we daren't go near either Herrera or Doña Mercedes,' he said. 'So we're just going to have to concentrate on the man we can go for – Luis.'

Chapter Twenty-Two

From where he was standing by the phone booth on Serrano, Paco could see the window of the *salon* where he had interviewed Doña Mercedes and Don Carlos. He wondered if she was in there now, shielded from the world by the heavy velvet curtains and her husband's influence.

'I'll get you,' he said softly. 'If you're the one who killed María, I'll get you.'

He picked up the receiver, and when the operator came onto the line, he asked to be connected with the Herrera apartment. After he had inserted a coin, there was a ringing tone, then a male voice said, 'Speak to me.'

'I want to talk to Luis,' Paco said.

'You're talking to him.'

'This is Ruiz.'

There was a pause. 'Inspector Ruiz?' Luis asked, and Paco could almost see the sneer on his face. 'Or perhaps I should be calling you Ex-inspector Ruiz?'

That's right you bastard, have your fun while you can, Paco thought. 'I need to talk to you,' he said.

Luis sighed theatrically. 'When are you going to give up, Ruiz?' he asked. 'When are you finally going to admit you're beaten?'

'You mean, how many more attempts on my life will it take before I'm frightened off?' Paco asked.

'Attempts on your life? I don't understand.'

'Don't you?'

'Of course not.'

'I still need to talk to you,' Paco said. 'Be in the bar on the corner of the block in five minutes.'

'I've nothing to say to you.'

Was he wrong? Paco asked himself. Was María's second visitor not Luis, but someone else entirely? Or even if it was Luis, had the purpose behind his visits been entirely innocent? He took a deep breath. 'How would you like your master to know you've put the horns on him?' he asked.

120

'I don't know what you're talking about,' Luis said, just a little too quickly.

'Bullshit!' Paco told him. 'The dead girl in the park was called María Sebastián. She was Don Eduardo's mistress. He was paying her rent, and you were sleeping with her whenever you got the chance.'

'You can't prove that,' Luis said shakily.

'Can't I?'

Another pause. 'You said the bar on the corner?'

'Yes. In five minutes.'

'I'll be there,' Luis promised.

*

There was no swagger in the ex-boxer's walk as he approached the table at which Paco was sitting. He looked instead like a man who had had the rug pulled from beneath him – a man who saw his whole life crumbling before his eyes. He sat down opposite Paco, ordered a brandy from the waiter and gazed into the middle distance. Only when the brandy had arrived and he'd taken a generous slug of it, did he turn to Paco. 'I've served Don Eduardo faithfully for thirteen long years,' he said.

'Faithfully!' Paco said. 'Do you call screwing his mistress being *faithful*?'

Luis shrugged. 'The master gave me his old shirts when he'd finished with them. I don't see this was much different.'

'Are you saying he'd finished with her?' Paco asked.

'No,' Luis admitted. 'But he didn't know, and so it didn't hurt him.' He took another gulp of his brandy. 'You won't tell the master, will you?' he asked, with a look of genuine panic in his eyes.

'You've got more to worry about than Herrera finding out you've been cuckolding him,' Paco said. 'You're right in the middle of a murder investigation.'

'Nothing is more important than serving the master,' Luis told him. 'Besides, I had nothing to do with María's death.'

'Can you prove that?' Paco asked. 'Do you have an alibi for the time she was killed?'

It was a trap, but if Luis was guilty, he wasn't falling into it. 'I don't know whether I had an alibi or not,' he said, 'because I don't know when the murder took place.'

'Sometime during the afternoon of the ninth.'

Luis thought about it, or perhaps only pretended to. 'It was my day off,' he said finally. 'I went to the bulls.'

'With someone else?'

'No, I was alone.'

'Did you meet anyone you knew?'

'No.'

Somewhere in there he had told a lie, but Paco couldn't put his finger on what it was. 'You were in love with María, weren't you?' he said.

Luis laughed. 'In love with her? Of course not. I enjoyed sleeping with her, but that was as far as it went.'

'But she was in love with you?'

'Not that either,'

'Then why did she go to bed with you?'

Luis shrugged again. 'Why do people go to bed with each other? For pleasure.'

But that didn't sound like María. Desperation had forced her into being Herrera's mistress, but Paco didn't think she was the kind of girl who would sleep around. Unless . . . 'What hold did you have over her?' he asked.

'Hold?' Luis said, as if he didn't understand.

Paco stood up. 'You're wasting my time,' he said. 'I think I'll go and phone your master.'

The look of panic was back in Luis's eyes. 'Sit down again,' he begged. 'Sit down and I'll tell you the truth.'

Paco lowered himself back into his chair. 'Go on,' he said.

'She told her mother she was working in a shirt shop.'

'I know that.'

'And I told her that if she didn't sleep with me, I'd tell her family what she actually did for a living. You may not like it, but that's the truth.'

'You really are a complete bastard, aren't you?' Paco said angrily.

'She'd already given herself to one man; it was no great strain to give herself to another,' Luis said, with apparent indifference.

I'm conducting a murder investigation, Paco thought, as he fought back the urge to throttle the valet. I'm conducting a murder investigation, and I must stay calm. 'How would Herrera have reacted if he'd discovered María had been seeing someone else?' he asked.

Luis looked shocked. 'You don't think the master killed her, do you?'

'Why not? You know how passionate these Andalucians can be.'

'He could never have done it.'

'Because he's the great Don Eduardo Herrera, and he wouldn't stoop to anything as low as murder?' Paco sneered.

'No, because he's not physically capable of it,' Luis replied.

'Come off it!' Paco said. 'I've seen him. He's a big, strong man.'

'Have you seen his hands?' Luis asked.

No, Paco thought, as a matter of fact, I haven't. Because when he'd appeared in the doorway of his apartment block, accompanied by a servant who was carrying his briefcase, he'd been wearing gloves, even though it was already a boiling hot day.

'What about his hands?' Paco asked.

'He's very sensitive about them. That's why he wears gloves.'

'For God's sake, man, stop playing games!' Paco exploded. 'What's wrong with his bloody hands?'

'He's got advanced arthritis,' Luis said. 'It's more than he can do to open a wine bottle. He'd never have been able to strangle María.'

*

Paco sat at the café table long after Luis had returned to the Herrera apartment. How far had he advanced his investigation? he asked himself, and decided he had not advanced it very far at all. Luis had said he hadn't been in love with María, but he could have been lying. Certainly he had no alibi for the time she was killed. The valet had also told him Herrera had arthritis – which was probably why he'd given up horse riding – but though he couldn't have killed the girl himself, it would have been easy enough for him to persuade someone else, one of his loyal followers, to murder her. And then there was Doña Mercedes; she was far from in the clear.

He had to talk to Herrera face-to-face, he thought. But how should he go about it? And then he remembered that in less than an hour's time, they would be burying Calvo Sotelo.

Chapter Twenty-Three

The East Cemetery was a sprawling necropolis criss-crossed by roads, just two kilometres from the bullring. Inside its walls, tombs stretched as far as the eye could see – some large, some small, but almost all of them elaborate. It was a vast, gothic city of the dead, a monument to the frailty of all flesh.

From his vantage point on the high ground in the centre of the cemetery, Paco watched the crowd gather around what would be the final resting place of José Calvo Sotelo, the murdered hero of the Spanish monarchists. There were hundreds of people there, perhaps thousands. Dressed in their mourning clothes and standing shoulder to shoulder, they formed a swaying sea of blackness, broken occasionally by the bright blue of a Falangist shirt.

What business had the Falange attending the funeral? Paco wondered. They had never had much time for Calvo Sotelo when he was alive. Why honour him now? Because, he supposed, this wasn't so much a show of respect as a show of strength. There were prominent politicians by the graveside, and if even they couldn't stop armed members of the Falange from attending, then it was, indeed, a force to be reckoned with.

His gaze shifted from the crowd to the small group of *Asaltos* who were sheltering from the heat in a clump of trees some way from the grave. They'd probably been to a funeral themselves, that of the lieutenant whose death had led to Calvo Sotelo's assassination. Now, like the fascists, they were there simply to be seen – to demonstrate the fact that no one was going to intimidate them.

A white Rolls-Royce entered the cemetery through the main gate, and Paco felt his pulse quicken. The moment he'd been waiting for had finally arrived: Eduardo Herrera was in striking distance.

Paco walked down the steps, skirted the growing crowd, and made his way to the road. The Rolls was just pulling up smoothly in front of a tomb which was crowned with a large, indignant-looking angel.

'Right, you bastard,' Paco said softly. 'Now you're going to have to talk to me.'

The back door of the Rolls swung open, but it was Carlos Méndez, not his brother-in-law, who stepped out. Méndez saw Paco immediately, and a look which was half-way between panic and annoyance came to his face. He poked his head back into the car, to consult the illustrious politician who was still sitting there. When he emerged again, his expression was much more certain.

He had heard his master's voice, and now knew what to do, Paco thought.

Méndez nodded twice – once over Paco's shoulder, and then at Paco himself. As if by magic, two large men appeared from out of nowhere, and took up positions on each side of Paco. 'It's bad taste to cause trouble at a funeral,' the one on the left said.

'It's bad taste to strangle girls and then dump their bodies in the park,' Paco replied.

The one on the right laughed. 'I like a man with a sense of humour,' he said, 'but if you try to get any closer to Don Eduardo than you are now, I'm going to have to kill you. Understood?'

'Wouldn't killing me be regarded as a little tasteless, as well?' Paco asked.

The man on the right did not laugh this time. Instead, he grabbed hold of Paco's arm. It felt like it was being clamped in a vice. 'It would all be so easy,' he said. 'I am carrying a spare gun, and if I have to shoot you, it will be found on your body. You will be just one more would-be assassin who has come to a sticky end. You don't want that, do you?'

'No,' Paco agreed. 'I don't want that.'

'Then you're going to behave?'

'I'd be a fool not to.'

Carlos Méndez had been watching the whole incident. Now, when the bodyguard nodded, he went back to the Rolls-Royce and opened the door. Paco wondered what it must be like to be him – to be the lackey who always went ahead to clear up whatever crap lay in the Great Man's way.

Herrera stepped out of the car, not even acknowledging his brother-in-law. He was wearing an expensive black suit with accompanying black gloves, and on his face was an expression of suitably dignified grief. He did not close the door behind him – Carlos Méndez was there to perform such functions – but instead stepped clear of the Rolls. Immediately, he was surrounded by a group of large men with wary eyes. If José Calvo

Sotelo had had that kind of protection around him, the policeman in Paco thought, they wouldn't be burying him now.

By the time Herrera had reached the edge of the crowd, two of his bodyguards had already started to create a path through it. It was a fascinating process to watch: no one seemed to be being treated roughly, yet a gap appeared through which Herrera could pass without rubbing shoulders with the common herd. The politician walked regally towards the grave, with Méndez following at his heel.

'Do you like your work?' Paco asked the bodyguard on his left.

'It pays well,' the man replied flatly.

A murmur ran through the crowd. The coffin was coming! The coffin was coming! Heads turned and people stood on tiptoe to get a brief glimpse of the last journey of one of Spain's most important political figures.

As the coffin passed through it, the crowd roared at the top of its collective voice, and many people gave the fascist salute. Then, starting at the middle and spreading out to the edges, an unnatural quiet fell.

Paco looked around him. The *Asaltos* had left the shade of the trees, and were fanning out around the edges of the crowd. He was not the only one to have noticed them. Several of the blue-shirted Falangists had moved away from the grave and were heading for positions from which they could outflank their enemies.

In the centre of the mourners, a man with a rich, powerful voice had begun to make a speech. 'I take an oath, before God and Spain, that the murder of this very great man will not go unavenged . . .' He relinquished each word as if it were as valuable as gold.

The Falangists and the *Asaltos* were getting dangerously close to one another. Trouble was almost inevitable, and Paco wanted no part of it. 'Am I free to leave?' he asked the bodyguard on his left.

'Yes, you can go,' the man answered. 'But be warned – the next time you make any attempt to get close to the *jefe*, we won't be so gentle with you.'

Paco turned and walked briskly away, towards the car park near the main gate. The orator at the graveside had called for revenge, he thought, and the crowd was roaring its approval. But who was there to demand that María's death be avenged? Who was there to call for justice for the peasant girl who had been driven by poverty into the arms of a rich, married politician, and forced by blackmail to give into the demands of his lecherous servant?

'Felipe and me!' Paco said aloud. 'There's only Felipe and me.'

He heard the rapid footsteps behind him, getting closer all the time, but only when he felt the tap on his shoulder did he stop and turn around. Carlos Méndez was standing there, looking slightly breathless. 'Yes?' Paco said.

'Why won't you leave my family alone?' Méndez asked, almost apologetically.

'What are you?' Paco demanded. 'The messenger boy?'

'Your investigation is making Eduardo angry,' Méndez said, choosing to ignore the insult. 'And when he's angry, it is those around him who are made to suffer.'

'You're saying he's making *you* suffer?'

'Me – and others,' Méndez admitted.

Paco put himself in Don Carlos's position – a penniless aristocrat who was forced to eat shit on a daily basis. And though he had an instinctive dislike of the class, he almost felt sorry for the man. 'I have no choice but to carry on with my inquiries,' he said. 'Your brother-in-law is involved in a murder.'

'You're wrong,' Don Carlos said. 'Yes, María was Eduardo's mistress, and I admit we made a mistake by not telling you that from the start. But why should he want to kill her?'

'Jealousy?' Paco suggested. 'Because he found out she'd been seeing someone else?'

Méndez laughed. 'You make it sound like he was in love with her.'

'And wasn't he?'

'Have you seen the apartment she lived in?' Don Carlos asked.

'Yes, as a matter of fact, I have. The rent must be quite high.'

'It is,' Méndez agreed. 'Anywhere within walking distance of our apartment would have been quite expensive, and that was one of Eduardo's requirements – that she was in easy reach. But what about the furniture? What did you notice about that?'

'Cheap, mass-produced,' Paco said. 'Did the girl choose it herself?'

'No, I chose it,' Don Carlos said, with just a hint of bitterness creeping into his voice. 'And given the pitiful budget Eduardo allowed me, I think I did quite well.'

'What's your point?' Paco asked.

'When you love someone, you want to give them the best of everything, not cast-off dresses and sub-standard furniture,' Don Carlos said. 'Eduardo didn't love María; she was just someone he liked to screw. And even that was beginning to pale on him. He'd have kicked her out weeks ago and moved in a replacement, but I talked him out of it.'

'And why did you do that? Because you were sleeping with her yourself?' Paco asked nastily.

Don Carlos looked down at the ground. 'No, I was not sleeping with her,' he said. 'My tastes lie in another direction.'

'So why . . .?'

'Because I felt sorry for her,' Don Carlos said, lifting his head again, and looking Paco squarely in the eyes. 'Because I didn't want to see her thrown out onto the street.'

'All right, so he didn't love her,' Paco said, getting the conversation back on track. 'But he may have had other reasons for killing her?'

'Such as?'

'Perhaps she'd threatened to go to the newspapers with her story.'

'Eduardo has enough influence to prevent most of the papers printing it. And as for the rest – the yellow, left-wing press – no one of any importance would believe them. And even if it was believed, do you think that the Spanish people don't know that politicians – even Catholic politicians – keep mistresses? If it had done anything to Eduardo's popularity, it would only have increased it.'

Méndez's words had a ring of truth about them which Paco found depressing. 'Maybe he was afraid his wife would find out,' he said, advancing his other theory. 'Or maybe she did find out, and had María killed herself.'

A look of what could only have been genuine surprise came to Méndez's face. 'You think she didn't know?' he asked.

'Did she?'

'Not about Eduardo giving María her old dresses, I'll grant you. They had a blazing row about that. But that he had a mistress – of course she knew.'

'And she didn't mind?'

Don Carlos resumed his examination of the ground. 'My brother-in-law has certain tastes which might best be described as . . . er . . . bizarre,' he said. 'María satisfied his yearnings and saved my sister from having to turn him down. Believe me, Señor Ruiz, Mercedes was at least as satisfied with the arrangement as Eduardo was.'

Paco pictured Mercedes Méndez in his mind. Yes, he decided, she was hard enough and cold enough to be happy that her husband was taking his pleasure elsewhere. 'What about Luis?' he asked.

'Luis?'

'Did you know he was sleeping with her, too?'

'Yes,' Don Carlos said, with a hint of shame in his voice. 'I knew, and I did nothing about it.'

'Why not, if you felt sorry for her as you claim you did?'

'By the time she told me, the damage had already been done. Suppose I had told Eduardo about it. He would have dismissed Luis, and Luis, to get his revenge, would have gone to see María's mother. So the poor girl would have made her sacrifice for nothing.'

'You could still have ordered Luis to leave her alone in future,' Paco said.

Don Carlos laughed again, hollowly this time. 'You seem to have a high opinion of my position in the household,' he said. 'I wish to God everyone else did.'

'You're frightened of him!' Paco said.

'Yes, that too,' Don Carlos admitted.

'Frightened enough to shield him even if you knew he was a murderer?'

'Luis didn't murder María.'

'He has no alibi for the time of her death.'

Don Carlos shook his head in contradiction. 'He has no alibi he's prepared to produce,' he said.

'And what does that mean?' Paco asked.

'Check the records of the police station nearest to the bullring, and you'll find out for yourself,' Don Carlos told him.

So Luis had some kind of alibi, Don Eduardo didn't care enough about María to murder her, and Doña Mercedes actually approved of her husband having a mistress. If all Don Carlos had said was true, he had effectively eliminated the three main suspects with one fell swoop.

But there was one big question which was still unanswered. 'If no one from the household had anything to do with María's death, why is someone trying to get me killed?' he demanded, and without waiting for a response, he turned on his heel and strode towards the park gates.

*

Paco covered nearly a kilometre and had almost reached his car when he heard the gunfire coming from the part of the cemetery he had left. He

129

wondered, briefly, who had started it. But it didn't really matter. *Asaltos* or Falangists, Falangists or *Asaltos* – what was the difference? This was not a fresh quarrel, merely a re-enactment of an old war – a war between the left and right which had plagued Spain for at least a century. A simple policeman like him couldn't do anything about it, even if he wanted to.

There were more shots. Paco got into his car and drove away.

Chapter Twenty-Four

The *Taverna* walls were decorated with the blue and white tiles of the south of Spain. Legs of mountain-ham hung from ceiling beams, and strings of garlic from hooks behind the bar. There was cured cheese in olive oil on the counter, and the smell of cooking floated enticingly through the air. It was a cool, pleasant place to be. But for all Paco noticed of his surroundings, it might as well have been the seediest bar in the seediest street in Madrid.

He checked his watch anxiously, for the tenth or eleventh time. Felipe had been gone for over an hour. Even with heavy traffic, it shouldn't have taken him that long to get back to the bar. So what the hell had happened to him?

'I should never have got him involved,' Paco told himself. 'When he gave me all that partnership shit, I shouldn't have listened.'

But the problem was, it wasn't shit, not to either of them. Paco thought back to some of the investigations he'd worked on over the years. The headless corpse in the metro. The tobacco smuggler's murder. The university professor who'd been discovered floating on the lake in the Casa de Campo. On all those cases, Felipe had been by his side, letting Paco bounce ideas off him, tolerating his boss's occasional bouts of irrationality, always steering a clear – if rarely inspired – course. To have cut Felipe adrift after what they'd been through together would have been both hurtful and insulting, and he deserved better than that.

The bar door swung open, and two people entered. One was a fat man in a shabby suit, the other a little mouse of a thing who had country girl written all over her. Paco breathed a heavy sigh of relief.

Paco watched as the fat constable guided Belén – the maid from the apartment opposite María's – between the tables. The girl seemed reluctant to be there, and but for the fact that Felipe had a firm grip on her arm, would probably have tried to run away. This wasn't going to be easy.

'What took you so long?' Paco asked.

'She was out shopping when I got there,' Felipe told him. 'I had to wait till she got back.'

Belén looked up at Felipe. 'You told me we were going to the police station,' she said accusingly.

'It's more comfortable here,' Paco said.

'Is this the man you've brought me to see?' Belén asked, and when Felipe nodded, she turned to Paco. 'Last time I met you, you said you were the landlord's agent, now it turns out you're a policeman. I don't know what to believe any more.'

'I *am* a policeman,' Paco assured her, 'and if I lied the last time, it was only because, in our line of work, deception is sometimes necessary.'

'I still don't like it,' the girl said, looking longingly over her shoulder at the door.

'Why don't you sit down?' Paco suggested.

'Don't want to sit—'

'We can talk better when you're sitting down,' Paco said, gently but firmly.

The maid sat, but only on the very edge of the chair. '*He* told me that María's dead,' she said, pointing at Felipe.

'I'm afraid it's true. Her body was discovered in the Retiro a few days ago. She'd been murdered. That's why we need you to answer a few questions for us.'

The girl's eyes had started to water, but she bit her lip and clenched her hands tightly on the table in front of her. 'What do you want to know?'

'You were a friend of hers, weren't you?'

A hesitation. 'I knew the señorita,' Belén admitted.

'I think it was more than that,' Paco said, as Felipe eased his large frame into the third chair. 'A minute ago, you called her María, and I bet that's what you called her to her face, too. In fact, I think you were the only person in the whole city she could really talk to. Isn't that true?'

'Maybe.'

'And what did you talk about?'

Belén shrugged. 'This and that. Our villages. The city. What we'd do if we were rich.'

'But María was already rich, wasn't she?'

'No, she . . . she . . .'

'She what?'

'Nothing.'

'She must surely have been rich to afford that expensive apartment, mustn't she?' Paco said.

The girl looked down at the table. 'I suppose so.'

'And she didn't even have a job, did she? So where did her money come from?'

'I . . . I've no idea,' Belén stuttered.

'Yes, you have,' Paco said. 'You nearly always knew when she had visitors, didn't you?'

The girl nodded. 'I spend most of my time working in the kitchen. You can always hear when anybody comes down the hallway.'

Paco smiled. 'And you always look through the peep-hole in the front door to see who it is, don't you?'

The girl blushed, as if she felt she'd been caught out in something wicked. 'It's very boring being in the kitchen all the time,' she said, excusing herself. 'Seeing who's going by makes my life a little more interesting.'

'And how many people came to see her?'

'Only two.'

'Both of them men?'

'Yes.'

'And you're sure she never had any other visitors?'

'I'm sure.'

Paco took out his cigarettes, and lit one. 'Did either of the two men ever quarrel with her?'

'I don't know.'

'Surely, you'd have heard them if they had.'

'The walls are quite thick.'

Paco sighed. 'Did she ever have any bruises – as if one of them might have hit her?'

'No.'

'Did she ever tell you she'd quarrelled with either of them?'

'No.'

'So what did she say about them?'

'I think she quite liked the old man sometimes.'

The old man! Christ, Herrera was forty-five! Paco wondered when had been the last time he'd thought of forty-five as old. 'What do you mean, she quite liked the older man?' he prodded.

Belén shrugged. 'She didn't say it in so many words, but I got the feeling that he didn't just, you know, take her to bed. That he sometimes talked to her.'

'And the younger man?'

'He was never there for more than half an hour.'

Just enough time to screw her, Paco thought. It was looking as if Luis had been telling the truth when he said he hadn't loved her. 'María was often away, wasn't she – sometimes for as long as a week?' he asked, turning his line of questioning in a new direction.

'Yes, she was often away.'

'Do you have any idea where she went?'

'All over the country.'

It was so exasperating. Every scrap of information had to be dragged from this girl. 'Where exactly did she go?' Paco asked.

Belén frowned in concentration. 'Burgos, Valladolid, Granada, Leon . . . and Seville. She went to Seville three or four times.'

'Why did she make all those journeys?'

'I asked her that once. She said she'd like to tell me, but she couldn't.'

'Had it anything to do with her gentleman – the older man?'

'I don't know.'

'Perhaps she was lying to you about where she went,' Paco suggested.

Belén shook her head. 'She wouldn't do that. I was her friend. Anyway, she always sent me picture postcards from the places she visited.'

So either she really had travelled all over Spain, or she had constructed an elaborate fraud to fool Belén. But why would anybody go to the trouble of fooling a simple maid? 'Did you hear anything unusual on the night María disappeared?' Paco asked.

'When was that?'

'Four evenings ago.'

The girl counted back on her fingers. 'It was my day off. I went back to the village, and didn't return to Madrid until the first train the next morning.'

Paco sighed again. How he would have loved to phone the police stations in all the places María had visited, and ask them if they could add to his knowledge of the girl. But a policeman under suspension had no right to do that. And Felipe couldn't do it, either, because his only concern was supposed to be the two socialists who had been shot to death outside the *casa del pueblo*.

'Can I go now?' Belén asked, with an odd mixture of timidity and aggression.

Paco, whose mind was more on the dead girl's journeys than it was on the girl in front of him, nodded absent-mindedly. 'Constable Fernández will drive you back to your employers' apartment,' he said.

'I'd rather walk,' the girl told him.

'It's no trouble,' Fat Felipe said gallantly.

'The police are always trouble,' the girl replied. 'I'm nervous just being with you.'

'Give her the tram fare, Felipe,' Paco said.

'I don't want the tram fare,' the girl insisted. 'All I want is to be left alone to get on with my job.'

Yes, Paco thought. That's all any of us want.

*

They sat in silence for several minutes after Belén had left, then Paco said, 'Don Carlos hinted that Luis had some kind of alibi. Check on it, will you?'

'You think he might be our murderer?' Felipe asked.

'It's unlikely,' Paco admitted. 'But then it's unlikely that any of them did it. Luis could have María any time he wanted, and I'm pretty sure that he was pretty sure neither María herself nor Méndez would ever dare to tell Herrera about it. Doña Mercedes didn't care what her husband did, as long as he left her alone. Which leaves us with Herrera himself. The trouble is, Don Carlos was right about him, too.'

'Right in what way?'

'About the fact that Herrera had no apparent motive for killing María. If he wanted to get rid of her, all he had to do was kick her out and she'd have gone scurrying back to her village with her tail between her legs. And even if she'd wanted to hurt him politically, she'd have had no idea how to go about it. So why run the risk of hiring someone to kill her?' Paco stopped suddenly. 'Unless . . .'

'Unless?'

'Unless he had her killed for some reason totally unconnected with their affair.'

'For example?'

Paco slapped his forehead with the palm of his hand. 'That's the problem,' he admitted. 'I've no bloody idea.'

Chapter Twenty-Five

He had never been a marked man before, and the knowledge that he now was changed his whole perception of the world around him. Streets which had been comfortably familiar to him for years seemed filled with menace. Shadows, which only the day before he would have ignored, took on the sinister aspect of lurking assassins. Even on Calle de Hortaleza, which came as close as anything did to being what Paco called home, he felt threatened with every step he took. And the worst of it was, he told himself, he didn't even know why he had been singled out for elimination – had no idea at all what it was that Herrera feared he might discover.

He reached the *Cabo de Trafalgar* without encountering any trouble, and once through its door, a feeling of security started to seep into him.

Bernardo was sitting alone at their usual table in the corner. Paco went over to join him. 'Where's Ramón?' he asked, as he sat down. 'It's not like him to be late.'

'Ramón won't be coming in tonight,' Bernardo said, a sheepish expression on his face. 'Or any other night, for that matter. Nacho told him to find somewhere else to drink.'

'Did they have an argument or something?'

'No, it's just that his face doesn't fit in here.'

'It's fitted well enough for the last twelve years,' Paco said, feeling anger bubbling up inside him. 'I'm going to have a word with Nacho about this.'

He started to rise to his feet. Bernardo reached across the table and pulled him down again. 'Before you talk to Nacho, I think *we* should have a talk,' the big market porter said.

'All right,' Paco agreed. 'But make it quick.'

'The political situation's worsening by the hour,' Bernardo said. 'The right-wing newspapers have been suspended. So has the parliament. There was a gun-fight at Calvo Sotelo's funeral . . .'

'I know. I heard it.'

'. . . four people were definitely killed, and fuck knows how many more were wounded—'

136

'We were discussing Ramón – our friend – not the state of the country,' Paco reminded him.

Bernardo shook his head, wonderingly. 'You still don't understand, do you? Spain's being split right down the middle. There was a time when the Carlists wouldn't have been seen dead with the Falange, but now they're acting like they're the best of friends. And we, the socialists, have taken the communist militia into our ranks – something I thought we'd never do.'

'Get to the point,' Paco said impatiently.

'Once, there was room for all shades of opinion,' Bernardo told him. 'But that time's past. You're either black or white, and since Ramón isn't white, he has to be the other thing. So talk to Nacho if you must, but it won't make any difference. Even if he wanted to let Ramón come back, he wouldn't dare to do it. He'd lose most of his other customers if he did.'

'What about me?' Paco demanded. 'Does my face still fit in here?'

Bernardo shrugged. 'Everybody knows you're not political, Paco. But even you'll have to come off the fence eventually.'

'And if I don't?'

'Then both sides will see you as the enemy.'

Why did everyone always have to make things so complicated? Paco wondered. For a second he was on the point of walking out, then he remembered why he had gone to the bar in the first place. 'I need a couple of favours, Bernardo,' he said, 'and I think you're the only one who can help me.'

'You've been a good friend to me,' the porter replied. 'So if you want something, you know you only have to ask.'

Paco leant forward, until his mouth was almost next to Bernardo's ear. 'When they suspended me, they took my gun away,' he whispered. 'And in my present circumstances, it's not good for me to be walking around unarmed.'

'Are you telling me that you want me to get you a—?' Bernardo said, in a voice so loud that all the bar could hear it.

'Shh,' Paco warned him.

'You're saying that you want me to get you a pistol?' Bernardo hissed.

'That's right.'

'You're crazy.'

'It shouldn't be too difficult,' Paco argued. 'Don't tell me you don't have any in the *casa del pueblo*.'

'Oh, we've got some, certainly. But we don't have enough weapons to arm our own people, let alone handing them out to anyone else who wants one.'

Paco placed his hand on his old friend's arm. 'Someone tried to kill me this morning.'

'Kill you!' Bernardo repeated, finding it a strain to keep his voice down. 'But why would anybody want to kill *you*?'

'Because I'm working on an investigation involving Herrera.'

'Eduardo Herrera? The politician?'

'Yes.'

A shrewd, calculating look came into Bernardo's eyes. 'What kind of investigation are you talking about?' he asked. 'Could it do him any damage?'

'Very possibly,' Paco said. 'I can't prove it yet, but I'm almost sure he's involved in a murder case.'

Bernardo whistled softly. 'That could really hurt him – even in these times,' he said. 'All right, I'll see you get your gun first thing in the morning. But you said two favours. What was the other one?'

'They didn't just take my pistol off me. They took my warrant card as well.'

'So?' Bernardo asked.

'I need some other kind of official document to replace it.

'A UGT membership card?' Bernardo said in amazement. 'That's what you want, isn't it?'

'If things fall apart like everyone expects them to, a union card will be the passport I need to get me into a lot of places I might have to visit.'

Bernardo grinned. 'And to think that only a few minutes ago I accused you of not being political,' he said. 'You've got more cunning than I ever imagined.'

Which was a reassuring thing to be told, Paco thought, because at the moment, cunning was the only thing he had on his side.

Chapter Twenty-Six

It took some courage to leave Bernardo and the comparative safety of the *Cabo de Trafalgar*, but it had to be done sooner or later, and at a little after one in the morning, Paco said his good nights and stepped out onto the street. It was, as always, full of people, and he recognized many of them. But what about the ones he didn't recognize? The young man in the overalls lounging outside the jeweller's store might be a disguised fascist. The middle-aged man who was walking a few steps behind him could, even at the moment, be reaching into his pocket for a pistol. If one of them was an assassin, there was nothing he could do about it!

It was almost a surprise to reach his own front door in one piece. He clapped his hands – though even doing that made him feel as if he were drawing unnecessary attention to himself – and the *sereno*, keys jangling from his belt, soon appeared.

'Have you let any strangers in tonight?' Paco asked, as the night watchman inserted his key in the front door.

'Strangers, Don Francisco? Now why should I have done that?'

Paco shrugged. Because you were bribed or intimidated into it, he thought. Because after the failure of their last attempt, they would make sure that the man they sent after him this time had enough intelligence to talk a simple night-watchman into doing what he wanted. But aloud, he said, 'I just wondered whether anyone in the block had had visitors you didn't recognize.'

'I've let no one into the house who didn't belong in it,' the night-watchman said, in a way which suggested that his dignity had been bruised.

'I'm sure you didn't,' Paco said, giving him a tip and stepping into the hallway.

As he made his way up the first few of the seventy-two wooden steps which led to his apartment, Paco felt his heart beating against his chest so loudly that he was certain anyone waiting for him would be well warned of his approach. He would have felt safer with a gun in his pocket. Tomorrow morning, Bernardo had promised, he would have one. But by tomorrow morning, he could already be dead.

He climbed another few steps, avoiding the spot on one of them which he knew creaked. He could go away, he told himself. He could get into his car and drive to Malaga or Soria, perhaps even across the border into France or Portugal. Once he had put some distance between himself and Madrid, he would be safe from the men in the blue shirts who wanted him dead. But he knew that he would not go away – that he was incapable of leaving a job half-finished.

He had passed the second-floor landing and already had his feet on the first step leading up to the third floor when he heard the door click open behind him.

He swung round. Knowing that it was pointless. Understanding that a hail of bullets in the front would do just as much harm as one in the back. Wondering why he had ever been so foolish as to return to his own apartment. Hoping that, against all odds, he might manage to survive. Accepting that . . .

'I've cooked a paella,' said a voice.

'You've done what?'

'My *sangría* was such a success with you that I thought I might as well try out a paella.'

Paco fought to control his breathing. There was no gunman standing there, only Cindy. Cindy, dressed in a short skirt and a thin sweatshirt which, for some inexplicable reason, had the number eighteen on it.

'How old are you?' he said.

'What makes you ask that?'

'I don't know.'

He didn't. The question – which had popped into his head in the middle of a whirlwind which was half-panic, half-relief – had come from no logical source that he could identify.

Cindy put her hand on her hip. 'It's not very gentlemanly to ask a girl's age,' she said, 'but if you must know, I'm twenty-nine.'

'I'm sorry. I didn't mean to . . .'

She held up her hand to silence him. 'Oh, I know it's rather late to be a graduate student,' she continued, 'but you have to remember I'm from the boonies. I'm the first person from my part of the state to even finish college, let alone go in for any further study.'

140

He was feeling an unexpected surge of happiness, Paco realized, and the source of that surge was the knowledge that, despite them being separated by a cultural gap as wide as the Straits of Gibraltar, she was only seven years younger than him.

She was looking at him strangely, as if she was trying to work out what was going on in his head. 'I didn't mean to be rude,' he told her. 'You really don't look twenty-nine.'

Cindy raised an eyebrow. 'It's too late to start playing at being gallant now, Ruiz. You've already revealed yourself in your true colours.'

It was not something a Spanish woman would ever have said, and he did not know how to take it. 'I never intended to insult you,' he told her, feeling his response was far from adequate.

Cindy threw back her head, and laughed. 'Oh, for heaven's sake, Paco, come inside before I burn the rice,' she said.

*

The paella was not the best he had ever tasted, but it was by no means the worst either, and so he compromised with the truth a little, and told her she was a brilliant cook.

'Liar!' Cindy said. 'But thanks anyway.'

She brushed away a strand of hair which had strayed into her right eye. He found it very hard to believe that she was nearly thirty. 'You're very beautiful,' he said.

'I might have passed for beautiful back home, but now I've seen the Spanish girls and I realize my limitations,' Cindy said, without bitterness.

'Yes, Spanish girls can be beautiful, too,' Paco agreed. 'But in a different way.'

Cindy mopped her plate with a piece of bread. 'I know you're a policeman, but you still haven't told me what kind,' she said. 'Who do you work for? If I had to bet, I'd put my money on your being on the Homicide Squad.'

The accuracy of her guess shook him. What had made her choose that above all other branches of police work? he wondered. Did he look like a man who was obsessed with killing? Did the spectre of death cling to him like an invisible cloak? He suddenly felt badly in need of a scalding shower.

'I'm right, aren't I?' Cindy said.

'Er . . . yes. As a matter of fact, you are.'

Cindy grinned. 'I thought so. Somehow I just can't see you watching for pickpockets or arresting petty thieves. You'd have to be involved in something more important – something that really altered people's lives.'

So, at least as far as she was concerned, there was no stink of death about him after all. Paco felt a sense of relief which was so deep it almost frightened him.

'I've done all those things,' he said, talking normally, trying to lower the emotional temperature of the room. 'I've followed pickpockets on the metro and arrested burglars, just like every other cop.'

'But that was never more than a hurdle you had to get over,' Cindy said, 'a step further towards what you really wanted to do. You were born to be a homicide cop, Paco Ruiz. I can tell that just by looking at you.'

Which was much what Captain Hidalgo had told him a couple of days earlier, Paco thought. And both the captain and Cindy were right, because here he was – with no official status, with a gang of murderers on his trail – and he was still being a cop.

Cindy poured them both another glass of Rueda. 'You want to talk about it?'

'What?'

'Your latest case?'

'No,' Paco said automatically.

'I don't mind,' Cindy told him. 'Really I don't. Whatever you're working on, it's obviously preying on your mind. It might help to talk about it to someone who isn't involved.'

'Perhaps you're right,' Paco confessed, and almost before he realized he was doing it, he was spilling out the details over the last of the wine.

*

They had made love, and now they sat on the bed, smoking. And naked. Paco tried to picture himself and Pilar in a similar position and failed. His wife had always considered it practically a mortal sin for her to move during intercourse. The last time he had slept with her, she seemed almost ashamed to have sex at all.

'The main question is – why did she do it?' Cindy said.

'I beg your pardon?'

'María. Why did she do all that travelling? From what you've said, she was very much the country girl.'

'That's right.'

Cindy blew two streams of grey smoke through her nostrils, and Paco found himself becoming aroused all over again.

'Country girls don't travel,' Cindy said.

With effort, Paco pushed the thought of sex to one side. 'María came to the city,' he said. 'Isn't that travelling?'

'No, it isn't,' Cindy told him. 'Let me tell you what it's like to be a boonie . . .'

'Don't forget, I'm from the countryside, too.'

'But you're a man, and that's different. Men have always been peddlers, or soldiers, or drovers – any number of things which caused them to travel about – but until recently, the woman's place has been in the home.'

Paco smiled at her confidence, her Yankee self-assuredness. 'Go on,' he said.

'If you're a boonie girl, you go to the city because you really want something badly – a better life or higher education. You're terrified by the size of everything, but slowly you get used to it, and finally you start to feel comfortable. But two worlds is enough for you to conquer. You either stay in your new home, or go back to your old one. Itchy feet are for people brought up in sophistication.'

'You're here in Madrid,' Paco pointed out. 'Doesn't that disprove your theory?'

'I'm here for the sake of my higher education,' Cindy said, brushing his objection aside. 'I needed to be here. And even then, even though I'd been working towards this for a long, long time and was real excited about it, I had to force myself to walk up the gangplank of the boat that brought me to Spain.'

She was waving her hands as she made her points, and her breasts were shaking gently. They were nice breasts, Paco thought, round and not too large. In fact, everything about her was nice.

Cindy laughed. 'Stop lusting after me and keep your mind on the subject,' she said.

'What subject?'

'Why María travelled around so much.'

'Well, if she didn't do it for pleasure . . .'

'And I'm sure she didn't.'

'. . . then she must have been on business. But whose?'

'Not her own,' Cindy said firmly. 'She had no training and no money. Maybe it was part of her job as Herrera's mistress, to keep him company wherever he was.'

'You're assuming that Eduardo Herrera makes a lot of trips himself,' Paco said.

'And doesn't he?'

'No, he's a very active deputy in the *Cortes*. His speeches are in the papers nearly every day. There simply isn't any way he could leave Madrid for weeks at a time.'

Cindy lit another cigarette from the butt of her first. 'All right, then. If she went alone, maybe she was doing for Herrera what he couldn't do for himself.'

'You mean, she was his partner?'

'Why should he make a peasant girl his partner? If she was anything, she was simply his courier.'

Paco shook his head in admiration. 'You're a very smart woman,' he said.

'Of course I am,' Cindy agreed. 'Some day, I'm going to be a doctor of philosophy.'

The sound of footsteps on the staircase below exploded like thunder in Paco's head.

'But the question is . . .' Cindy continued.

'Quiet!' Paco whispered.

'Why should I . . .?'

He clamped his hand over her mouth. The footsteps got louder, reached the landing outside Cindy's front door – and stopped.

At least there was only one of them, Paco thought. He might be able to take just one of them, even if the son of a bitch had a gun. Making as little noise as he could, he slipped off the bed, padded to the kitchenette, and picked up a carving knife.

You shouldn't have come here! his angry brain screamed at him. You should never have put Cindy at such risk.

Outside, a man coughed, said, '*Joder!*' and then began to ascend the stairs again. Paco realized that Cindy was standing beside him, trembling.

'Who was it?' she whispered.

'Señor Lopez. My neighbour from across the corridor. He's not as young as he used to be. Nowadays, he needs to stop for a rest at every landing.'

'So why did he scare you so much?' Cindy asked. 'Or were you expecting someone else?'

'In troubled times like these, you can't be too careful,' Paco said.

Cindy frowned. 'You told me all about María, so why don't you level with me on this?' she said.

'I will,' Paco promised, walking back into the bedroom and reaching for clothes. 'But not tonight.'

'You're going?' Cindy said, the disappointment evident in her voice.

'I have to,' he replied.

Had to because, if he was going to get killed, it would be in his own apartment or somewhere else which didn't endanger Cindy.

He stepped into his trousers, and wished he already had the gun.

Chapter Twenty-Seven

In the pleasant morning light, the fears of the previous evening seemed foolish, but Paco did not con himself into thinking that the threat had gone away. Still, he had at least survived the night, and now he was sitting in a Galician bar on Calle Fuencarral, drinking strong black coffee with Felipe.

'If there's one thing left-wingers hate more than the fascists, it's each other,' Felipe was saying. 'There were gunfights all over the city last night, and most of them were between the socialists and the anarchists.'

Paco nodded absent-mindedly, and wondered why the girl had chosen to be murdered in such chaotic times. Or perhaps he was examining the problem from the wrong angle. Perhaps it was because of the chaos that she'd had to die.

'With all this trouble, the military's bound to take over soon,' Felipe said gloomily. 'Even if that miserable bastard General Mola doesn't do something, that little shit Franco will.'

Paco looked around him. There were a number of customers sitting at the cast-iron tables, having a mid-morning snack of coffee and *churros*. At the bar, two workmen were drinking 'sun and shade', an intoxicating mixture of brandy and anis. Outside, a shoeblack was plying his trade, and a lottery-ticket seller was shouting that he had the day's lucky numbers. How could everything seem so normal when, in fact, Madrid was nothing but a vast lunatic asylum which the inmates seemed about to take over?

'Did you check up on Luis's alibi?' he asked Felipe.

'On the day of the murder, Luis went to see the bulls,' the fat constable said, in his best witness box manner.

'That's what he told me. Was he alone?'

'No. He went with a bunch of mates from his boxing days.'

So that was one lie at least the valet had told. 'Why is this down on record?' he asked.

'Because he got in trouble even before the first *corrida* had started.'

'What kind of trouble?'

'He met one of his old rivals. They were both drunk. They had an argument, then started throwing punches. Somebody called the cops, and by the time they arrived, things had turned really nasty. Luis and the other man were arrested.'

'And charged?'

'No, the local cops didn't want the paperwork. They threw the two of them into the cells to sober up. Then, the next morning, they let them out with a warning.'

If Luis had such a watertight alibi, why hadn't he produced it? Paco wondered. But he thought he already knew the answer. The valet had been terrified that his master – his precious master – would find out he'd been in trouble with the police, and dismiss him.

'Being in gaol doesn't put him in the clear,' Felipe said. 'He could have arranged for one of his pals to kill María.'

Paco shook his head. 'He might have set his mates on me,' he said, 'but if he had killed María out of jealousy, he'd have wanted to do it himself.' He paused to light a cigarette. 'Did you check on Carlos Méndez as well?'

'Yes, but only because you asked me to,' Felipe replied. 'I couldn't see the point myself.'

'He *is* one of the family,' Paco reminded his constable. 'What did you find out about him?'

'There are strong rumours that he's a nancy boy. One of the constables I talked to even thinks he remembers Méndez being arrested once, in a general sweep of queers. But since he's got influence, he was soon released and the paperwork went missing.'

Paco nodded. He could well believe Don Carlos was a homosexual; the man had admitted as much in the cemetery the previous day. 'What else?' he asked.

'His official title is Herrera's private secretary.'

'And what does that entail?'

'From what I can gather, whatever Herrera wants it to. Booking the halls for meetings, answering his less important letters, screening his appointments . . .'

And closing the car door after his boss had stepped majestically out of the vehicle, Paco thought. 'Is that all you've got?' he asked Felipe.

'No,' the constable said cautiously. 'I've been thinking about these trips María took.'

'What about them?'

'Well, she travelled all over Spain, as we know, but the place she went to most often was Seville.'

'So what?'

'So this morning, I found out that Herrera just happens to own a big business there.'

'What kind of business?'

'A silk factory.'

Maybe Cindy had been right, Paco thought. Maybe Herrera had been using María as a courier. But if he had, what had she been carrying? Money? Confidential documents? Would he have entrusted such important matters to a peasant girl?

'You haven't uncovered any connection between Herrera and the rest of the places that María visited, have you?' he asked, without much hope.

'He's got party offices in most of them, but then he's got offices in nearly every big town in Spain, including the ones that María didn't visit.'

Why was she killed? Paco asked himself for the thousandth time. María had mostly stayed at home when she was in Madrid, and had only been visited by two men. Rule out blackmail and sexual jealousy as motives, and what was he left with? Something which happened on one of her trips. 'It looks like I'm going to have to go down to Seville myself, and do some checking,' he said.

Felipe massaged his treble chin. 'I know I was the one brought Seville up,' he said, 'but even so, it seems like a long way to go on what might turn out to be a wild-goose chase.'

'What other kind of geese do I have to chase?' Paco asked.

'Very true,' Felipe agreed.

*

The two detectives stepped through the doorway and out into the street. The light in the bar had been pleasantly subdued, but outside it struck the pavement with force, then bounced back to blind them. Paco lifted his hand to shield himself from the second half of the attack – the direct sunlight overhead.

'It's going to be another hot one,' Felipe said.

His eyes adjusting to the brightness, Paco checked the street. The lottery-ticket seller was still there, as was the shoe-shine boy. And just a few metres up the road from the bar, a young knife-grinder had stopped his hand-cart and was blowing on his pipes to announce his arrival.

'We should close down the police stations for the summer,' Felipe said, passing his hand across his brow. 'We should close them down and piss off to the coast, where it's a bit cooler.'

148

'And who would catch the criminals if we did that?' Paco asked, his mind more on the street than on what his partner was telling him.

The knife-grinder was looking in their direction. No, more than that – he was watching them. And there was something else. Though Paco couldn't quite place his face, he was sure that he had seen the man before.

'The criminals could come to the coast as well,' Felipe said. 'The rest would do them good.'

The knife grinder was still blowing on his pipes, but the whole picture looked unconvincing. It was almost as if he were merely playing a part – as if standing next to a cart was a new experience for him, and the overalls he was wearing felt so unnatural against his skin that they were making him itch.

'I mean, just think about it for a minute,' Felipe continued. 'We could nick a few villains in the morning, before it got too hot, then in the afternoon . . .'

The knife-grinder raised his right arm and pointed it at the two detectives. But he wasn't just pointing, Paco realized, with sudden horror – he was fingering them!

Paco turned and looked down the street. A black Hispano-Suiza was making its way slowly towards them. He turned again. The knife-grinder had abandoned his cart and was walking rapidly but stiffly away down the road.

Stiffly? Of course! That was where he'd seen the boy before, outside María's apartment. He'd been the one with the knife – the one Paco had kicked in the groin.

The black Hispano-Suiza had started to pick up speed. '. . . and if we could all of us agree to have a siesta at the same time . . .' Felipe was saying.

'Down!' Paco screamed.

Fat Felipe looked at him as if he'd lost his mind. 'Down?' he repeated.

There was no time to explain – no time to do anything but act. Paco kicked Felipe's legs from underneath him and by the time the constable hit the pavement, his boss was already pulling his gun free of its shoulder holster.

There were three young men in the Hispano-Suiza, one driving and two leaning out of their windows with pistols in their hands. Paco ignored the gunmen, and aimed at the driver. The shot rang out like the crack of a mule driver's whip, the windscreen shattered – but the car kept on coming.

To Paco, it seemed as if every noise had suddenly been magnified. The car's engine screamed, and the echo of the shot was like thunder as it bounced from one side of the street to the other. Even Felipe's laboured breathing, as he began to recover from the shock of being thrown to the ground, had the intensity of a lion's roar.

Paco fired again, still aiming at the driver. The Hispano-Suiza swerved violently. Paco felt a bullet zing past his cheek, and heard a second thud into the wall behind him. The car was almost level with him now. He fired a third shot, and saw one of the gunmen jerk violently backwards.

And then it was all over. The car was past them, speeding down towards the Red de San Luis, zig-zagging to avoid hay carts and shocked pedestrians.

Paco knelt down beside his partner, who was sprawled awkwardly across the pavement. 'Were you hit?' he asked anxiously.

Felipe groaned. 'Well, if I wasn't, this is a bloody awful attack of indigestion,' he said through clenched teeth.

It was then that Paco noticed a patch of red on his partner's chest – a patch which seemed to grow every time Felipe breathed out. 'We'll get you to hospital,' he said 'You'll be all right.'

Felipe groaned again. 'If one of us was going to be hit, it was bound to be me,' he said. 'My problem is, I'm such a fucking big target.'

Chapter Twenty-Eight

There had been several people in the white-tiled waiting-room, but one by one they had left, and now only two remained – Felipe's partner, and Felipe's wife.

Isabel sat serenely in a straight-backed chair, her hands folded neatly on her lap, but Paco paced the floor, lighting one cigarette after another.

'That won't help him,' Isabel said.

Paco turned to look at her. Who would ever have imagined that big, fat Felipe would have married such a thin, ethereal creature? he thought.

'It won't help him,' Isabel repeated, as if she were getting some twisted satisfaction from making the statement.

'Chest wounds can be tricky things,' Paco said. 'I'm worried about him.'

'The time for worrying is past,' Isabel told him. 'It is in God's hands, now.'

And who would have thought that Felipe, who was about as devout as a stray dog, could actually have made a life together with anyone so pious?

'He admires you, you know,' Isabel said.

'He what?'

'Admires you. For your honesty and your determination. He was always telling me that he considered it a real privilege to work with you.'

Oh my God, Paco thought. Not that! Not that!

Because the last thing he wanted at that moment was the extra burden of hero worship from a man who was lying on an operating table only because of him.

The waiting-room door swung open, Don Eduardo Herrera swept in, with Carlos Méndez following at his heel. Méndez seemed surprised, almost shocked, to see Paco standing there, but Herrera only gave him a cursory inspection, then, with the air of a man whose time is too valuable to waste, glanced at his watch.

He doesn't even recognize me! Paco thought. He's ordered my death – it *has* to be him – and he doesn't even recognize me! 'What are you doing here, you bastard?' he said angrily. 'Come to gloat?'

Herrera looked around, as if he found it impossible to imagine that the remark was being addressed to him. Then, seeing no one but Méndez, he turned to face Paco again. 'I know you from somewhere,' he said, looking closely at the inspector for the first time. 'I have it! You were parked outside my house the other day.'

'This is Inspector Ruiz,' Don Carlos said.

If the face hadn't meant much to Herrera, the name meant a great deal. He scowled with deep displeasure. 'So you're the man who refuses to keep his nose out of my affairs,' he said.

'And you're the man who's ordered his thugs to kill me,' Paco replied.

Herrera's face went blank. 'I don't know what you're talking about,' he said.

He was good, Paco admitted, but half the trick to being a successful politician was to learn how to act the innocent. 'Those Falangists on Hermosilla yesterday?' he said. 'The gunmen in the car this morning – the ones who shot my partner? You know nothing about them?'

'Nothing.'

'Then I repeat, what the fuck are you doing here?'

'We're here to visit some of my brother-in-law's loyal supporters who have been attacked—' Don Carlos started to explain.

'Don't talk to this man!' Herrera ordered his brother-in-law. 'Don't even give him the time of day.' He raised a finger and pointed it at Paco. 'I allow no one to speak to me as he has just done. He'll be made to pay for his words.'

Paco felt the urge to throw himself on the politician, to beat the man to a bloody pulp. But how could he do that with Isabel Fernández sitting there? How could he force her to witness such indignity when her husband was only a few metres away, fighting for his life?

'Get out of here!' he ordered Herrera, through clenched teeth. 'Get out of here while you still have the chance.'

'Listen, Inspector Ruiz . . .' Méndez began.

'I told you not to speak to that man,' Herrera said imperiously. 'We *will* leave, but not because some jumped-up official has told us to. We'll leave because I can't bear to be in the same room as him a second longer.'

He turned on his heel, and left as dramatically as he had entered. Carlos Méndez gave Paco one helpless, hopeless look, then followed his master.

'He's nothing but a bag of piss and wind,' Paco growled.

Yes, but Herrera was a dangerous bag of piss and wind, he reminded himself – a poisonous bag, with the power to issue orders which got people killed.

He turned to look at Isabel Fernández. Felipe's wife more than ever seemed to resemble Our Lady of the Sorrows, and if she had heard his angry exchange with Herrera, she gave no sign of it.

Paco lit another cigarette. The acrid smoke raked at his throat. He considered stubbing it out, but then what would he do with his hands?

The door opened, and a young doctor entered. 'Are you Señora Fernández?' he asked Isabel.

Isabel stood up. 'Yes, that's me,' she said, with considerable dignity. 'How is my husband?'

The doctor placed a comforting hand on her shoulder. 'We've done all we can,' he said. 'Now it's up to him. If he can somehow summon up the strength to . . .' He trailed off, knowing his words were inadequate, but having nothing else to offer.

'He's going to die, isn't he?' Isabel said.

'I'm afraid we must brace ourselves to expect the worst,' the doctor replied.

Isabel bent her head in meek obedience to God's will. Paco could have slapped her.

First an innocent girl had been murdered, he thought, and then his partner was at death's door. He would probably never find the man whose hands had choked the life out of María, nor the three who had gunned his partner down. And he didn't really care if he didn't, because they were just the instruments of the attacks – no more important than the pistols they had used. What he wanted was the man who had given the orders. And whatever it took, he would have him.

Part Two

Seville 16–18 July 1936

Chapter Twenty-Nine

The afternoon sun was at its height, and the countryside shimmered in a sickly heat haze. Paco took one hand off the steering wheel, and wiped the sweat from his brow. It was crazy to drive to Seville, he thought for the fiftieth time. So what if María had visited the city on several occasions. How was that going to lead him to her murderer? Yet if the solution didn't lie in Seville, where did it lie? Not in Madrid. And not in María's village in the mountains, either. He had got all he could out of those two places.

'I'll find the answer in Seville,' he told the parched fields which lay ahead of him. 'I *have* to find the answer in Seville. I owe that much to Felipe.'

He made good time on the first forty-seven kilometres of his journey, because he was travelling on the royal road, built at the time of the monarchy to connect the capital with the palace in Aranjuez. After Aranjuez, it was a different story. The road deteriorated almost immediately after he had left the town, and the further he drove into the open countryside, the worse it became.

As he avoided pot-holes and swerved across the road to overtake farm carts, Paco found his mind drifting back, inevitably, to Felipe. They'd been a good team, he thought, complementing each other's strengths, compensating for each other's weaknesses, and making – between them – one perfect investigator.

And now Felipe was as good as dead. Though Paco still found it hard to believe, the man who had been enjoying his coffee and bun only a few hours earlier was probably now lying on a cold morgue slab.

'I miss him already,' he said softly.

But there was more to it than that. Whatever was waiting for him in Seville, it was sure to be both complicated and dangerous, and without the reassuring presence of Felipe by his side, he was more frightened than he cared to admit.

*

It was evening by the time he reached Valdepeñas, but even the lethargic descent of the sun didn't do much to relieve the suffocating heat inside the

157

Fiat. An inn loomed ahead, surrounded by fields of vines. It was an old squat, stone building, which must have seen much history, yet seemed untouched by it. If Paco had had Felipe with him, he would have asked the fat constable what he thought about staying there for the night. As it was, he simply pulled up by the front door, and went inside.

The main room of the inn had a flag floor, covered with straw. A tap dripped continuously into the enamel sink, and the air was filled with a mixture of frying olive oil, cigarette smoke, and cow dung from the boots of the drovers who made up most of the clientele. Paco walked across to one of the tables and sat down, aware that every other man in the room was watching him.

A scrawny waiter with a wall eye and bad teeth appeared. 'Can I help you, señor?' he asked, giving Paco's smart suit a close inspection as he spoke.

'I'd like some food now, and after that I'd like a room for the night,' Paco told him.

'The food we can manage – rabbit with garlic – but we have no rooms spare,' the waiter said unconvincingly.

'None?'

'None.'

Paco reached into his pocket and pulled out the UGT membership card Bernardo had given him that morning. 'Are there any rooms free now?' he asked.

The waiter examined the card as if he suspected a trick. 'There might be one free,' he admitted.

'And can I have it?'

The waiter grinned. 'Of course, comrade. And now I will go and get your food for you.'

The waiter disappeared into the kitchen, and returned with a plate of rabbit, a flask of wine, and two glasses. After he had put the plate in front of Paco, he sat down and poured them both a drink. 'Where have you come from?' he asked.

Paco looked down at the rabbit. It smelled good, as country cooking always did, but there was not much meat on it. Still, it was better than nothing. 'I've come from Madrid,' he said.

The waiter took a sip of his wine. 'And how are things in the capital?'

'Things are very confused. No one really seems to be in control any more.'

'Are there many fascists there?'

Paco thought of the three young men in blue shirts who had attacked him outside María's apartment, and of the other three who had gunned down his partner. 'Oh yes, there are plenty of fascists,' he said.

The waiter nodded, as if that were the answer he had expected. 'There are fascists here, too. Not so many as in Madrid, but they swagger around as if they owned the place.'

Paco laughed. 'And don't they?'

The waiter looked at him suspiciously for a second, then joined in his laughter. 'I suppose the do own it – legally,' he said. 'The law has always been on the side of the rich. But their time is running out. We – the people – have suffered long enough. It is our country, and very soon we will take it back.'

Paco slipped another piece of the skinny rabbit into his mouth and wondered what the señoritos who controlled all the land around the inn would be eating that night. Wondered, too, what they would be wearing in the morning, when they rode around on their thoroughbred horses, watching the ragged peasants work their fields for them. 'They won't give up without a fight,' he warned.

'*Joder*! We know that,' the waiter exclaimed.

'And they will be better armed than you are.'

The waiter nodded gravely. 'It is undoubtedly true what you say. We're sure they've got weapons stored all over the place – in barns, bodegas, even buried in orchards – but our cause is just, and we are courageous.'

Paco sighed. How many times had he heard such brave, foolish talk in the army? 'You should tread carefully,' he said. 'I served with men in Morocco who thought it was a glorious thing to rush into battle. Most of them died there.'

The waiter poured him another glass of wine. 'What are you saying?' he asked, with a touch of hostility creeping into his voice. 'That we shouldn't fight?'

'It's always better not to fight if you don't have to,' Paco replied. 'But if you must fight, then at least plan in advance how you are going to do it. You can be sure that the fascists will.'

One of the drovers sitting near the door banged his glass on the table. 'More wine, Julio!'

'Coming,' the waiter replied, standing up.

'Remember,' Paco said, 'plan it in advance. Martyrs may have candles lit for them, but they never get to plough their own fields or see their grandchildren grow up.'

*

He was back on Calle Fuencarral with Fat Felipe. They'd just left the Galician bar, and were walking towards the Red de San Luis. The shoeshine boy was there. So was the knife-grinder who wasn't a knife-grinder at all. Paco wasn't going to be taken by surprise this time. Even as he spun round to face the Hispano-Suiza, he was reaching for his pistol.

Then he saw them! Reyes, his long-dead love from Melilla. And María, the girl who he'd never have known about if she hadn't been murdered. They were walking along arm-in-arm. And they looked so much alike that they could have been sisters!

Just over their shoulders, he could see the menacing black car with the two gunmen leaning out of the windows. He knew he should fire on it, but he couldn't. His hand was frozen above his shoulder holster, and though he tried to scream out a warning, the words wouldn't leave his mouth.

The black car drew closer and closer. Suddenly there was a hail of bullets – far more than could have come from just two pistols. María and Reyes began to jerk, as if they were being manipulated by a crazed puppeteer. Blood gushed from their bodies in jets. Paco felt the bullets whiz past him, but though there were hundreds of them, perhaps even thousands, none of them struck him.

The car was gone. The two girls lay in a tangled heap on the pavement. Fat Felipe had fallen just a couple of metres further on. A crowd had gathered, and accusing fingers were being pointed at the one person who had not been hurt in the attack – a man standing alone, up to his ankles in blood.

*

Paco awoke in an unfamiliar bed, drenched in sweat. Through the window he heard the sound of cows lowing, and men clearing their throats of early morning phlegm. Up the stairs wafted the smell of freshly roasted coffee and warm bread. For a second, he didn't know where he was. And then it all came back to him.

As he climbed out of bed, he realized that he was still shaking from the nightmare. It would come back to haunt him again, he was sure of that. And each time it did return, it would have the same ending – with his failure to protect the ones he loved – because it could have no other.

In the mountains north of Jaen, Paco's progress was halted by a flock of sheep. For over half an hour, the seemingly endless stream of animals formed a vast wave of dirty white fleece across the road. Perhaps if he'd blown his horn, the shepherds might have made a gap in the flock through which he could pass. But he didn't think so. They were wild, mountain men, almost as dirty as their charges, and to them, anyone wearing a suit and driving a car was their natural enemy.

Outside Montoro, he heard a bang, felt the Fiat lurch to the right, and realized he had a flat tyre. Under the blazing sun, he struggled with the tight wheel-nuts and pondered on what the third disaster might be.

The third disaster came on the edge of Cordoba, at the hottest part of the day, when his radiator boiled over. It took fifteen minutes to walk to the nearest house, where he was given an olive oil can filled with water. As he returned to the Fiat, he wondered what comment Felipe would have made if he'd been there.

He could picture the fat constable, watching him pour the water into his radiator, then scratching his backside reflectively, and saying, 'You don't perhaps think that somebody's trying to tell us something, do you, *jefe*?'

And Paco, in return, would have said, 'What exactly do you mean by that?'

'Well, it's obvious we were never meant to get to Seville, so why don't we just turn around and go home?'

Paco grinned for the first time since he'd had his nightmare. Yes, that was what Felipe would have said all right. He would have expressed the doubts, and allowed his chief to take the positive attitude. But now there was no one to react against, and any doubts Paco felt – and there were many – had to come entirely from within himself.

'I've no choice but to go to Seville, Felipe,' he told his colleague.

'It's the only chance I have of ever getting a good night's sleep again.'

It was early evening when he finally reached the outskirts of Seville. Ahead of him, dwarfing the rest of the city, was the Giralda Tower, a Moslem minaret which had been transformed into a triumphant acclamation of Catholicism by Hernán de Ruiz – who, for all Paco knew, could have been a long-dead ancestor of his. In the shadow of the magnificent tower stood the cathedral, looking as much a fortress as a place of worship. There were orange trees everywhere, and lush green palms which swayed gently whenever a little breeze blew up.

The streets were bursting with life. Dashing men and dark-haired women walked around in a way which said that though Madrid had the government, Seville had the style. Gypsies sang and danced on street corners, hoping to earn a few centimos. Gentlemen in black riding sombreros and fancy waistcoats trotted by on magnificent Andalucian horses. Dogs, worn out by the heat of the day, lay sleeping fitfully in gutters.

Paco booked into a cheap *fonda* on the Calle de Santiago. Outside in the street, life still called, but he wanted no part of it. He drank two brandies and went straight to bed.

Chapter Thirty

The mercury in the thermometer fixed to the bar wall had climbed up to thirty-five, but Paco was sure the real temperature was six or seven degrees higher than that. This was heat, he thought. This made Madrid seem almost temperate.

He looked around the bar. It was a long, narrow room with entrances both at the front and the back. There was a chipped gilt-framed mirror behind the counter, and fading bull-fighting posters hanging on the walls. The barman, who had volunteered the fact that his name was Alvaro, was somewhere around forty. His face wore a permanently aggrieved expression, and his hairline was receding. Paco was his only customer.

Paco turned to examine the building on the other side of the road – the main reason he'd come into the bar in the first place. It was a square structure with high, arched windows. And though it was smaller than the tobacco factory where Bizet's Carmen had worked and sung her arias, it shared some of the more famous building's neo-classical grandeur.

'So that's the silk factory,' Paco said.

'Yes, that's it,' Alvaro agreed sourly.

Paco counted the guards. There were two permanently stationed at the front door, and four more on patrol around the perimeter. It seemed excessive security for an industrial unit, but perhaps when you were as important as Don Eduardo Herrera Moreno, it was necessary to protect all your property from your powerful enemies.

'Another wine?' Alvaro asked.

'Might as well,' Paco agreed. He swung round so he was facing the bar. 'Could I ask you a question, Alvaro?'

'Depends,' the barman said, without enthusiasm. 'What kind of question have you got in mind?'

Paco reached into his pocket, took out the photograph of María, and laid it on the counter. 'I was wondering if you'd ever seen this girl around?'

Alvaro squinted at the picture, but did not pick it up. 'Who are you?' he asked. 'Some kind of cop?'

'I used to be a policeman,' Paco admitted. 'But that's all over. Now, I work for myself.'

Alvaro took the picture between his thick finger and thumb and held it closer to his eyes. 'What kind of work do you do?' he asked. 'Confidential inquiries?'

'Yes.'

The barman shook his head doubtfully. 'It's easy for you to say that. Anybody can claim to be anything. But how do I know you're not still a cop? Or, at least, working for them.'

'You're a cautious man,' Paco told him.

Alvaro scratched his chin. 'In times like these, I'd be a fool to be anything else.'

Paco took out the UGT card, and held it up in front of him. 'Ever seen a policeman with one of these?' he asked.

The barman examined the card for quite a while. 'It would appear that you really are an honest working man,' he said finally.

'And the girl?' Paco prompted. 'Have you seen her?'

'Might have,' Alvaro conceded. 'Why? What's she done?'

'She hasn't done anything,' Paco lied. 'I'm just trying to trace her for someone.' He lowered his voice, even though there was no one to overhear. 'I can't go into all the details, of course, but it's a question of a legacy.'

Paco could also see the peseta signs light up in Alvaro's eyes. 'And if I help you find her, will there be anything in it for me?' the barman asked.

'There's a finder's fee of one hundred pesetas for every single person who has provided useful information. But, naturally, it's only payable *after* the girl has been located.'

The barman hesitated for a second, then said, 'She looks a little bit different in the picture, but if she's the girl I think she is, she's been in here for a coffee several times over the last year or so. A nice girl, she is. No swank to her.'

Paco lit a cigarette. 'And did she tell you what she was doing in Seville?'

Alvaro's eyes narrowed. 'What's her reason for her coming here got to do with finding her?'

'Isn't it obvious,' Paco responded. 'The more people I meet who've had contact with her, the more chance I have of finding her.'

'And the reward?'

'You get the same hundred pesetas whether you're the only person I talk to, or if I see fifty more.'

'She told me she was here on business,' Alvaro said. 'Didn't look like a business woman to me – more like a girl from the village who's had a few of the rougher edges rubbed off her. But there you are, that's what she said.'

'You don't happen to remember the last time she was here, do you?' Paco asked.

'I do, as a matter of fact. It was my birthday, you see.'

'And when exactly was that?'

'A week yesterday. The eighth. She was here in the morning.'

Just thirty-six hours before she was killed. There were moments during most cases when Paco felt a tingle which told him that, though he was still like a man blundering around in a dark room, he was finally getting near to the light switch. And he had that tingle now.

'Did she happen to mention to you what kind of business she was in?' he asked.

Alvaro shook his head. 'But I know she visited the silk factory, because I could see her walking across there from the window. So maybe she's a buyer from one of the big shops.'

'There's another possibility,' Paco said, watching the other man closely. 'Perhaps she was working directly for Don Eduardo Herrera Moreno.'

A look of pure loathing came to Alvaro's face. 'If I'd thought she was involved with Herrera, I'd never have served her a drink, as nice as she was.'

'I take it you don't like Herrera,' he said.

'I hate the son of a bitch. We all do. But not as much as we hate that bastard Méndez.'

Don Carlos? The private secretary? The opener of car doors and booker of halls? 'Why should you hate Méndez?' Paco asked.

'Because Herrera might own the silk factory, but it's his brother-in-law who runs it.'

That made no sense at all, Paco thought. Herrera was the businessman. Méndez was nothing more than the bankrupt son of a patrician family. 'You're sure Méndez's in charge?' he asked.

'He's certainly the one who's done all the negotiating,' Alvaro told him. 'Or maybe I should say lack of negotiating.'

'You're not making a lot of sense,' Paco said. 'Maybe you should tell me the whole story.'

Alvaro leaned on the counter, as if the narration of his grievance was going to be a long and exhausting process. 'Remember the troubles of '34? Remember Asturias?'

'Yes, I remember it,' Paco said.

Of course he did. How could any Spaniard ever forget it? It had been a bloody business. The miners of Asturias had risen against the right-wing government in Madrid, and taken over almost the whole of the province. They'd been well organized, and armed with rifles and dynamite, but still proved no match for the legionnaires and Moorish troops used by General Franco to crush the revolt. The campaign of pacification had been swift and brutal, and by the time it was finished, 1,300 people had lost their lives – many of them killed after the fighting was officially over.

'Well, Asturias wasn't the only place to give the government a headache,' Alvaro said, with obvious pride. 'Any number of factories went on strike down here, the silk factory among them.'

'That can't have pleased Méndez,' Paco said.

'That's where you're wrong. Oh, I'm not saying he was over the moon about it, but – considering he'd only just been put in charge of the factory – it didn't really seem to bother him, either.'

Timing was so important in this investigation, Paco thought. He felt instinctively that it was no coincidence that María had been killed when the country was teetering on the edge of collapse, and he was sure that it was not merely chance that had caused Méndez to take over the factory at the start of the troubles of '34. 'How can you be so sure it didn't bother Méndez?' he said.

'Because most of the owners and managers tried to negotiate with their workers, but all Méndez did was to chain up his doors. And they stayed chained up until around the fifth day of the strike, when the builders arrived.'

Paco's tingle was growing stronger. He still didn't know where the light switch in this particular case lay, but he sensed that he could almost reach out and touch it. 'So while the strike was on, Méndez took the opportunity to call the builders in,' he said.

'That's right. They were in there for days. Made one hell of a racket, as well.'

Paco examined the building again. The windows were set high in the wall – to let in light, not to be looked through. 'What exactly were they doing?' Paco asked.

'I've no idea,' Alvaro confessed.

'Weren't you curious? Didn't you ask any of the workers about it, once the strike was over?'

'I would have done – if any of the workers had ever got back inside to take a look.'

The tingle was still there, the switch was almost screaming at him to touch it, 'You're not telling me Méndez employed a completely new labour force, are you?' Paco asked.

'That's exactly what he did,' Alvaro said in disgust. 'And they're not even Spanish.'

'So where do they come from?'

There was a rumbling sound in the distance. Alvaro looked up at the wall clock as if to confirm a suspicion. 'Where do they come from?' he said. 'You'll see for yourself, if you wait a minute.'

Three open lorries pulled up outside the main door of the factory. On the back of each one were a couple of dozen dark-skinned men wearing knitted woollen caps.

'Second shift,' Alvaro said.

Two of the factory guards took up a position facing the top of the street, a second pair facing the bottom. The remaining two released the tailboards of the lorries. The dark-skinned men clambered down and disappeared into the factory. It wasn't exactly like watching prisoners being transferred from one gaol to another, but it wasn't that far from it, either.

'What are they?' Paco asked. 'Moroccans?'

'Could be. But to know for sure, you'd have to talk to them, and nobody around here ever has.'

'Nobody's talked to them?' Paco repeated, incredulously.

'Nobody.'

The guards were still in position, and now a second group of men was emerging from the silk factory and climbing onto the backs of the lorries.

'First shift going home,' Alvaro said.

The tailboards were fastened, and the lorries roared away. The whole operation had taken less than five minutes.

'Where do they live?' Paco asked.

167

'Herrera owns this old army barracks on the edge of town, and Méndez's Moors doss down there. I shouldn't be surprised if they live like pigs in shit, but again, nobody knows for sure. It's guarded day and night.'

'They must come out sometimes,' Paco said.

'Only to work. Everything they need, including their food, is taken to them.'

'They're almost like slaves,' Paco reflected. 'And I'll bet Méndez's paying them a fraction of what he gave to the old workers. Even with the cost of the guards, he must be saving Herrera a fortune.'

Alvaro shook his head condescendingly. 'You don't understand the man. He's not doing it to save money. He's doing it out of spite.'

'Spite?' Paco said doubtfully.

'The old workers dared to strike, and now he's not having them back in the factory at any price.'

'I would think that, working for Herrera as he is, saving money would be the main con—'

'He's not saving money,' Alvaro interrupted, obviously annoyed by Paco's scepticism. 'Look, one of the first things the Popular Front did when it took power last February, was to declare an amnesty for everyone who'd been punished for taking part in the troubles of '34.'

'I know that.'

'Which meant that any worker who'd been sacked for political reasons had to be recompensed for the wages he'd lost, and be given his old job back. Well, Méndez wasn't having any of that.'

'He refused to cough up the back-pay? So what? That's a commercial decision again. He probably realized that it would take the workers years to get the money back through the courts.'

Alvaro grinned, as if he'd just scored a point. 'Méndez didn't refuse to cough up. He gave all the workers the two years' wages he owed them. He didn't refuse to employ them again, either. He just wasn't having them back in the factory.'

Herrera was a shrewd businessman. He'd never have built up his empire from nothing if he hadn't been. And he was tight with his money: he took a girl from the country as his mistress, and clothed her in his wife's cast-off dresses. Would he really have allowed his brother-in-law to indulge himself in such expensive vindictiveness? 'Let me get this straight,' Paco said. 'Méndez is paying the workforce their full wages for sitting at home.'

'Exactly. And what's that, if it's not spite?'

Something very, very different, Paco thought. He looked across at the silk factory. The two guards on the door were as vigilant as ever, the ones on foot patrol were just turning the corner. They were all hard cases who looked as if they would not hesitate to use their weapons. Yet even as his stomach turned to water, Paco knew that if he were ever to turn up a motive for María's death, he was going to have to find a way past them and into the factory.

Chapter Thirty-One

The overhead fans whirled listlessly round, the radio on the bar counter blasted out strident *Sevillanas* which told of love and death. It was half-past eleven, and though it had been dark for some time, the city was coated with a layer of sticky heat.

Paco was in the corner, crouched over the phone and trying to compete with the general noise level of the bar. 'Is that the hospital of *Nuestra Señora de la Calatrava*?' he shouted into the instrument.

'Yes, it is,' replied a crisp, no-nonsense female voice, which sounded as if it was used to dealing with anxious calls.

'Can you put me through to a doctor? I want to ask about one of the patients.'

'I have all the information. Are you a relative?'

'No, but—'

'Bulletins on the state of patients' health can only be given to relatives.'

'The man I want to ask about is my partner!' Paco said desperately.

'You're in business together?'

'No, no. I'm a policeman and—'

'You're ringing about Constable Fernández?'

Paco sighed with relief. 'Yes, I am. Is he going to be all right?'

'As I said, if you're not a relative . . .'

'You can surely tell me whether he's going to live or to die, can't you?' Paco pleaded. 'Or . . . or if he's dead already.'

'If you came into the hospital and asked to see his doctor . . .' said the voice, giving nothing away.

'I'm in Seville,' Paco told her.

'In that case, I'm afraid there's nothing I can do.'

'I want to know!' said Paco, in a shout which was almost a scream.

'I'm sorry,' the voice said, with what sounded like genuine regret, 'but we have our procedures. It wouldn't be fair to the others.'

'I don't care about the others!' Paco said, but he was already talking to a dead line.

He walked across to one of the empty tables, and sat down. A waiter came across to him. 'What can I get you, señor?' he asked. There was not much enthusiasm in his words, but who could expect enthusiasm in a place where the air was almost hot enough to bake bread?

'I'll have a cognac,' Paco said. 'A Fundador, if you've got it.'

'Anything to eat?'

'Nothing.'

The waiter nodded, and made his way lethargically back to the bar. If Fat Felipe had been with him, they'd have been ordering something to eat, Paco thought. Felipe could not have come to Seville without doing the complete gourmet tour.

He pictured his partner sitting opposite him, and it was almost as if he was.

'So you're going to break into the silk factory, are you, *jefe*?' asked this figment of his imagination.

'That's right,' Paco agreed.

'Even though it's guarded by six armed men who'll probably kill you before you even get through the door?'

'That won't happen. I've got a plan.'

The imaginary Felipe chuckled so hard that his big belly wobbled. 'A plan? You call that a plan? You really must be desperate.'

'I am,' Paco agreed. 'I have to do it for you and María. And for Reyes, as well.'

'It's just about the craziest thing I've ever heard. Still, if there's one man in Spain who can make it work, the man is you.'

'Thank you, Felipe,' Paco said to the empty chair on the other side of the table.

The waiter returned with a glass and a bottle of Fundador. He placed the glass on the table, and unscrewed the bottle cap.

'Half the normal measure,' Paco said.

The waiter looked at him strangely. 'I shall have to charge you the full price.'

'That doesn't matter.'

The waiter poured the drink and left. Paco looked down at his glass. He'd got the amount just right, he thought – enough to give him courage, not so much as to make him lose his edge.

*

171

The later it got, the hotter it seemed to be. Paco checked his watch. He'd been sitting at the table for over half an hour, and most of his frugal brandy was gone.

The wireless on the bar counter was still playing *Sevillanas*, but most of the customers no longer had the energy to even tap their feet in time to it. Then, suddenly, in the middle of a song about a gypsy girl who fell in love with an aristocrat, the music stopped.

'I was enjoying that,' complained a man at the table next to Paco's. 'What's the matter? Has something gone wrong with your wireless?'

The waiter walked to the counter, and examined the machine. 'It's still lit up,' he said.

'You ought to keep a spare in case the one you're using breaks down,' the customer grumbled.

But the wireless hadn't broken down. It crackled, and then a second later an official-sounding voice said, 'Stand by for an important announcement.'

A young woman at a corner table reached over and nervously took her boyfriend's hand. A group of middle-aged couples looked questioningly at each other. Two old men went into an urgent whispered conference. The bar was suddenly filled with a tension even more overpowering than the heat – because while everyone suspected they knew what the announcement would be, few hoped that they would be right.

The announcer coughed. 'There has been a revolt within the Army of Morocco . . .' he said.

There was instant pandemonium.

'A revolt!'

'I told you it was coming!'

'Well, I don't believe it!'

'It wouldn't be on the radio if it wasn't true.'

'Shut up, all of you!' someone called out. 'I want to hear the rest.'

The noise subsided slowly, though some people continued to speak in whispers.

'. . . Melilla, Ceuta and Tetuán are temporarily in rebel hands,' the announcer said, 'but Tangier and Laranche have remained loyal. The government has already taken decisive action, and the situation is well under control. Please await further developments.'

Another pause, and then the music started again. All signs of lethargy had left the bar. Customers waved their hands excitedly and argued at the top of their voices.

The revolt would spread to the mainland.

Of course it wouldn't. How could it when the government still controlled the navy?

The army would rise in Seville itself.

The soldiers stationed in Seville were all loyal to the Republic.

It was about time somebody did something about the crisis.

Maybe, but an army take-over wasn't the right way to go about it.

Paco paid for his drink and left. All along the route back to his hotel, the bars had their radios on full volume and the same message was being repeated again and again.

'. . . the situation is well under control . . .'

'. . . under control . . .'

'. . . under control . . .'

He thought about Madrid, where fascists and socialists were killing each other every day, where blue-shirted Falangists flaunted their weapons on the Puerta del Sol and at Calvo Sotelo's funeral.

The government had the situation under control, did it? What bullshit that was! If it couldn't even control the warring in the capital, what chance would it have against the army?

Chapter Thirty-Two

The narrow alley was dark and hot and smelled of urine, but at least as long as he stayed there, he was safe. The problem was, he couldn't stay there, not if he was to find out what he needed to know. To get that information, he had to cross the dangerous open space between the alley and silk factory. And not just once, but twice.

Footsteps. Paco stepped back further into the darkness. Two of the factory's guards passed by on the other side of the road. Paco counted to five, then tiptoed to the top of the alley. The guards were walking towards the main entrance, where two other guards were permanently posted. And coming from the opposite end of the factory were another couple of security men.

He'd been standing there long enough to know this was their regular routine. One team went clockwise, the other anti-clockwise. The circuit around the building took them six minutes, which meant that in just over three minutes, both teams would be as far away from the entrance as they ever got.

The workman's overalls he'd slipped on over his suit made the heat of the alley even worse, but at least he wouldn't have to put up with them for much longer – they were only necessary for the first phase of the operation, and that, for better or worse, would soon be over.

Paco reached into the cloth bag he was carrying, and checked his equipment by feel. One brick. One bottle. One cigarette lighter.

And one chance, he told himself. If he missed his target the first time, he had missed it for ever.

The guards began their new circuit, and Paco started to count down the seconds. 'One hundred and eighty . . . one hundred and seventy-nine . . . one hundred and seventy-eight . . .'

As he reached double figures, he raised his hand to his forehead and discovered that his fingers were as cold as ice. By the time he was down to twenty seconds, his heart was trying to batter its way out of his rib-cage.

'. . . three . . . two . . . one!'

He sprinted diagonally from his hiding place towards the right-hand edge of the building. To his own ears, his footfalls echoed as loud as thunder, but the permanent guards by the door didn't seem to have noticed him. Yet.

He had reached the pavement. He stopped, pulled the brick out of the bag, and took careful aim.

'Only one chance!' he gasped.

Only one chance – and this was it. He hurled the brick at one of the high windows.

As his hands dived into the bag again, he heard the sound of breaking glass and a voice from the main entrance shouting, 'What the fuck . . .?'

He flicked back the hood of the lighter and held the flame to the crude fuse which was sticking out of the bottle. When he was sure it had caught, he threw the bottle at the smashed window.

He could hear the guards coming, running down the street at a furious rate. He began to run himself, heading for the alley which lay beyond the one in which he'd been hiding.

'Long live the Republic!' he screamed over his shoulder. 'Down with the fascist Herrera!'

He was ten metres from the alley when the first bullet whizzed past him and buried itself in the brickwork, five when the second hit the ground in front of him. And then he was safe, shielded from their pistols by a solid brick wall.

But only temporarily safe. It would take him at least another ten seconds to reach the next street, and if the guards arrived at the top of the alley before he'd managed to reach the bottom of it, he'd be a sitting target.

He raced on up the alley, kicking up dirt and sending tin cans flying. His lungs were on fire, yet he knew it would be fatal to slow down.

'Keep going,' he urged himself. 'Keep going for just a little bit longer.'

He could see the light of a street lamp shining on the pavement of the road which ran parallel to the one in front of the silk factory. He had only to reach that, and he would have a fighting chance.

There was a loud explosion from the other end of the alley. Paco threw himself to the ground a split second before the bullet flew by over him. He was crawling on his belly now, less than half a metre from the bottom of the alley. Less than quarter of a metre. There was another shot, but by then he had wriggled around the corner.

He climbed quickly to his feet. His car was still where he had left it, parked just beyond the street lamp. He rushed to the far side of the vehicle, pulled out his revolver, and crouched down.

'Come on, you sons-of-bitches, come on!' he gasped. 'Let's see how you do when somebody's shooting back.'

But there was no sound of pursuit, and after a minute had passed, he knew they had given up the chase. Part of him, the rational part, had always expected this – had understood that catching an anarchist would be of secondary importance to putting out the fire that the anarchist had started. But there had been no room for rationality when he'd been running down the alley, trapped like a wooden duck at a shooting range.

He checked his heart. Beating fast, but that was only to be expected after all that running. He looked down at his hands, and saw they were trembling. Well, weren't they entitled to tremble? He'd just been shot at, for Christ's sake.

He stripped off the overalls and threw them on the back seat of the car. Paco-the-anarchist-fire-bomber's part of the plan was over. The next phase called for a very different Paco, who had to be much more respectable.

'It's my last chance to walk away, Felipe,' he told the warm night air. 'If I go through with the next part of the operation, there's no turning back.'

He checked his heart again, and found it had slowed down a little. That was one good sign, anyway. Slipping his pistol back into his jacket pocket, he made his way back up the street.

The moment the guard at the main entrance to the silk factory saw the man in the trilby turn the corner, his hand automatically went down to his holster. The man's progress was irregular, the guard noted. For a few steps he would walk perfectly normally, then he would stagger slightly to the left or the right. Drunk, the guard decided – drunk, but trying to pretend that he wasn't.

The man in the trilby drew level with the entrance. He stopped, and swayed slightly. 'Bewiful night, isn't it?' he said. 'Really bewiful, bewiful night.'

'Fuck off,' the guard answered.

The man in the trilby drew himself to his full height. 'Theresh no need to take that attitude,' he said, with drunken dignity. 'Here I am, making pleasant conversation about wha' a bewiful night it is, and there's you . . .'

The guard took a step forward to push him away. Paco pulled the pistol out of his pocket by the barrel, and brought the butt down hard on the other man's head.

For a split second, the guard just stood there, a look of surprise on his face. Then his legs gave way, and he fell in a crumpled heap on the pavement. Paco bent over him, opened his jacket, and found his wallet. There were a couple of bank notes inside. Paco slipped the money in his pocket and threw the wallet down on the ground next to the unconscious guard.

The door was shut. Paco prayed it wasn't locked from the inside – prayed he hadn't risked his life for nothing. He turned the handle and gave a gentle push. The door opened slightly. He gave a second push, and stepped through the gap.

The scene inside the factory was almost surreal. The area by the door was in near darkness, but the far end of the room was lit up by a ravenous fire which was gorging itself on two wooden looms. And standing around the looms, glowing in the flames like demons from hell, were the five guards, cursing at the tops of their voices as they tried to deaden the blaze by beating it with pieces of sacking.

Paco looked around the long, eerily-illuminated room. Nearest to him were the reeling machines. Beyond them were the water baths and dyeing tanks. On tiptoe, he moved quickly to the nearest water bath, and squatted down behind it.

Perhaps a minute ticked by, the light growing fainter all the time. The thwacking of the sacks on the looms was becoming less regular, too. Then it stopped altogether.

'If I could get my hands on the son-of-a-bitch who threw that fucking bomb . . .' said a voice in the darkness.

'There's no chance of that,' said a second man. 'He'll be long gone by now.'

Beams of light cut through the air, and there was the sound of five sets of footsteps as the guards made their way back to the door. Paco held his breath.

'We're not going to get into trouble for this, are we, Miguel?' one of the guards asked worriedly, as they passed less than a metre from Paco's hiding place.

'I don't know,' Miguel replied, equally concerned. 'You know what Don Carlos is like when he gets into one of his rages.'

Don Carlos again! Back in Madrid, Méndez had seemed a pale figure, constantly under the shadow of his sister and brother-in-law, but here in Andalusia, he appeared to be a force to be reckoned with.

'It's . . . it's not as if the anarchist bastard had fire-bombed the other side of the building,' the first guard argued.

'True enough,' Miguel agreed, sounding as if he was attempting to reassure himself as much as the others. 'Like Arturo says, that would have been a real fucking disaster – specially since the lorry for Madrid's making a pick-up tomorrow night.'

The footsteps stopped. Paco heard the door swing open, then one of the guards shouted, 'Roberto's on the ground! Somebody's shot him!'

'Nobody shot him,' Miguel said. 'But he's been attacked all right. I can feel a bump on his head the size of a duck egg.'

'So what happened? Did that anarchist arsehole come back?'

'He must have done.'

'Then he could . . . he could be in the factory! He could be right inside the fucking factory!'

'What are you doing, Miguel?' asked Arturo.

'I'm going to turn the lights on.'

'You know it's policy not to . . .'

'I don't give a shit about policy. And neither will Don Carlos. If the anarchist's in there, I want to see him.'

Paco edged his way around the water bath. Suddenly, the room flooded with light, blinding him.

'He's not here,' said Arturo.

'He's here all right,' Miguel told him. 'I can almost smell the bastard.'

'But I can't see—'

'You don't expect him just to give himself up, do you? He's hiding – behind one of the water baths or the dyeing tanks.'

His heart back in overdrive, Paco slid his pistol out of his holster. His vision had returned to normal now, but he only had six bullets and there were five guards. It wasn't very good odds by anybody's standards.

'Roberto's been robbed,' said one of the guards who hadn't spoken before.

'He's what?' Miguel asked.

'Roberto's been robbed. Look, this is his wallet.'

The man on the pavement groaned. 'Bastard took me by surprise,' he said.

'The anarchist?' asked the worried guard.

'No, not the bloody anarchist. Some bloke in a suit and a hat. Didn't look like a robber – that's how he was able to catch me off-guard so easily.'

'Where'd he go?' Miguel asked.

'How the hell am I supposed to know that? From the moment he hit me, I was out cold, wasn't I?'

'We'd . . . we'd better help him up,' said Arturo.

'Yes, help me up,' Roberto said. 'And you can close that fucking door as well.'

The factory was plunged into darkness again, and there was sound of the door being slammed shut.

Paco took a deep breath. Phase Three of the operation had been completed, and he was still alive. He wondered how much longer his luck would last.

Chapter Thirty-Three

Paco came cautiously out of his crouch and stretched his cramped muscles. It had been over ten minutes since the guards had closed the main door, eight minutes since he'd heard footsteps as the two teams had resumed their patrols around the perimeter of the building. All of which meant that it was about as safe for him to make his move as it was ever going to be.

The brief glance he'd had in the light of the blazing looms had been enough to tell him that the silk factory took up about two-thirds of the building. But it wasn't this factory which interested him. He'd risked his life to discover what lay beyond the brick dividing-wall – a wall which almost definitely hadn't been there before the silk workers' strike of '34.

Walking on tiptoe, with his torch pointing at the floor, he slowly picked his way between the reeling machines, towards the end of the silk factory. There was only one door in the dividing wall, he discovered. The lock did not look complicated. But then why should it? With six armed guards on duty outside, any intruder should have been stopped before he ever entered the factory, so why bother with any extra security inside?

Paco took a handkerchief out of his pocket, unwrapped it carefully, and extracted his set of skeleton keys. Holding all but one tightly in his left hand, he inserted the remaining key into the lock with his right. He turned gently. It was obvious immediately that the lock was not going to budge.

The second key did not work, either. Nor the third. He was trying the fourth when he heard the lock click. He froze and listened. There were no shouts of alarm from the guards. No sound of movement at all. He wrapped the keys up in his handkerchief, returned the bundle to his pocket, and eased the door open.

He didn't dare shine his torch in a sweeping movement round the room, for fear it would be seen outside. So, instead, he explored little by little, creating one small island of light, examining what was caught in it, and then moving on. At the end of half an hour he had covered the whole room and, having all the pieces of the jigsaw puzzle in his mind, fitted them together to make a complete picture.

There were no looms or water baths in this second room. Instead there were metal-working benches and industrial lathes, wood-shaping equipment and lengths of steel piping.

What he had seen told him why Méndez had refused to let the workers back into the factory.

'And it tells me something else, Felipe,' he whispered into the darkness. 'It tells me why María had to die.'

*

He had his answers at last, but as long as he was effectively a prisoner in the building, he couldn't make any use of them.

'Should have thought about how to get out before I got in, shouldn't I, Felipe?' he said.

But he knew that if he'd done that, he might well have lost his nerve.

He considered his options. Leaving the way he'd entered was clearly out of the question, so he'd have to escape through the back. He glanced up at the high windows. They looked as if they'd be big enough to squeeze through, and with any luck he could drop to the ground without hurting himself.

He waited until the foot patrols were round at the front of the building, then quickly placed a ladder against the wall and climbed up to one of the windows. He groped around for the catch, and couldn't find one.

'Shit!' he said, under his breath.

The window was solid bloody glass – no opener at all!

Though he examined the rest of the windows in turn, he knew, after he'd found no catch on the third one, that they'd all be the same.

He sat down on one of the work benches. He badly needed a cigarette to calm his nerves, but even though the risk that the smell of his smoke would drift to the men outside was minimal, it was a risk he couldn't take.

Could he break the thick glass? he wondered. Perhaps – but even if all the guards were around the front, they'd be bound to hear the noise, and by the time he'd cleared all the shards away and got down to the street, they'd be on him. If he'd had someone on the outside to cover him – if Felipe had been out there – he'd have risked the glass. Alone, it was impossible.

He looked at his watch. It was nearly half-past four. It would be light soon. He wondered what time the workers reported for duty, and wished he could have a cigarette.

*

The sun was already starting its daily climb. At the top of the ladder, Paco held his chisel against the mortar which held the window frame in place, and tapped it gently with his hammer. He worked for exactly half a minute – the half-minute the guards on patrol would be furthest away from the window – and then stopped.

He had been doing the same thing for nearly an hour. Half a minute's chiselling, five and a half minutes' rest. Half a minute's chiselling, five and a half minutes' rest. Even with just thirty seconds, there was a chance the guards might hear him, but balanced against the fact that the workers might arrive at any moment, he didn't have a choice.

He stopped tapping and examined what he had achieved. There was still one hell of a lot of mortar still in place. He would kill for a cigarette.

*

The lorries rumbled up the street, and came to a halt in front of the silk factory. While two teams of guards watched the street, the remaining team unchained the tailboards. Once the tailboards were down, the dark-skinned men climbed off the lorries and headed for the factory's main door. Another day's work was about to begin.

In the hidden factory behind the partition wall, Paco lifted the hammer in his sweating hand, and chipped away the last piece of mortar.

The factory's main door swung open, and the Moors streamed in. When they saw what had happened to the looms, they all started talking at once.

Paco tried to ease the window free. There was nothing to hold it in place now, but the bloody thing still refused to budge.

'Now listen to me, you ignorant foreign bastards,' Miguel the guard shouted at the jabbering Moors, 'I know we can't make any more silk until we get some new looms, so half of you are going to have an easy day of it. But that's no reason for the others – the one's who are doing the real work – to start slacking. So stop fucking talking and get fucking working.'

After all its initial resistance, the window came away from the wall with such unexpected ease that Paco almost lost his balance. But it was out, thank Christ – at last it was finally out. He was just starting to descend the ladder when he heard the key being inserted into the lock in the door that divided the silk factory from the secret one.

The Moor tried the key once more to check that it was working properly, then said something to his companion in Arabic.

'What's wrong now, you idle bastard?' Miguel called from across the room.

'Door not open.'

Miguel sighed. 'Bloody hell, do I have to do everything for you sodding monkeys?' he asked. He strode across to the door. 'Give the key to me. I'll soon have it open.'

Paco had reached the bottom of the ladder, and laid the window carefully on the floor. How long would it take Miguel to realize that the reason the door wouldn't open was because it was bolted from the inside? he wondered. And what would the guard do once he had worked it out?

Miguel turned the key. 'See? No problem,' he said.

'Door not open,' the Moor persisted.

'Door not open,' Miguel mimicked. 'Of course the door will bloody open now I've unlocked it.' But when he pushed, it remained resolutely shut. 'Funny,' he told the Moor. 'It should be opening unless . . . Bloody hell! That anarchist bastard!'

Paco's legs and trunk were already out of the window, but however much he twisted and turned, his shoulders refused to go through. He was caught like a rat in a trap, just waiting for the guards to come and find him. And when they did find him, would they shoot him in the head, or through the balls?

'Go and tell one of the other guards to come here,' Miguel told the Moor.

'No understand.'

'I want to speak to one of the guards outside. It's very important!'

'Still no understand.'

'Bloody hell, there's no getting through to you people. I go, you stay here. If anybody unbolt door from other side, you come tell me, damn quick.'

A final twist did it. Paco was free of the window, and falling to the ground. The impact jolted his spine, but the second his feet made contact with the pavement, he began running.

He'd left it too late, he told himself as he ran. He should have chipped at the mortar one full minute out of six. Even forty-five seconds instead of thirty would have made a difference. He wondered, briefly, if he'd hear the shot before it hit him, or if he'd just suddenly feel as if he'd been struck in the back by a runaway lorry. And all the time, he kept running . . . running.

He had covered nearly a kilometre before he could bring himself to accept that the alarm hadn't been raised in time – that he had actually got away. He clutched a lamppost for support, and decided that what he wanted most in the world was a drink.

Chapter Thirty-Four

As he stood on the bank of the River Guadalquivir and looked down at the soothing water, it seemed incredible to think that only hours earlier he had been within seconds of death. In fact, the whole of the previous night seemed like nothing more than an unpleasant dream. But there had been nothing imaginary about it. What he'd found at the back of the silk factory had been frighteningly real.

Paco looked at the river again. The morning sun beat down on it, turning the blue water into a stream of liquid gold. The river had played an important part in making Seville the great city it was. Without the Guadalquivir, it wouldn't have been in Seville that Christopher Columbus announced the discovery of the New World. If the river hadn't been there, the *conquistadores* of South America would have set off from somewhere else, and returned with their ships weighed down with treasure to a different town. The golden river had made Seville a golden city in the Golden Age of Spain. Paco wondered whether there would ever be a golden age for his country again.

He lit a cigarette. He'd had one night without sleep, and after what he'd heard the guards in the silk factory say, he knew he could look forward to another one. So the smart thing would be to go to bed – to grab a little rest while he had the chance. But even though his body ached with tiredness, he knew that his mind wouldn't let him rest.

He kept walking, wrapped up in his own dark thoughts of a murderer who just might get away with his crime. He hardly noticed where he was going, and it was with some surprise that, a little after eleven o'clock, he realized he had reached the Plaza de San Fernando. There was a pavement café, at the opposite end of the square to the civil government building, and since chance seemed to have brought him to it, Paco decided he might as well have a drink.

Several of the tables were free, and Paco chose one next to a middle-aged man in white overalls, who had several pots of paint at his feet, and was reading the newspaper.

A waiter, in a smart green jacket, appeared. 'What can I bring you, señor?' he asked.

'A Fundador,' Paco said. 'And a big glass of iced water as well.'

A young man dressed in overalls sat down at the painter's table. 'Morning, *jefe*,' he said.

The painter put down his paper. 'Morning,' he replied. 'Have you heard the latest?'

'You mean about the army take-over in Melilla?' his young assistant asked.

The painter snorted. 'Melilla! That's old news now.'

'So what . . .?'

'They occupied Laranche just before dawn. That means they've got the whole of Spanish Morocco now. And that's not all. General Franco's gone and declared martial law in the Canary Islands.'

Paco remembered the radio broadcasts the previous evening, spilling out of every bar he passed: 'The situation is under control . . . under control . . . under control . . .'

What a hollow claim that was already turning out to be.

He looked round the square – at the elaborate Plateresque civil government building, at the shops, at the people going about their business. Everything seemed so normal, and yet less than 200 kilometres away, across a narrow stretch of water, the army had set up its own state.

'D'you think there'll be any risings on the mainland?' the younger painter asked his boss.

'I shouldn't be at all surprised.'

And neither would I, Paco thought, as the waiter placed his brandy and water in front of him. After what he'd seen during the night, he would only be surprised if the risings *didn't* occur.

A distant rumbling sound made Paco turn his head. A convoy of army lorries was coming, slowly but surely, up the Calle de San Fernando.

The painters had seen it, too. 'They're going to attack the civil government building,' the older one said. 'The rotten stinking sons-of-bitches!'

The lorries reached the square and began to fan out around the civil government building. Now they were closer, Paco could see that each of them was dragging a heavy field-gun.

A grey-haired man in a smart suit tapped Paco on the shoulder. 'You don't mind if I sit myself down at your table to watch the show, do you?' he asked.

'Be my guest,' Paco told him.

The man sat, and took a packet of cigarettes out of his pocket. 'Do you know the first thing the army did after it had taken control of Melilla?' he said.

'No. What?'

'It rounded up everybody who might possibly be against it, and I mean everybody – socialists, communists, trades' union members, the lot – and shot them all. Just like that! Without even a trial. And you mark my words, it'll be the same here. I'm only glad I've never supported the left.'

There would be a great many people in Seville who would suddenly claim never to have supported the left, Paco thought, noticing that the two painters – who were probably union members – had gone without finishing their drinks.

Gunners were swarming out of the backs of the lorries, uncoupling the field guns and aiming them at the civil government building. How many soldiers would it need to take over a city with a population of a quarter of a million? Probably rather less than it would take to control a herd of a quarter of a million sheep – because people learned by the example of what had happened to others.

'I can't say that I entirely approve of what the army's doing,' the man in the smart suit said. 'But really, it was time somebody took decisive action.'

Apart from the soldiers, no one on the square was moving. Paco stood up and walked to the entrance of the bar, where the waiter and a group of customers stood, their eyes fixed on the civil government building. 'Do you have a public phone?' he asked.

The waiter blinked. 'What did you say, señor?'

'Do you have a public phone?'

'It's . . . uh . . . in the corridor next to the toilets.'

Paco forced his way through the crowd, and headed for the corridor. But had he left it too late? Had the lines already been cut? He picked up the phone. There was a ringing sound, then the operator said, 'Can I help you?'

'I'd like to place a call to Madrid,' Paco said.

'What number, please?'

Paco gave her the number of the *casa del pueblo*, praying there was not already an army officer standing next to her, checking a list to see if it was a proscribed number.

'Trying to connect you,' the operator said, and Paco noticed that his hands were trembling again.

It took two minutes to make the connection and a couple more before Bernardo could be found and brought to the telephone. 'You sound very distant,' the big market porter said. 'Where are you?'

'Seville.'

'Seville!' Bernardo repeated. 'And what the devil are you doing there?'

'Working on a case.'

Bernardo snorted with disbelief. 'Paco, there *are* no cases, any more,' he said. 'There's no justice, either, unless you count revolutionary justice.'

'Or military justice,' Paco corrected him, remembering what the man in the smart suit had told him about the executions of left-wingers in Melilla.

'They said on Radio Madrid this morning that the uprising has been confined to Morocco,' Bernardo said. 'How do things look where you are?'

'Even as we're talking, the army's about to take over Seville.'

Bernardo snorted again, with disgust this time. 'When are those bastards in the government going to realize that it's time to start telling us the truth?'

'What's the situation like in Madrid?'

'Terrible. The army's still loyal, but who knows how long that's going to last? We marched on Sol – just like they did in 1808 – and demanded that the government arm us.'

'And?'

'They refused point-blank.'

'But haven't you got weapons already?'

'We have about 8,000 rifles. You can't defend a whole city with as few weapons as that – especially when you've got enemies inside as well as out.'

He was right about the enemies inside. Practically the whole of the Barrio de Salamanca would be on the side of the rebels. Paco wondered if he should contact his chief and tell him what he'd found out.

'Have the police—?' he began.

'Don't you understand what's going on?' Bernardo interrupted. 'There aren't any police any more – or if there are, they don't dare show their faces. It's the militias who are keeping order. They're the only ones with either the will or the means.'

Somebody had once said that the first casualty of war was the truth. The second, Paco thought, was the judicial system. 'Where will you be tomorrow night?' he asked.

'Tomorrow night?' Bernardo echoed. 'I haven't got a fucking clue where I'll be tomorrow night. *Ostias*, Paco, the way things are going I don't even know where I'll be an hour from now.'

With his free hand, Paco fumbled for a cigarette. 'I need to be able to reach you,' he said. 'It's very important.'

'You're not still going on about this stupid bloody case of yours, are you?'

'No. This is something else.' Paco stuck the cigarette in his mouth, and flicked his lighter open. 'Something very important to you and your comrades.'

'Important to me and my comrades? What does that mean? Be a little more specific, Paco.'

Paco took a long drag on his cigarette. More specific? On an open line? In a city which was about to fall to the military? 'I can't give you any more details now,' he told his old friend.

'You're the limit!' Bernardo exploded. 'You won't tell me what you're up to, but at the same time, you expect me to make myself available whenever you want to . . .'

'I can help you,' Paco said. 'I can really help you. But you've got to trust me.'

There was a pause, then Bernardo said, 'I'll tell you what I'll do. I'll let whoever's on the switchboard know where I am. Is that good enough for you?'

'It'll have to be.'

In the background, at the other end of the line, Paco heard some shouting, 'The car's just pulled up outside, comrades,' then Bernardo said, 'I have to go now. *Salud.*'

Salud, not *adios*, Paco noted. No one on the left said 'Go with God', any more, because if God existed at all, he was now the merest irrelevance.

He returned to the bar. Most of the customers were still crowded in the doorway, but sitting at one of the tables was a pair of *guardias civiles* – a private and a corporal. Paco wondered what would have happened if one of the *guardias* had decided to go to the toilet while he was on the phone to

Bernardo, and heard him use the word 'comrades'. He'd have to be more careful in future, at least until he'd closed the case.

'Put the wireless on, Oscar,' a man called from the door.

The barman reached up to the shelf on which the wireless stood, and turned the knob. It took a few seconds for the set to warm up, but when it had, the whole bar was filled with the voice of an agitated announcer.

'The army is threatening the Republic,' he shouted. 'Even now, the civil government building is surrounded by soldiers. Brothers, do not allow this to happen to us. Arm yourselves! Show the fascists what you, the workers, are made of . . .'

The two *guardias civiles* exchanged glances, then the corporal stood up and walked over to the counter. 'Turn that shit off!' he said to the barman.

'But I want to hear it,' the barman protested. 'We all want to hear it.'

The *guardia* reached down to his holster and unfastened the flap. The butt of his pistol glinted menacingly in the sunlight which shone in through the window. 'If you don't turn it off, I'll put a bullet through the wireless,' he said. 'And while I'm at it, I just might put one through you as well.'

The barman blanched, then, with a trembling hand, he reached up and clicked the switch.

The second *guardia* had now joined his partner at the bar. 'Listen to me,' the corporal said. 'Only Reds would think of listening to filth like that – and you know what's going to happen to Reds from now on, don't you?'

The barman gulped, and nodded.

'We've got some important business to attend to,' the *guardia* continued, 'but we'll be back, and if I hear you've switched that wireless on again, you'll be for it.'

'I . . . I swear I won't . . .'

'Well, you'd better not.'

Without even offering to pay for their drinks, the two *guardias* swaggered towards the door. The crowd parted to let them through. Not one of the men standing there complained about the corporal ordering the barman to switch off the wireless. The military take-over had only just begun, but its effects were already evident.

*

Just to be on the safe side, Paco gave the two policemen five minutes to get out of the area before paying and leaving the bar himself. The crowd did not part for him, as it had for the *guardias*, and he had to jostle and elbow his way out through the door.

On the square, the army had completed its deployment. The field guns formed a semi-circle around the front of the civil government building. Gunners were crouched down behind each weapon, and an officer was strutting self-importantly from one position to another.

Paco looked at the windows of the besieged building, half-expecting to see a rifle barrel pointing from each one, but he saw only faces pressed against the panes.

A sudden cheer went up from the soldiers, then they were on their feet, slapping each other heartily on the back and pointing at the roof of the building. Paco lifted his own eyes. A large piece of white material – probably a tablecloth – was being raised up the flagpole.

'They've surrendered!' somebody behind Paco shouted.

'Just like that,' said another man.

'Without even a single shot being fired,' exclaimed a third.

Paco wondered if the workers in the outlying *barrios* would give in quite so easily. He hoped they wouldn't.

'Better to die on your feet than live on your knees,' he said softly, thinking, even as he spoke, that that didn't sound like him at all.

Chapter Thirty-Five

Soldiers – mostly young conscripts – stood in pairs on every street corner, holding ancient rifles in their nervous hands, and looking around constantly, as if they were expecting trouble. *Guardias civiles* passed from nearly-empty bar to nearly-empty bar, checking and re-checking the papers of the few customers who had been brave enough – or foolish enough – to pretend that nothing had changed. And the Falangists, whose moment had come at last, roamed the streets in packs, searching for communists. Or anarchists. Or anyone who might once have voted liberal. If the great heart of the city had not quite stopped beating, it had at least been slowed down by the military jackboot.

It was an entirely different story in the working-class suburbs. The radio announcer had urged left-wing supporters from the surrounding countryside to come to the aid of their comrades in the *barrios*, and there'd been a constant stream of them all day. Now, as darkness fell on the first day of the military take-over, the churches out of the reach of the army burned, and the workers who'd set them on fire crouched behind their hastily erected barricades, and waited.

*

The hay cart had been turned sideways, so that it blocked one end of the bridge. There were a dozen men standing round it, but only three of them appeared to have rifles. Paco brought his Fiat to a halt about five metres from the wagon, opened the door, and, with his hands raised, slowly got out of the car.

Two of the unarmed men stepped forward. The three men who did have guns didn't move, but trained their weapons on Paco, because, even if he was wearing a boiler suit, he was also driving a car and that marked him down as one of the enemy.

The militiamen had reached the Fiat. One of them held out his hand. 'Papers!' he demanded.

Paco lowered his arms, reached into his pocket, and produced his UGT card. The militiaman looked at it suspiciously, then shrugged his shoulders, as if to say it seemed genuine, so he supposed that meant Paco was all right. 'What business have you in this *barrio*, comrade?' he asked.

'I've been ordered to take this vehicle to the socialist militia's headquarters,' Paco lied.

'You'd have been more welcome if you'd brought a few guns with you,' the militiaman said, 'but I suppose we might need some transport once the real fighting starts.'

He signalled to the other men, and putting their shoulders to the cart, they pushed it until there was a gap large enough for the Fiat to get through.

Paco got back into his vehicle. 'Good luck,' he said as he slid out of neutral. 'You're certainly going to need it,' he added silently to himself, as he eased the car past the road-block.

*

He parked on the street parallel to the one which ran past the silk factory, and entered Alvaro's bar by the back door. The owner was standing behind the counter, washing glasses. There was no one else in the room.

Alvaro looked up from his work. 'Oh, you're back again, are you, señor private detective?' he said. 'And wearing overalls this time, I see.'

Paco grinned. 'It seemed a lot safer than walking around in a business suit.'

'In this *barrio*, you're probably right.' The barman took the glasses out of the water and placed them on the draining board. 'Anyway, what brings you here tonight?' he asked. 'Have you, perhaps, found the girl, and come to give me the hundred-peseta reward that you promised me yesterday?'

Paco shook his head. 'I'm afraid not.'

The barman grimaced philosophically. 'Have a drink, anyway,' he said, pouring a white wine and sliding it across the counter. 'Where've you just come from? The centre of the city?'

'That's right,' Paco agreed.

'Is it true that the army's in control there?'

'Yes, it's true.'

'Bastards!' Alvaro said, pouring a drink for himself.

'How are things on this side of the river?' Paco asked.

'We've been showing them what we're made of, and make no mistake,' Alvaro told him. 'Everybody's been on strike. Everybody, that is, except for those sons-of-bitches in there.' He flicked his thumb contemptuously in the direction of the silk factory.

Paco looked across the street. The number of guards on the main door had been doubled, but that was only to be expected after the events of the previous evening.

But what if the break-in had other consequences? he fretted. What if it meant they'd cancelled the planned shipment to Madrid? Then he'd never be able to bring the murderer to justice.

'I expect you're wondering why I'm not on strike myself,' Alvaro said.

'What?'

'I said, I expect you're wondering why I'm not on strike myself.'

'Why aren't you?'

'The commander of the militia asked me personally if I wouldn't mind staying open,' Alvaro said proudly. 'It's a hot night, and there is nowhere else in the whole *barrio* where the militiamen can get refreshment.'

Paco smiled. 'And whatever's happening, Spaniards always need a place to get refreshment.'

'Of course! It's part of our tradition. In other countries, they get drunk, but here in Spain, we just drink.' He poured Paco a second wine. 'You want to hear what they're saying on the wireless?' he suggested.

Paco shrugged. 'Why not?'

Spain had discovered the New World and invented bull-fighting, he thought. Now there was something else for which it would be famous: it would be the first country ever to hear of its own destruction over the air waves.

Alvaro flicked the switch. There were a few seconds of military music, then a voice made thick with too much sherry broke in. 'This is General Queipo de Llano speaking to you from the heart of Seville.'

'The bastards have gone and captured the bloody radio station!' Alvaro said.

'Spain is in safe hands once more,' the general thundered from the wireless. 'Most of our enemies are in flight. The rabble who have stayed and still resist us will be shot like the dogs they are. Victory is ours. Victory is Spain's . . .'

Alvaro pulled out the plug, and the wireless went dead. 'If only we had more weapons,' he said gloomily. 'Give us a few more weapons, and we might just have a fighting chance.'

There was the noise of a lorry approaching. The guards at the door of the silk factory were suddenly more alert, and Paco felt his sinking hopes start to revive.

The lorry pulled up in front of the main doors. It was a long distance truck, with a canvas hood over the back, on which were written the words, 'The United Fruit Company of Seville'.

'Never heard of them before,' Alvaro said. 'And anyway, why should they be delivering fruit to a silk factory?'

'They're not delivering anything,' Paco told him. 'They're making a pick-up.'

Two men in overalls climbed out of the cab of the lorry. On the pavement, the four guards had now been joined by two others, and all of them were scanning the street for any sign of the militia. Satisfied that the coast was clear, one of the guards rapped on the door with his knuckles.

'What the hell's going on?' Alvaro asked.

'You'll see,' Paco assured him.

The door opened, and two Moroccans emerged, carrying a long wooden packing case between them. Another pair followed, and then a third.

'What a son-of-a-bitch Méndez is,' Alvaro said in disgust. 'We're virtually at war, but he still keeps selling the bloody silk as if nothing was happening.'

Paco didn't speak. Instead he watched the Moroccans load the crates into the lorry, go back into the factory, and come out again with two more. After ten minutes loading, they went back inside and closed the doors behind them.

About half the stock of the factory-within-a-factory was now on the lorry, Paco estimated. He wondered where they intended to send the rest. Probably to Badajoz or Granada, to await the arrival of General Franco.

The driver and his mate were climbing back into their cab. Paco put a peseta down on the counter. 'I have to be going,' he said. He walked to the back door, stopped, and turned around. 'If you and your comrades need weapons,' he told Alvaro, 'you'll find plenty in the silk factory.'

He stepped out onto the street just as the engine of the truck which belonged to the United Fruit Company of Seville burst into life.

Part Three

Madrid 20 July 1936

Chapter Thirty-Six

The early morning sun was already beating down on the two tractors which formed the improvised roadblock, but for the moment at least, the heat was bearable.

Bernardo took a packet of cigarettes out of his overall pocket, and offered it to Paco. 'When was the last time you had a decent sleep?' he asked.

'I had a siesta the day before yesterday, just after I called you,' Paco said. 'And I managed to grab the odd half-hour while I was on the road.'

'So you've slept for perhaps five or six hours in the last seventy-two?'

'Something like that.'

'Well then, no wonder you look like a piece of dried dog shit,' Bernardo said, scanning the empty road ahead of them. 'You're sure that they're coming?'

'They're coming,' Paco said, with more conviction than he felt. 'The last time I checked on them, they'd stopped in a bar in Aranjuez for a coffee.'

Bernardo lit Paco's cigarette, and then his own. 'What I don't understand is how, on a thirty-hour drive, they wouldn't have noticed you were following them.'

'They didn't notice me following because I wasn't,' Paco said tiredly. 'At least, not all the time. The one advantage that I had over them was that I knew where they were going. So sometimes I'd hang back for a couple of hours at a time, and sometimes I'd drive well ahead and wait for them to catch me up.'

'Still, they might have made the connection . . .'

'No,' Paco said. 'If they had spotted me, they'd have taken diversionary action long before Aranjuez.' He checked his watch, nervously. 'I've missed all the news while I've been travelling. Where have the army been successful?'

'All over the place,' Bernardo said despondently. 'Córdoba, Granada and Cádiz in the south. Segovia, Soria, Burgos and Valladolid in the north.' He looked at the eager young militiamen who were manning the road-block.

'These lads think it's all going to be a great adventure. But it won't be. It'll be a bloody business which we won't recover from for the next fifty years.'

Paco turned to face Madrid. 'What about back home? Are the fascists causing you any trouble in the city?'

'They'd like to, but we've got them pinned down in the Montaña barracks.'

Paco gave an involuntary shudder. God, how he hated those bloody barracks which had been, for him, the gateway to hell called Morocco. He didn't have to see the place to be reminded of it. It was always with him. However much he tried to deny the fact, he was the person it had made him.

'Are you all right, Paco?' Bernardo asked. 'You look as if you've seen a ghost.'

'I'm just exhausted,' Paco said. 'What about all those rifles you were demanding? Did the government finally see sense and issue them to the militias?'

Bernardo laughed bitterly. 'Oh, they've given us the rifles, all right. 55,000 of them. The only problem is, only 5,000 of them have got bolts.'

'But a rifle without a bolt is useless!'

'Exactly. That was the thinking behind it. Keep the rifles and bolts separate, and it wouldn't matter if one or the other fell into the wrong hands.'

'So where are the bolts now?' Paco asked.

'Think about it,' Bernardo said. 'What is the one place, in the whole of Madrid, where we couldn't get at them?'

A parade square, surrounded by gaunt three-storied buildings! A factory which turned out people ready to kill without question or compunction!

Paco groaned. 'They're not in the Montaña barracks, are they?'

'That's right. In the Montaña barracks. 50,000 rifle bolts and who knows how many fascists.'

Would the shadow of the place never leave him? Paco wondered. Sometimes, it seemed to him as if he was destined to die there. 'Jesus Christ!' he said. 'It's a real fucking mess, isn't it? What are you going to do about it?'

'We'll get the bloody bolts,' Bernardo said resolutely. 'Whatever it takes, we'll get them.'

'And then you'll have all the weapons you need?'

Bernardo shook his head. 'We'll never have all the weapons we need. Not while we're fighting almost the whole bloody army.'

There was the sound of an engine in the distance, and a lorry appeared round the bend. 'Is that it?' Bernardo asked.

'That's it,' Paco said, breathing a sigh of relief.

Bernardo stepped out into the middle of the road and held up his hand. The lorry slowed, then came to a halt.

Paco and Bernardo, flanked by two militiamen, walked over to the lorry. The driver wound down his window and smiled. 'Good morning, comrades,' he said. 'How's the situation in Madrid? I hope you've shown those fascist bastards a thing or two.'

'Would you and your mate please get out of the cab,' Bernardo said, flatly.

The lorry driver's smile stayed in place. 'I'm a member of the UGT, comrade,' he said. 'Look, here's my union card as proof.'

'My friend here's got a card, too,' Bernardo said, looking at Paco, 'but he isn't a member of the union.'

'What's that supposed to mean?' the driver asked, with a hint of annoyance creeping into his voice.

Bernardo nodded to his two militiamen, who swung their rifles from their hips, so that the barrels were pointing directly at the two men in the cab.

'What it means,' Bernardo said, 'is that I'd like you and your mate to get out of the lorry.'

With a show of patient, but martyr-like, reluctance, the driver and his mate climbed out of the cab. Two more militiamen walked over from the tractor road-block.

'So what have you brought up, all the way from Andalusia?' Bernardo asked.

'Can't you read the canvas, comrade? Fruit. Or to be more specific – oranges. We've been driving all night to get them to the market on time. If we're late, we won't sell them until tomorrow, and by then half of them will have rotted.'

Bernardo pointed to the back of the lorry. 'Untie the flap,' he told two of his men.

'Really, comrade, there's no need at all to go and . . .' the lorry driver protested.

'Untie it,' Bernardo repeated.

Two of the militiamen opened the canvas cover at the back of the lorry. The vehicle was piled almost to the roof with sacks of Seville oranges.

'I told you that's what we had on board,' the driver said. 'They're vital supplies. Now that the Republic's fighting for its life, Madrid's going to need all the oranges that it can—'

Bernardo looked questioningly at Paco, who nodded. 'Clear out the oranges, and let's find out what's underneath,' he told his men.

*

The sacks of oranges formed several small mountains on the ground. The back of the lorry was empty.

'Looks like you've made a mistake, Paco,' Bernardo said heavily.

But he couldn't have! He had seen the crates being loaded, and Alvaro the barman had as good as assured him that the United Fruit Company of Seville was a fake. So the guns just had to be there.

Unless a switch had been made! Unless they'd been on to him since he entered Alvaro's bar, and this lorry had never been more than a diversion.

'I'm sorry to have delayed you, comrade,' Bernardo said to the lorry driver. 'My friend here is sometimes a little over-zealous.'

The other man nodded. 'No real harm done. Now if you and your men would just help us to load up the lorry again . . .'

'Of course.'

The lorry driver shouldn't have let that look of triumph and relief come into his eyes, Paco thought – not even for the split second it had been there. 'I want to take a closer look at the back of the lorry,' he told Bernardo.

The big market porter sighed. 'Give it up, Paco. It should be obvious by now, even to you, that there's nothing—'

'It won't take me more than half a minute to check this out,' Paco said, climbing over the tailboard.

He ran his gaze over the back of the lorry. He had seen a large number of crates being loaded, but there was no evidence of them now. So maybe he had misread the driver's eyes. Perhaps a switch had been made after all, when he was waiting for the lorry to catch him up or deliberately holding back.

'Well?' Bernardo asked.

'There's nothing here,' Paco admitted. And then he moved slightly to the left, and heard one of the floor boards creak. 'A false bottom!' he shouted. 'The fucking thing's got a false bottom!'

The driver and his mate – existing somewhere in the twilight zone between freedom and arrest – stood to one side and watched the first of the packing cases from under the false floor being laid on the ground. The driver wore the expression of a man who desperately wants to believe he can still talk his way out of trouble. His partner, in contrast, had the blank eyes of someone who has already given up.

Bernardo took a small crowbar out of his pocket, slid it under one of the boards, and levered. As the plank splintered, Paco saw the glint of metal.

With one plank out of the way, it did not take Bernardo's large hands more than a few seconds to tear the rest away, and expose the dozen rifles which were lying in the case. He turned to the lorry driver. 'Know anything about these?' he asked.

'They . . . they must have been put there before we picked up the lorry,' the other man said unconvincingly.

'And I suppose they'd have been removed without you knowing anything about it, either.'

'That's right! We were just told to deliver the lorry, then our job was done.'

Bernardo took one of the rifles out of the case, and checked the mechanism with the assurance of a man who knew all about guns.

'What are they like?' Paco asked.

'Basic,' Bernardo told him. 'Basic but effective. You could kill a man as well with one of these as you could with any other rifle.'

'We didn't know that they were in there,' the driver repeated hysterically.

Bernardo looked as if he were suddenly very tired of the whole situation. 'Take these two back to the city and lock them in the *casa del pueblo*,' he told his militiamen. 'I'll deal with them when I have time.'

Four militiamen moved in, each taking an arm of one of the arrested men.

'I tell you I'm innocent,' the driver screamed, as he and his mate were led away. 'I swear to you on my dead mother's grave that I'm innocent.'

'There are no innocents any more,' Bernardo said. He turned back to Paco. 'Thanks for the rifles. And if there's ever anything I can ever do in return . . .'

'There is. I need another favour right now.'

'This is to do with that murder case of yours again, isn't it?' Bernardo said.

'Yes, it is.'

The big market porter shook his head in exasperation. 'You're like a dog that's got its teeth clamped onto somebody's leg,' he said. 'You won't let go until somebody breaks your jaw for you.'

'True,' Paco agreed, thinking that the captain had said something similar to him only a few days earlier. 'But you did admit you owed me a favour.'

'We're fighting a war, Paco,' Bernardo said. 'Hundreds of people – good people – were murdered in Morocco last night, and here you are concerned with just one death.'

'I can't do anything about what happened in Morocco,' Paco told him, 'but a crime was committed here in Madrid, and it's my duty to go after the guilty party.'

Bernardo looked up at the sky, as if seeking the divine guidance of a god he no longer believed in. Then he turned to Paco and grinned. 'All right, you bastard, what do you want?' he asked.

'Not much,' Paco said. 'Just a red armband and the use of two of your lads for a couple of hours.'

*

There was something missing from the streets, Paco thought as he drove up Calle Velazquez – something which had been there when he left the city three days earlier, and now was gone. And then he had it. The señoritos in the smart blue shirts, who had been so much in evidence before the military rising, had completely disappeared.

He pulled up in front of the apartment block where the Herrera family lived. The last time he'd visited it with Felipe, there'd been a uniformed doorman who'd shown by the expression on his face that he didn't care that they were policemen, because in his job, he had many powerful patrons. There was no sign of him now, as Paco looked around a lobby in which all the expensive pot plants had been overturned, the leather sofas ripped open, and the carefully painted walls desecrated by crude left-wing graffiti daubed in red paint.

'Now that the people finally have the power, the rich are on the run,' said Antonio, one of the young militiamen Bernardo had assigned to help him.

'Death to the capitalists, and to the priests who are their willing lackeys!' said Mauricio, the other militiaman. 'The victory of the people is certain.'

They are nothing but children, Paco thought, children passionately mouthing political slogans they only half-understand, but which, for them, have all the force of magic.

The three of them crossed the lobby and took the lift up to the third floor. The blue corridor carpet had gone, leaving the bare parquet exposed. Who had taken it? The socialists or the fascists? Whoever had been responsible, the reason behind it was bound to be political, because, as Bernardo had rightly said, everything was political.

They had reached Herrera's door, and Paco rang the bell.

'They'll be long gone,' Antonio said.

'Perhaps,' Paco agreed.

There were footsteps in the hallway, then the sound of bolts being drawn back. The door opened, and Luis the valet was standing there, dressed, as always, in an immaculate striped waistcoat.

The servant ran his eyes over the detective's boiler suit, somehow making Paco feel as if he was not only dressed shabbily, but had also done something shabby. 'You again!' he said contemptuously.

Paco felt a sneaking admiration for the man. The world in which Luis had lived – the values to which he had dedicated his entire life – had collapsed before his eyes. Yet he knew that he still had his master's approval and trust, and could continue to be as haughty as if nothing had changed.

'Do we arrest him, comrade?' Antonio asked, his voice filled with youthful enthusiasm.

'No, we don't,' Paco said. He turned his attention back to Luis. 'Who else is here, apart from you?'

'No one. The other servants have all been sent to their villages. They will not return until order is restored.'

He meant military order, Paco thought. 'And what about the family?'

'The master and mistress have gone to Burgos.' Luis paused, as if he thought Paco might have gained the wrong impression of their motives. 'The master will be of more use to the Cause in the north, under General Mola's protection, than he could be here,' he explained.

'That's treason!' Antonio exploded.

'Shut up!' Paco told the young militiaman.

So the Herreras had fled. Well, that didn't really matter to him one way or the other. But there was one other member of the family who mattered very much indeed. 'What about Méndez?' he asked, dreading the answer. 'Has he gone north as well?'

Luis shook his head. 'No, Don Carlos is still in Madrid,' he said, pronouncing Méndez's first name with a respect which would have taken the policeman by surprise a few days earlier, but which now seemed like only the señorito's due.

'If he's not at home, where is he?' Paco said.

But even as he was asking the question, he realized that he already knew the answer. There was only one place where Méndez could be – a place which had been haunting Paco's thoughts and dreams for half a lifetime, and a place fate seemed to be pointing him towards however much he resisted it.

Luis had still not spoken.

'He's in the Montaña barracks, isn't he?' Paco said. 'Come on, man, you might as well admit it.'

The servant nodded. 'That's right,' he agreed. 'Don Carlos is in the Montaña barracks.'

Chapter Thirty-Seven

The shots being fired around the Montaña barracks were little more than gentle pops in the air from the Gran Via, but by the time the three men had reached the Plaza de España, they sounded more like the distant explosion of fireworks.

Paco parked the Fiat, and, flanked by his escort, walked across to the obelisk which dominated the square. He stopped directly in front of it, and looked up at the seated statue of a bearded man in a ruff. Miguel de Cervantes. How wise the old man looked, how well aware of human weakness and fallibility.

The shooting had intensified, and Paco sensed Antonio twitching by his side.

'We'd better go and see what we can do, *jefe*,' the young militiaman said excitedly.

'In a minute,' Paco said, lowering his gaze from the great man to the smaller statues of his two most famous creations – Don Quixote and Sancho Panza. The knight sat on his bony horse, holding his lance in his hand and ready to charge the windmills he believed were giants. His squire, by contrast, was astride a donkey. His broad peasant face said more clearly than words that he wasn't about to mistake flocks of sheep for armies, or galley-slaves for oppressed gentlemen.

The visionary idealist and the practical realist – there was a bit of both of them in all Spaniards. Paco rested his eyes on the knight's right hand, which was raised in the air and seemed to be pointing him towards the place he dreaded – the Montaña barracks.

'Shall I follow you one last time?' he asked the statue.

*

Paco remembered sitting at the pavement café, with Felipe, and looking up the grassy slope which led to the Montaña barracks. That had been only a few days earlier, but it had also been in a different world. Then, the only people in the park at the bottom of the hill had been strolling gentlemen of leisure, and uniformed nannies pushing prams. Now, the park had been overrun by a mob of workers in overalls.

There were thousands of men here. Some hid behind park benches or trees. Others just crouched close to the ground. There were men with rifles, men with knives, and men with nothing more than fists to shake at the fortress.

The air was filled with the sharp crack of shots – both from and towards the barracks – and by the reek of cordite. Paco brought his escort to a halt just short of the park – close enough to watch the drama, far enough away to be comparatively safe. He looked up at the fortress. There was a rifle at every window.

'What do we do now, *jefe*?' Antonio asked.

What should they do? Climb the steep steps up to the barracks main entrance and ask to see Carlos Méndez? They wouldn't get half-way there before the fascists – or the socialists – cut them down.

'*Jefe* . . .?' said the young militiaman.

'Now,' Paco said, trying his best to ignore the knot of tension in his stomach, 'we wait.'

A low-flying plane appeared in the distance. A murmur of unease ran through the mob at the foot of the hill. Was it the fascists? Were they about to bomb the park? Then someone shouted, 'It's one of ours!' and everyone cheered.

The plane swooped lower over the fortress. Paco did not see the bomb drop, but he heard the explosion and felt the ground under his feet shake. There was more cheering from the men in the park, but as the plane flew away again, the fortress looked as invulnerable as it ever had.

The cheering continued anyway. Some of the men in the park, forgetting caution in their excitement, stood up and began to dance around. Fresh shots rang out from the barracks. One of the dancing men clutched his stomach and fell to the ground – and the atmosphere was sombre once more.

'Should we get closer, so we can take a shot at them, *jefe*?' Mauricio asked.

Paco shook his head. 'It'd only be a waste of bullets.' He lit a cigarette. The man who'd just been shot had thrown his life away. How many more men would do the same thing before the day was over?

A group of *Asaltos* arrived in a lorry, bringing with them a single field-cannon. In their eagerness, hundreds of people swarmed over the back of the truck, trying to help with the unloading. Once it was on the ground, the cannon shot a few shells at the barracks, but it seemed to have no more effect than the aeroplane's bomb had done.

The rifle fire continued. Sometimes a bullet would hit its target, and a man on one side or the other would jerk violently backwards; but most of the shots were wasted, doing no more than chip the brickwork of the fortress or thud harmlessly into the thick trunks of the park trees. Paco lit a fresh cigarette from the stub of the one he'd been smoking, and wondered if Carlos Méndez was feeling as frightened as he was himself.

*

At exactly eleven o'clock, the firing from the barracks suddenly stopped, and the rifles were withdrawn from the windows. A wave of anticipation ran through the crowd.

'The fascists have stopped shooting!' somebody shouted, though it was already obvious to everyone there.

'They've given up!' a second man bawled.

'Victory is the People's!' called a third.

All eyes focused on the flagpole. The Spanish flag was being lowered. The mob scuffled and fretted, wishing whoever was winding the flag down would work faster.

Perhaps the right-wingers inside *had* given up, Paco thought. Perhaps fate was letting him off the hook. But he didn't really believe it. He couldn't force into his mind an image of himself still climbing the seventy-two steps to his apartment when each step represented a year of his life gone.

The flag had disappeared completely. The crowd continued to stare at the space it had occupied. No one seemed to be breathing. And then a new flag began to climb the pole – a white one. The mob in the park roared. Instantly, men who had been lying on the ground were jumping to their feet, and those who had been sheltering behind trees broke cover. Paco threw his cigarette to the ground and, before he could give himself a chance to change his mind, joined in the rush towards the Montaña barracks.

The advance took on a life of its own. It was a great, inexorable wave, in which each individual who helped to compose it played only a small, helpless part. Men fell, sometimes in heaps of four or five, and were trampled by those who followed them. Nothing, it seemed – neither divine nor man-made – could stop this huge force whipped into being by the sight of the white flag.

Paco gasped and strained and told himself he smoked too much. He had no idea how deep or wide the crowd was, but it filled his whole world. He looked up at the Montaña barracks, which was getting closer by the second. It seemed a hundred years since he had examined the body of the girl in the Retiro, but soon, one way or another, it would be over.

The slope slowed the advance down a little, but still the mob pressed on relentlessly. Those in the lead had now reached a high stone parapet separating the barracks' upper terrace from its lower one. Men in danger of being flattened against the parapet pushed and shoved to reach the steps which ran up the centre – and all the time the pressure from behind continued unabated.

Paco was half-way up the steps when the machine-gun opened fire. At first the people around him couldn't believe it. The garrison had surrendered! they shouted. They'd seen the white flag for themselves, so the gun couldn't be shooting at them! But it was: its unmistakable rattle continued, spraying terror even faster than it could spray its lethal bullets.

Retreat was impossible. The front lines were both hemmed in from the sides and being pushed from behind. So there was no way but forward, even if forward meant death.

Dozens of men fell, some dead before they hit the ground, others merely wounded. They were all, alive or dead, trampled by the advancing mob behind them.

There were rifles at every window of the fortress now, making their own contribution to the carnage. People were screaming and clawing in the air. Begging for mercy. Praying that the bullets would miss them. And still the attack moved forward.

Paco ploughed on through the nightmare, his mind focused on the next steep step, then the one which followed. And suddenly, he had reached the top of the parapet and was free of the narrow confines of the staircase.

Ahead of him, the surviving part of the front line had already reached the barracks door, and fifty or more men, blind with rage, were battering at it with their fists, or else throwing their bodies at this one last barrier between them and their enemies.

The door splintered and gave way. The mob streamed in. Paco weaved his way forward, skidding on pools of blood, almost tripping over bodies, yet somehow managing to stay upright.

By the time he reached the barrack yard, the shooting had stopped and militiaman occupied all three tiers of the galleries which ran around the square. The air was filled with madness, excitement, fear, despair, and the stench of death. Paco saw a terrified soldier running around the second tier, pursued by half a dozen men. When he fell, they were on him like mad dogs – kicking, punching, hacking at him with knives. He could not possibly have survived more than a few seconds of such an attack, yet they slashed and pummelled for over a minute.

A huge militiaman appeared on the top gallery. His thick arms were extended over his head, and in his hands he held a soldier who looked little more than a boy.

'Here the son-of-a-bitch comes!' the big man shouted to his comrades below.

He swung his arms, and the soldier was flying through the air, then plummeting towards the ground. He hit the courtyard with a sickening, bone-crushing thud.

'Wait there, and I'll get you another one,' the big man promised, disappearing through a doorway.

Guns were being handed out from the armoury – old rifles, and pistols so new they were still in their boxes. Men danced and sang and shot their weapons pointlessly into the air, drunk on blood and the miracle of their own survival.

Two militiamen appeared at the edge of the square, dragging a bloody, beaten Carlos Méndez between them. One of them slammed him against the wall, and the other took a few paces backwards and raised his rifle.

Paco stepped between Méndez and his would-be executioner. 'Don't kill him, comrades!' he shouted.

A dangerous, half-mad look came into the second militiaman's eyes. He drew his pistol and pointed it at Paco's head. 'Why shouldn't we kill him?' he demanded. 'Friend of yours, is he? Because if he is, you know what that makes you.'

'Do I look like a fascist?' Paco asked.

'There's a lot of fascists who don't look like fascists any more,' the militiaman growled, his finger tightening against the trigger of his weapon.

Paco felt the now-familiar sensation of his heart thumping against his ribs. The militiaman intended to shoot him, he was sure of it, and with all the killing going on around them, no one was likely to object to one more death. He felt a sense of loss. He didn't think he was afraid to die any more, but it would be tragic to have come so far only to be killed before he could achieve his objective.

The militiaman's eyes said, as clearly as any words, that he was within a second or two of giving the trigger the final squeeze. Strangely calm now that his moment had come, Paco wondered if there was anything he could do to save himself. And then he realized that while he couldn't do a thing, there was a person who could prevent his death – Carlos Méndez.

'Am I a friend of yours, Méndez?' he asked the man who was leaning against the wall.

Carlos Méndez wiped a trickle of blood away from the corner of his mouth. 'I should have killed you myself, instead of putting my trust in others to do the job,' he said contemptuously.

'What's all this about?' the militiaman with the pistol demanded.

'You heard him,' Paco said. 'He tried to have me knocked off. Not something you do to your friends, is it?'

The militiaman lowered his pistol, though he did not put it back in his holster. 'Why did he want you dead?' he asked Paco.

'Because he knew if he didn't get me, I'd get him. His name's Carlos Méndez. He's a rich fascist from the Barrio de Salamanca . . .'

'So why'd you stop us shooting him? That's enough reason to kill him a hundred times over.'

'He seduced my sister . . .' Paco said.

'That's a complete lie,' Carlos Méndez screamed. 'I would never have anything to do with—'

The militiaman with the rifle stepped forward and slapped him across the face. 'Shut up, you bastard!' he growled.

'He seduced my sister,' Paco repeated, 'and if my family is ever to regain its honour, it is I who should take revenge, not you.'

The two militiamen exchanged a quick glance, then the one with the pistol said, 'If you want him, he's yours. He wasn't much fun, anyway. No fight left in him.'

The militiamen who'd hit Méndez, grabbed his prisoner roughly by the shoulder and swung him into Paco's arms. 'Let's go and find ourselves another one,' he said to his partner, and the two men disappeared back inside the building.

Méndez's knees had buckled slightly when Paco had taken hold of him, but now he seemed to be finding his feet again.

'Can you stand up on your own?' Paco asked.

'Yes.'

Paco released his hold, took a set of handcuffs out of his pocket, and clicked one of the cuffs on Méndez's right wrist. 'Carlos Méndez Segovia, I am arresting you for the murder of María Sebastián,' he said.

Chapter Thirty-Eight

Outside, in the street, there was the pandemonium and excitement of Carnival and the Festival of San Isidro rolled into one. Guns were being fired into the air as a salute to the victory. Complete strangers embraced or danced wildly in the centre of the road, holding up traffic which was only too glad to stop and watch the spectacle. The Montaña barracks had fallen! The right was vanquished and, finally, the workers were in control of their own destinies.

Inside, in a small room at the back of the *casa del pueblo*, two men sat facing each other across a plain wooden table. One had a battered face which had recently been bathed and then had a sticking plaster applied to it in a haphazard, uncaring way. The other chain-smoked, as if he had carried out all his labours of Hercules, and now didn't know what to do with his hands.

'We'll win in the end, you know,' Carlos Méndez said.

Paco took a long, deep drag on his cigarette. 'Perhaps you will,' he agreed.

'But I won't live to see it, will I?'

'I don't know. I've been told you're to be tried by a revolutionary tribunal.'

Méndez laughed. 'A revolutionary tribunal! What fine names these working-class rabble give themselves once they've got the power. And what do you think the verdict of this so-called revolutionary tribunal will be?'

'You're to be charged on two counts,' Paco explained. 'One: that on July 9th you murdered María Sebastián. And two: that you attempted to smuggle weapons into Madrid to arm the fascists who have remained. There should be a third charge: that you had my partner, Felipe Fernández, gunned down. But I can't prove that.'

'You can't prove I killed María, either,' Méndez said.

'Don't be so sure of that,' Paco told him. 'You had the motive, the means and the opportunity. I've got a lot of circumstantial evidence I could present if I had to. But,' he shrugged, 'that won't be necessary. They'll

213

convict you on the arms charge, and that will be enough. You're not going to deny you tried to smuggle weapons into Madrid, are you?'

'No, I would never deny that,' Méndez said fiercely. 'I'm proud of what I've done for the Cause. My only regret is that the guns didn't get through.'

Paco stubbed his cigarette, lit a new one, and offered Méndez the packet. The señorito shook his head, as if to say that he wanted nothing which had been provided by his enemy.

'Why are you still here?' Méndez demanded. 'You've handed me over, and now your job's finished.'

'I'd like to talk about María for a while,' Paco said.

'Why?'

'Because I'm still a policeman, and it will satisfy my professional curiosity.'

And because, somehow, he still couldn't quite force his mind to separate María from Reyes, the girl he had loved so long ago in Spanish Morocco.

'So you want to talk about María, do you?' Méndez asked. 'And if I refuse? What will you do then – have some of your thuggish friends come in here and beat it out of me?'

'No,' Paco said. 'If you won't talk, I'll simply go away. And you'll be taken back to your cell, where you'll have nothing for company but your thoughts.' The cigarettes still lay on the table. He looked down at them. 'For God's sake, have a smoke, Don Carlos.'

Méndez looked longingly at the cigarettes, then took one out of the packet, and lit it. Paco waited until he had inhaled, then said, 'How did María happen to meet your brother-in-law?'

Méndez sneered. 'Isn't it obvious? Anything that ever happened to Eduardo happened because I arranged it.'

'Why did you arrange it?'

'Because that was what he wanted. He was tired of spending money on prostitutes, and he told me to find him a mistress,' Méndez said with disgust. 'A cheap mistress. So I found him one. María was working in a sweat shop at the time—'

'I know. I talked to her sister.'

'She told me she was finding life very difficult in Madrid, but, like the fool that she was, she had too much pride to go back to her shack in the mountains.'

So only the rich are allowed pride, are they? Paco thought. But aloud he said, 'You decided that she fitted the bill, and set about corrupting her.'

Méndez shrugged. 'You make it sound so difficult. It wasn't. Women – all women – are natural *putas*. They'll sell their bodies at the drop of a hat.'

'Even your sister?'

'Even my sister,' Méndez said viciously. 'Eduardo's father used to bow when my father passed by. Do you really think my sister could have married a man like him – a man who came from nothing – for love? Of course not. If he hadn't been so filthy rich, she'd never even have looked at him.'

'And what about you?' Paco asked.

The question seemed to take Méndez completely by surprise. 'Me?' he repeated.

'Didn't you live off your brother-in-law's money as well? Didn't you fetch and carry for him? And doesn't that make you just as much a *puta* as everyone else?'

Méndez smiled a superior smile, one which indicated just how stupid he thought Paco was being. 'Whatever I did, I did for the Cause,' he said. 'Eduardo had the money and the influence, but he didn't have the stomach to do the real work. And so it was left to me to order the beatings and the political assassinations, to labour day and night to bring the so-called government down. And I have succeeded.'

'Have you?' Paco asked.

'Of course,' Méndez replied. 'What do you think caused the military revolt? All the hot air Eduardo spouted? Or the fact that there was no order in the country any more?'

There was no denying he had a point. Though he was undoubtedly claiming more credit than he was due, it was people like him, not Herrera, who had convinced General Franco that the army must take over.

'I had you fooled, didn't I?' Méndez demanded aggressively. 'You thought I was just an impoverished aristocrat living off his rich brother-in-law's hand-outs. Watered-down stock! I could see it in your eyes the day you came to the apartment. "Look at the way he jumps to his feet to obey his sister's commands," you said to yourself. "See how she interrupts him as if he were a nobody." Why, you even thought I was afraid of Luis, a lackey who would gladly have laid down his life for a man of my quality.'

Yes, it had been a good act, Paco thought, but even so he should have seen through it – if not before, then at least on the day of Calvo Sotelo's funeral. Don Carlos had run after him and begged him to leave the family alone. First he had argued that his brother-in-law had no reason to kill the girl, then that his sister also lacked a motive. And finally he had spoken of Luis.

'*He has no alibi for the time of her death,*' Paco had said.

Don Carlos had shaken his head. '*He has no alibi he's prepared to produce.*'

'*And what does that mean?*'

'*Check the records of the police station closest to the bullring, and you'll find out for yourself.*'

And because he'd been fixated on the murderer being one of his three prime suspects, Paco had missed the obvious point. Luis would never have told Don Carlos about being arrested, any more than he would have told Eduardo Morreno, so how had he found out? There was only one way: someone had reported it to him. And once you saw him as a man who was reported to, then the whole act of insignificant brother-in-flaw collapsed like a badly built domino tower.

'When the history books are written, there will be pages and pages on me. Eduardo will be only a footnote,' Don Carlos said, cutting into his thoughts.

'Let's get back to María, shall we?' Paco said. 'Whose idea was it to use her as a courier?'

'Mine,' Méndez told him, proudly. 'We needed to communicate with our supporters in other parts of Spain, but we knew they were being watched, both by the so-called government and by the left. That's why María was so perfect for the job – she wasn't just acting the part of a simple country girl, she actually was that girl. No one would ever have suspected her of being a part of a sophisticated political conspiracy.'

'Did she know what she was doing?'

'Of course not! I told her she was just helping with Eduardo's business dealings.'

'And she believed you?'

Without asking, Méndez lit a second cigarette from the butt of his first. How easy it was, having once compromised your pride, to go on doing it, Paco thought.

'Until that last trip down to Seville, she believed me,' the señorito said.

'What happened then?'

'You know what happened.'

'Tell me anyway.'

'She delivered things to the silk factory. Sometimes it was just messages, at other times it was money. On her last visit, one of our people must have been careless and left the door to the arms workshop open. She only got a brief glance of what was going on inside – but it was enough.'

'And then?'

'She had enough sense not to say anything at the time, but the second she got back to Madrid, she phoned me up. She didn't know what to do, she said. She didn't want to get Eduardo into trouble, but on the other hand, she was afraid that if she didn't report what she'd seen to the police, she'd land in trouble herself.'

'So she rang you for advice,' Paco said, a hard edge slipping into his voice. 'Because she trusted you.'

'I expect that was it,' Méndez answered, indifferently. 'At any rate, I told her not to worry. I said that there was a perfectly innocent explanation for what she'd seen, but it was too complicated to go into over the phone . . .'

'Then you went round to her apartment and strangled her . . .' Paco could see Méndez's thin, but strong hands clamping on to her white throat; could imagine the look of astonishment in María's trusting eyes, a look which changed to pure terror when she realized all this was real and she was going to *die* '. . . strangled her and dumped her body into the Retiro.'

'I should have thought about the dress,' Méndez said. 'I removed everything else which might have identified her, but I forgot about the dress.'

'Don't you feel any remorse at all for murdering her?' Paco asked.

Méndez turned the idea over in his mind. 'I come from a very old family with a long tradition of service,' he said finally. 'What I did, I did for Spain.'

Paco suddenly felt as if he'd laid a ghost to rest, felt that finally, in some way he couldn't quite define, he'd paid off a debt. Leaving his cigarettes on the table for Méndez, he stood up. 'We won't be meeting again,' he said.

He didn't hold out his hand, and was sure the other man would not have accepted it if he had. Yet from the troubled expression on Méndez's face, it was plain that there was something that the señorito wanted from him.

'I've answered all your questions,' Méndez said. 'Now I'm going to ask a few of my own.'

It wasn't a request. Even now, in his prison, Carlos Méndez was issuing orders as if he owned the world. But why not answer his questions? A man facing death in a few hours was surely entitled to that. 'What do you want to know?' Paco asked.

'You could have been killed when you took part in the storming of the Montaña barracks, couldn't you?'

'That's true,' Paco agreed. 'A lot of people were.'

'Was your only purpose in taking part in that storming to arrest me?'

'Yes.'

'And when you found me in the courtyard, you realized that I was about to be shot?'

Paco laughed. 'The militiaman had his rifle pointing at you. It was pretty obvious what he intended to do with it.'

'So you put your life at risk again in order to stop that from happening.'

'My life was really in your hands, not theirs,' Paco pointed out. 'You've wanted me dead for quite a while, but when you had your opportunity – when all you had to do was say I was your friend – you wouldn't take it. Why?'

'It was too high a price to pay,' Méndez said coolly. 'But that's not important. I am asking the questions now, not you. And what I want to know is this. If you were intending to hand me over to people who would execute me anyway, why try to stop those militiamen? Was it because you thought they'd just meekly hand me over?'

'No,' Paco said. 'I could see they were out of control. I wasn't surprised when one of them pulled a gun on me.'

'So I repeat: why take the risk when without your intervention, the result would have been exactly the same?'

'You wouldn't understand.'

'I'm not stupid,' Méndez said angrily.

'No, you're not,' Paco agreed. 'But you're as incapable of seeing the world through my eyes as I am of seeing it through yours.'

'Try me,' Méndez challenged.

Paco sighed. 'It would have been wrong to let those two half-crazed militiamen kill you,' he said. 'You had to be dealt with by the proper authorities.'

'The proper authorities!' Méndez repeated. 'Do you call the rabble who run this place the proper authorities?'

'Yes,' Paco said. 'The government has recognized them as such so they must be.' He walked to the door, then turned to look at Carlos Méndez one last time. 'It may not be much of a system of justice I'm handing you over to,' he told the señorito, 'but in these troubled times, it's the best I can do.'

Chapter Thirty-Nine

Felipe had half a dozen tubes running in and out of his body. He looked down at them with disgust. 'This is how they feed me,' he said. 'Liquids! And there's not even any kick in them. What I wouldn't give for a plate of *chorizo* and a decent glass of Rioja.'

Paco smiled fondly at his partner. 'You're looking a lot better than you were the last time I saw you,' he said.

'I'm losing weight,' Felipe complained. 'I must be.'

'You can afford to drop a few kilos,' Paco told him.

'I've got used to being fat,' his partner countered. 'Try saying Thin Felipe. It just doesn't sound the same, does it?'

'No, it doesn't,' Paco agreed.

'Still, when I'm back on my feet, we'll do a tour of the bars,' Felipe said, cheering up. 'A few *raciones*, a couple of *platos del día*, maybe a little seafood and a couple of generous helpings of *empanada*, and I should be my old roly-poly self again.'

Paco wondered if there'd still be the *raciones* Felipe dreamed of when he got out of hospital – or even the bars to serve them. 'I'll go now,' he said, rising from his seat. 'Give you a chance to rest.'

'You showed them, though, didn't you, *jefe*,' Felipe said. 'You showed all those fancy señoritos that they can't push *us* around.'

'Yes, I showed them,' Paco replied, opening the door and stepping out onto the corridor.

*

A small crowd had gathered on the corner of Hortaleza and San Mateo, and the people who composed it – mostly old men – were gazing up at the rooftops of the other side of the street.

One of the onlookers on the edge of the crowd was a bald man with a loaf of bread tucked under his arm. Paco tapped him on the shoulder. 'What's been happening here?' he asked.

The bald man turned briefly to look at him, then returned his eyes to the roof, as if he were frightened of missing something. 'There's a fascist sniper somewhere up there,' he said out of the corner of his mouth. 'Just shot three people further down the street. But don't worry – the militia are after him. He won't get away.'

The old man's words bounded around Paco's brain as the sound of bullets echoed around the narrow streets. '*Just shot three people further down the street. But don't worry – the militia are after him. He won't get away.*'

It didn't take long for war to twist the way people thought. The sniper's bullets had claimed three victims, but that didn't matter – because he'd be made to pay for it. And so it went on. Atrocities on one side led to atrocities on the other, and all that counted was getting even.

Paco could see the militiamen now. There were six of them. Three were picking their way slowly across the tiled roofs from the left, the others were carefully edging their way along the guttering from the right.

'They've got him caught like a rat in a trap,' the bald man said, with evident satisfaction.

Paco eased his way through the crowd. He had seen enough killing for one day. What he needed now was a drink.

The balconies along his route to the *Cabo de Trafalgar* were crammed with women – women fanning themselves, women drinking iced coffee, women knitting. All of them had their eyes fixed on the rooftops, and all had the same expression of excited anticipation they would have displayed at a bullfight.

'It's like a game to them,' Paco said to himself. 'Nothing but a fucking game.'

But it was a game in which real people spilled real blood and ended up dead. The siege of the Montaña barracks had shown that well enough.

The victims of the sniper's fire lay where they had fallen, at the corner of Calle Farmacia. As the bald man had told him, there were three of them. One was a middle-aged woman in a long black dress, the second a girl Paco recognized as one of the local flower sellers, and the third a white-haired man in a shabby blue suit. None of them wore an armband or any other indication of belonging to a political party. They hadn't been shot because of who they were, but because of where they were. They had died for having the temerity to live in a socialist *barrio*.

Two young militiamen were standing guard, their rifles at the ready, as if they were expecting someone to attempt to steal the corpses. Seeing Paco's red armband – and recognizing him as the old man of thirty-six that he was – they made a clumsy attempt to come to attention.

'At ease,' Paco said awkwardly.

The *Cabo de Trafalgar* was now only a couple of hundred metres away, and he could almost taste the drink he so badly needed. From the rooftops behind him came the sound of renewed shooting, but Paco did not stop to look. He did not even turn his head.

*

The *Cabo de Trafalgar* was normally full of thirsty workmen at that time of day, but when Paco pushed the door open, he saw that the only person inside was Nacho.

'*Salud*,' the barman said.

'*Salud*,' Paco replied, walking over to the bar, and sitting down on one of the big wooden stools. 'Where is everybody, today?'

'They've all gone to the mountains.'

'The mountains? Why?'

Nacho raised his eyebrows, amazed by the extent of Paco's ignorance. 'They've gone to fight the fascists, of course. Haven't you heard? The bastards have already got as far as Villalba and Guadalajara.'

It was hard to imagine the lads he usually drank with – Pepe the plumber, Eugenio the postman, and little Mauricio the cobbler – out in the sierra battling the army. 'What time did they set out?' Paco asked.

'About half an hour ago. Before they left, I cooked them a big *tortilla* to eat when they got there. And you can be sure I gave them plenty of wine to go with it.'

Paco remembered how the campaigns had been planned in North Africa – how the supply lines had been the most important part of any operation they were engaged in. And the lads from the bar had gone off to the mountains with nothing more than a potato omelette and a few bottles of wine.

'What will happen when the *tortilla* runs out?' he asked Nacho.

'I'll cook them another one.'

'And take it out to the mountains?'

Nacho snorted. 'Of course not. Why do that when they can come in here and pick it up themselves?'

For a second, Paco couldn't make sense of what the barman was saying. Then he understood. 'You mean to tell me they'll be coming back tonight?' he asked.

'Naturally. Why should they sleep out in the mountains when there's comfortable beds waiting for them at home?'

222

Paco shook his head in despair. 'Give me a wine, Nacho. No, better make it a brandy.'

The barman poured him out a large measure. 'Have you heard the latest news?'

'What latest news?' Paco asked wearily.

'They've arrested your friend Ramón.'

'He used to be your friend Ramón as well,' Paco said. 'Who's arrested him? And for what reason?'

'It was the anarchist militia who took him.'

'Are you sure of that?'

'They were wearing red and black handkerchiefs around their necks – what else could they have been? As to why they arrested him, you know yourself that he has some very right-wing views.'

'And since when has that been reason enough to deny a man his liberty?'

Nacho shrugged. 'Not long. Only since the Montaña barracks fell.'

Chapter Forty

Through the blazing afternoon heat, Paco trudged the streets, looking for Ramón. At anarchist headquarters – where only a few days earlier, his red armband would have earned him a bullet – he was greeted as a comrade, but not given much help. They had never heard of the man he was looking for, they told him. Was he sure it was the anarchists who had arrested his friend? Yes, he was sure. Then perhaps he should try one of the branches nearer to his home. The situation was still very confused, and each group was using its own initiative.

The anarchist post nearest to Calle Hortaleza was housed in a sacked church. The man in charge took Paco down to the crypt and showed him the prisoners they had arrested earlier in the day. Paco recognized a few of them.

There was a coalman, still covered with black dust. 'It's true I once gave the fascists ten pesetas,' he babbled, 'but I didn't know who they were. They were wearing suits, so I thought they'd come from the town hall, and it was some kind of tax they were after.'

There was the shoe-shine boy who normally worked on the corner of Gran Vía. 'Let me out of here!' he pleaded. 'I had to clean the rich men's shoes. They were the only ones who could afford to pay.'

And there was a shrunken old man in a dark-blue suit. 'It's my nephew who's denounced me,' he said sadly. 'He thinks that this way he won't have to pay back the money he owes me.'

All in all, there were around twenty prisoners – poor, shivering wretches, each loudly proclaiming his own innocence. Ramón was not among them.

'Perhaps your friend was arrested by the branch closest to his ministry,' the anarchist gaoler suggested.

'Perhaps he was,' Paco agreed.

But Ramón was not being held at that branch, nor at the three or four others Paco tried. So maybe it wasn't the anarchists who'd arrested him after all. Or maybe they'd arrested him and then let him go. Or were lying when they said they didn't have him. It was even possible that Nacho had got the story wrong, and he hadn't been arrested at all. Whatever the case, as darkness began to fall Paco realized he'd hardly slept for four days and that he was too mentally and physically exhausted to do any more that night.

*

Paco dragged his aching body up the first eighteen of the seventy-two stairs which led to his apartment, rested for a moment, then ploughed on. He had just passed the second-floor landing when he heard a door click open, and a surprised voice behind him say, 'Paco, is that you?'

He turned. Cindy was standing in her doorway. She had a towel wrapped around her head, and was wearing a blue cloth dressing gown which stopped just above her knees. He didn't think he had ever seen her look more beautiful.

An amused smile played on her lips. 'It really *is* you,' she said.

He wondered what she found so funny, then realized that it must be the fact that, though he was now so used to them that they felt like a second skin, he was wearing overalls.

'It's good to see you, Cindy,' he said.

'It's good to see *you*,' the girl replied. 'Where've you been? I knocked on your door several times, but nobody answered.'

'I was in Seville. Working on a case.'

Cindy shook her head. 'Isn't that just like you? History's been made right here in Madrid, and you were in Seville, working on a case as if nothing at all was happening. The militia stormed the Montaña barracks this morning, you know.'

He could have told her he'd been there himself, but he didn't want to talk about it – was too tired to explain why he'd been there. So instead, he just said, 'Yes, I know.'

Cindy held out her hand to him, and he took it in his, 'Would you like to come inside?'

'Very much.'

He followed her into her salon. 'Would you like a drink?' Cindy said. 'A glass of wine? Or a brandy?' Then she slammed her hand down on the table, as if she were angry with herself. 'Oh hell, Paco, let's forget the social crap. I've missed you so bad it hurts, and now you're back all I want to do is go to bed with you. And isn't that what you want too?'

Paco shook his head. 'I'm too exhausted,' he said. 'I just wouldn't be up to it.'

Cindy smiled, and ran her tongue over her lips. 'You might think that now,' she said, 'but once I've got you in the bedroom, you'll find the strength from somewhere.'

And he did.

*

Afterwards, lying in each other's arms, they talked about the future.

'When are you leaving for the United States?' Paco asked, trying to hide his sadness.

Cindy propped herself up on one elbow. 'Leaving for the States?' she repeated. 'Now whatever made you think I'd want to do a thing like that?'

Paco shrugged. 'Isn't it obvious? There's fighting in the sierra, not more than thirty kilometres from here.'

'I know. It was on the radio.'

'The lads who left Madrid today think it will be all guts and glory, but it won't. I saw how the army operated in Seville. The militiamen with their *tortillas* and bottles of wine won't stand a chance against professional soldiers.'

'Don't underrate them,' Cindy said. 'They managed to take the Montaña barracks.'

'Yes, but at what cost. There's a limit to the amount of blood which can be shed in any cause – even in the cause of freedom.'

Cindy smiled. 'Do you know, I've never heard you talk that way before,' she said.

'What way?'

'So abstractly. "The cause of freedom". Indeed! Whatever happened to the hard-headed policeman who only cared about his job?'

'Like so many other things, my job no longer exists,' Paco said. 'But we were talking about you. You have to leave.'

'And miss the most exciting event of the century?' Cindy said. 'Not a chance.'

Paco shook his head, as he seemed to have done so many times that day. 'It isn't a game,' he said.

'I know it isn't. That's why I volunteered my services at the hospital this afternoon. And maybe, when I've got a little experience of nursing, they'll send me up to the Front.'

'You won't have to go anywhere,' Paco said. 'Within a matter of weeks, the Front will be right here.'

'What about you?' Cindy asked. 'What will you do?'

'Join one of the militias.'

'Even though you think they're doomed?'

'Yes.'

'But why?'

'Because I've closed my last case, and it's time to stop being Don Quixote. What Spain needs now is more Sancho Panzas.'

Cindy smiled. The smile was a little sad, as if she'd just realized she'd lost something of value. 'What's brought about this sudden change?' she asked.

'I was with Bernardo this morning, when he arrested a couple of gun-runners. One of them was screaming that he was innocent. And do you know what Bernardo said?'

'No. What?'

'He said that there are no innocents any more. And he was right. The fascists have done some wicked things – this afternoon I saw the bodies of three people who'd been killed by one of their snipers – but do you really think the left is going to come out of this without blood on its hands?'

'No,' Cindy said seriously. 'No, I don't.'

'So all I can do is choose one side, and hope it's less wrong than the other. And the side I've chosen is the left.' He ran his hand through Cindy's hair. 'Let's not talk about that any more. I'm glad you're staying – even though I still think you should go.'

Cindy grinned impishly. 'You'd miss me if I went home, would you, Paco?'

'Yes.'

'And what would you miss most? My conversation? Or taking me to bed?'

'Both those things and much more,' Paco said. 'I think I'm in love with you.'

Cindy's grin stayed in place, but it had become awkward and lopsided. 'You don't love me,' she said.

'How can you be so sure of that?'

'You were in Seville, working on this case? Right?'

'Right.'

'Tell me honestly, Paco, while you were chasing this murderer of yours, did you ever – even for a second – stop to think of me?'

'No,' Paco admitted. 'My mind was on the investigation, and nothing else. But I still think I love you.'

'Just what I need,' Cindy said. 'A romantic-idealist-turned-practical-realist, who can be so single-minded that he doesn't think of the object of his desires for days. A man who can offer me no future because he's married, and, even if he wasn't, will probably be killed within the month.'

'Are you telling me you don't want to see me again?' Paco asked.

Cindy shook her head. The grin was more natural now, almost mischievous again. 'No, I'm not saying that. We don't have a real great basis for a relationship, but I'm sure we can work something out.'

Paco put his arms round Cindy and hugged her to him. He thought back to the horror of Morocco, and knew that worse – much worse – lay ahead of him.

He imagined fighting under the hot Castilian sun and in the cold snow of winter. He could already hear the noises of battle and smell the stench of burning corpses. Blood, rivers of it, flowed before his eyes and . . .

Cindy ran her hands up and down his back. 'Don't think about it,' she urged, reading his mind. 'For an hour or so more, let's pretend none of it exists.'

She was right, he thought. He brushed his lips against hers, then hugged her to him. 'I *do* love you,' he said.

'And I – God help me – *do* love you,' Cindy whispered back.

There was a sound of distant shooting drifting, almost lazily, on the evening breeze. But they refused to hear it.

Printed in Great Britain
by Amazon

38274205R00137